I Am Mr. Poe

I Am Mr. Poe

A NOVEL

by

Elle Powers

ROYAL
RAVEN
BOOKS

Royal Raven Books
20 Hedge Lane
Afton, Virginia 22920
royalravenbooks.com

For Edgar

"I cannot say to you weep not, mourn not, but I do say,
do both, for he is worthy to be lamented."

Elmira Shelton to Maria Clemm
October 11, 1849
Richmond, Virginia

A Note of Caution—

My dear Reader,

Is my being dead going to be a burden to you?

My deepest apologies, friend, but this is no way to begin a tale, is it? Forgive me for being brusque, and before proper introductions, but I must know forthright. And so I ask again: Is the state of my being a stumbling block? A show-stopper? A tear in the fabric of your reality?

If so, I give you leave to close the book. If you are still in the bookshop, then all the better. Set it back on the shelf and do not think about wasting any of your hard-earned coin on this manuscript. (Believe me, I know about the cost of living. Consider the money better spent elsewhere.)

The last thing I want is my condition coming between us. Perhaps I am—openly, selflessly—giving you a significant detail regarding my untimely demise. Alas, I foresee in your biased reading something important slipping past because you cannot let go of this perceived character flaw.

And then, "This from a ghost!" you declare. "How very unreliable."

Go away then, I say. Close the book. Leave it on the bench. Return it to the shelf. It is not for you, friend. For once in my pitiable existence, I do not want you to read my story and would rather you forget about me.

No, no, no. I do not mean that. Do not forget me, but rather revert your impressions to the myth you made up about me. That will do just fine.

As for the rest of you, hear me out.

I know the popular narratives and gossips have painted me an unreliable, unstable character—weak, disgraceful, immoral, mad. Drunken blackguard at best and demon-possessed fiend at worst.

I, however, would have you believe me vulnerable, ill-starred. A flawed human being. A victim of circumstances. No better, no worse than any man. Mad, you say? Show me a sane man who lived through all that I did and did not do himself in or find himself committed to the lunatic asylum.

For this brief history, I ask your cooperation. Read carefully every word, for the signs are hidden within, and if you commit yourself diligently, you will decipher the mystery herein. I will tell all in pure truthfulness. I do not lie. None of this is self-serving. How can it be? How can I be affected now?

No. It is all for you, dear Reader.

Once in my life, I said that to transform all human thought, it would be necessary to write and publish a little book titled *My Heart Laid Bare*. I said also that it must be true to its title to attain its end.

Unable to do so while I still lived and breathed in this world, I present it to you now, without repression. Here it is: My Heart Laid Bare—for you.

Will there be horror? A bit, unfortunately. Certainly there will be fear, to which man is contrarily attracted and sickened. As inevitable to sublunary life, none of these can be edited out. My state makes me invulnerable to these attractions and aversions, but it is not without compassion that I record such realities. I give you this account with all the sensitivity of a doctor telling his patient he has developed some incurable disease and has only weeks to live.

"But you yourself are dead!"

What? Oh, that claptrap again. Have you never read anything written by a ghost? Now think before you answer that question. We dead men of letters seem incapable to rest our pens, as well as our souls. It is time to move on from that bit of old news and make your choice.

As I've already said, this testimony is not for the weak-minded, feeble-hearted, living, breathing man or woman.

It is for the curious. For the insightful. The outsider. For he who might look beyond himself and the material world and wonder, *Why?* For God's sake, why is life so bitterly cruel and unfair?

I am as inclined as ever to tell this tale if you will listen. Forget that I am dead. Forget that I am famous. Remember this only:

I am an orphan.

Respectfully & truly,
Your Narrator,

Edgar A. Poe

b. January 19, 1809–d. October 7, 1849

PART ONE:

The Orphan

Chapter One
1815

—⁙—

"In speaking of my mother you have touched a string to which my heart fully responds. To have known her is to be an object of great interest in my eyes. I myself never knew her—and never knew the affection of a father. Both died (as you may remember) within a few weeks of each other. I have many occasional dealings with Adversity—but the want of parental affection has been the heaviest of my trials." —Edgar

"He was very beautiful, yet brave and manly for one so young." —Thomas Ellis

Lothair

Atlantic Ocean

Ah, I am pleased to see you are still with me. Coming along then?

Let us go now, if you will, to my earliest definable memory, in which you will meet the character who most dominated my young life—*dominated* being the crucial word here. Indeed, his mark can be seen on the whole of my forty years.

See there, that small boy on the sea? The pale lad with the over-large gray eyes and dark curls?

Yes, that is me, six years old, all alone, amidship, on the North Atlantic.

What's that? Not alone? That big man there, you say? "Who is he?"

Ah, yes. That is John Allan, from whom we derive the initial *A* in my name.

You should know, I never meant "Allan" to be central in my nom de plume. That was a Griswold blunder—my erstwhile biographer. But enough about him for now. At this age, I am content to be young Master Allan; Poe sounds like *poor*, or worse, the Scottish expression for "chamber pot": *chanty po*.

Mr. Allan is not particularly big, though bigger than me at this time—big frown, big beak, big chin. That chin, how it haunts me. Mighty, one would say of John Allan, and booming too, in speech, temper, and opinion—an imposing Scotchman in personality and stature.

"Is he your father?"

My father? I see why you might assume so. He sits me on his knee and reads to me, quite attentive and tacitly fond.

How rare. John Allan is most often distracted by business and airs. That is how we find ourselves on this vessel in the middle of summer, 1815. But I suppose on the ocean there's not much worry can do about one's profits and losses.

When my stomach is settled, we practice in the cabin with *Murray's Reader* and *Speller*. But he reads to me here, on deck, I think because I am unnerved by confined spaces, and we both crave the open air.

John Allan is my father by fostering, not by birth.

My foster mother, Frances Keeling Valentine, or Mrs. Allan as it were—young and fetching and sentimental—

is below decks, seasickness having sent her to bed. She is always a bit frail, my Ma, and I am thoroughly devoted to her.

I am *her* pet, not John Allan's. He tolerates me for a while, and at first, I think he takes pride in me. Or perhaps he is proud of his charitable nature, which obligated him to take me in and lend me his name. He is an orphan too, but that doesn't earn me any sympathy.

Since every tale must have a villain, most suggest my foster father for the part. Disguised as a gentleman and patron, he is in fact autocratic and shallow. Allan is flesh, however, not a monster or a demon. But for the sake of tradition and simplicity, we will cast him as the antagonist for the time being.

My deficiency in Allan's mind is that I am the son of *strollers*. That is what he calls the parents of my birth, actors who traveled with a troupe. To hear him say it in his rolling Scotch conjures a grotesque image of debauchery and squalor: *strrrolll-errrs*.

They died of consumption, my parents. At least I think so. My father somewhat disappeared first.

Frances Allan, who had called on my mother during her final illness, brought me home to her and Mr. Allan's stately brick in Richmond's business district like a troublesome stowaway. I was not yet three years old.

Now, in my sixth year on earth, I have departed Virginia, setting out from the James River, fixing a course to Hampton Roads, and from there onwards to England by boat. I am up for an adventure, but this ocean voyage unsettles me.

The only significant attachments I leave in Virginia

are my playmate Catherine (my "sweetheart," to whom I was married in the nursery upon leaving for this expedition); Judith, the negro woman who takes care of me; and Tom, the Ellises' young son.

One of our man servants has come with us, as well as Ma's sister, Miss Nancy Valentine, who is also in bed and queasy. They, along with Frances and John Allan, comprise what I think of as family, even if the bond is flimsy. For a boy with dead parents, I hold on to it with all the ignorance and tenacity I possess.

Yet I do not feel safe. I cannot remember ever feeling safe.

See how Allan doted on me then? Why, he looks positively smitten. His affection shocks me even now, that I could once make him grin so liberally.

"Och, come on, Ned. There's naught to be afraid of now. There're no wars. No pirates." He scoops me up in his arms and bears me to the railing as I kick and fuss.

"See? It's water, is all. It's not going to hurt you."

Once I'm righted and secure between the wooden side of the boat and John Allan's sturdy legs, I settle, looking down at the water as if in a trance.

Mind yourself, Master Allan. It is like serpents slithering under a dark silken veil. What hides within that chilly blue abyss? Something immense, surely....

I shiver at this inner voice. It's one I have heard before . . . I recall its first emergence a year or two ago and
how it disturbed me. It must be my imagination, but it
sounds so very old.

I didn't think of it then, but now I'm reminded that
my mother sailed this route when she was a girl. Only
she was going towards the New World, not away from it.
She had left the London theatre of her mother's gener-
ation for the playhouses of the Colonies, to travel from
one stage to another and back again, finding a new-old
costume, a new-old dialogue, and a new-old dingy room
in which to wither away. Over and again. The American
audiences adored the delicate English starlet—my mother, Eliza, the ghost.

"Pa? You sailed this way before?"

"Aye. On bigger ships than this. But she's a sturdy
wee vessel," he says, patting the gunwale of the pilot
boat *Lothair*. The salty wind stiffens his hair into untidy
waves. "She'll get us there soundly."

The sides of the boat groan as it wobbles. I cannot
tell that it advances at all, only that it plunges and shud-
ders. It is the water that travels, dancing its serpentine
curl. My mind conjures tales of shipwreck and peril at
sea, told by the merchants and ship captains who dine
with us at the Allans' home in Richmond.

I hear the Voice again:

*This is where the spirits of the dead
reside.*

"Thomas says they's monsters down there."

Grim creases score Allan's brow. "*Therrrrre*—'Thomas

says *there are* monsters.' Do not start talking like them, lad."

I know better. At only six years of age, I know how to speak properly, but I also know how to mimic what I hear. *Thomas says, "They's monsters down there."*

"They're afraid of the water is all," Allan is saying. "But you don't have to be afraid. Tell Thomas you don't believe in devils and spirits. Guinea-folk superstition. . ."

I don't reply but frown at the roiling sea below. I quite like Thomas's and Judith's ghost stories, carried over from a wilder continent, which both terrify and delight, and in hindsight are probably intended to keep me from mischief. Being afraid keeps me out of trouble, but it also feeds my excessive imagination.

Chapter Two
1815–16

"Edgar is growing wonderfully & enjoys a good reputation and is both able & willing to receive instruction." —John Allan

"My voice was a household law when few children were not out of leading strings." —Edgar

Ayrshire
Scotland

"Pa, say something for me. Say I was not afraid coming across the sea."

Writing to Charles Ellis, his partner in the tobacco-export business, John Allan corroborates my story when I ask him. You see? He can be generous when so inclined. I also send a kiss to wee Tom Ellis and my sister Rosalie. (Pa includes Rose's foster mother, whereas I neglected her.)

"Very good, Ned, I'll write it. Quiet now, and let Mrs. Allan give me her tidings. Franny, I cannot think much less write when he's underfoot. Thomas, do something with him."

When we reach Liverpool, John Allan conducts his business dealings, then moves us along to Ayrshire, his homeland in Scotland. In spite of the almost constant rain, being on stable land again brings out the wild monkey in me. The shaken seasick laddie did not disembark the ship with the rest.

Irvine, Kilmarnock, Greenock—this is Rabbie Burns country, and I hear a good deal of crowing about the Scottish bard from the masses of Allan relatives, who call my Pa Johnny.

Some of these cousins are children, with whom I romp over the damp and enchanted coast. We chase each other across muted beaches and watch ships come in and out of port, while I thank the gods I am not on one. And once in a while, the fog is so blinding, it buries me in its white nothingness. Ma and Aunt Nancy come nearly undone one evening after sundown when I cannot find my way to our door, much less discern which door is ours, until alas, I have missed supper. (Do not worry, dear Reader: their fraught kisses make my delay worthwhile.)

You see the fear (the Voice) hasn't abandoned ship. It is always there, in my chest, behind my eyes, like some shadowy stalker. And I find the best way to forget its presence is to become utterly absorbed in activity.

To please my foster parents, I consume every storybook I'm given. To please my new chums, I run faster, climb higher, and play harder than the rest. We find cobblestones to pound, puddles to leap, and mud to bring home on our boots. The lads I clobber, and the lassies I charm. When we ride through the village, I insist on sitting with the driver, imagining this creaky, plodding cart as a dragon, sweeping its tail along the doorsteps, knocking over wagons and barrels. Indeed, the books I read by the home fire kindle the boyish adventure of the following day.

And I know now why Bobby Burns wrote verse. It's not the voices of dead poets I hear here. This land, of secrets and mists, speaks to me in images only lyrics can paint properly. Even as a child, I suspect this ancient countryside a theatre of violence and romance, blood and desire. (For can you not have one without the other?)

The Voice tells me so.

The fairies steal unwatched children for their own and leave fairy children in their stead. Perhaps you are a changeling, Master Allan, and the fairies want you back.

The superstitions here would rival the slaves' back home. There are fairies and elves; bodachs, or bogeymen; castle ghosts; water spirits connected to rivers, lakes, and the like; and the Auld Black Divil himself. Such delicious torment. And we mustn't forget that I am exposed to the most colorful cursing and swearing I will hear in my whole lifetime.

Bridgegate House on High Street

&

The Old Grammar School at Kirkgatehead

Irvine

By Christ's cross and all the saints....

The Voice says John Allan is trying to be rid of me.

He wants to leave me with his sisters in Irvine while he
and Ma tour Glasgow and Edinburgh. Ma and her sister
Nancy protest on my behalf, and I'm permitted to attend. However, when it's time to set up house in London,
Allan prevails, despite the ladies' outcry, and I'm sent
back to his birthplace to live with Aunty Mary.

I am afraid I press Pa's sister Mary nearly to her
ruin. She is patient and well-meaning, but she is not
my mother, and I do not want to be here and make her
miserable for it.

To make matters worse, it rains almost every day, and
for an almost seven-year-old precocious boy, this is like
trying to confine a lion in the parlor. The wild animal
needs its wilderness, and the Allan family's two-story
Bridgegate House, maintained by the prim Mary Allan,
is no jungle.

At my antics, this otherwise gentle woman turns into
a shrieking, incoherent banshee.

"I'll skelp ye, ye wee rascal!"

I think she means *scalp*, which is the custom of the
natives in my country, who, so I hear, remove the tops
of their enemies' heads for trophies. I do not take her at
her word; she hardly looks fierce enough to me. And my
Pa, who could be severe in his own right, surely wouldn't
have me maimed.

As I refuse meals—only to steal food later at night—
and stomp out my displeasure, my Pa's aunt calls me an
imp and a devil, and although I cannot disagree with
her, I take offense.

My school day is tedious and crude. For lack of inspiration, the teacher sends me to the churchyard to copy the

inscriptions on the old gravestones. Although I go where I'm told, for the master here will not spare the rod, I refuse to perform any academic work. Instead, I make my dispute known at home, much to Aunt Mary's vexation. She threatens, she coddles, she cries, and I sulk.

You must fight this banishment, Master Allan. You belong with your mother. Fight this with all that is in you, or you will be left here on the coast of Scotland. Pa will forget about you, and he will make Ma forget you too. And then you will die and be buried in this kirkyard, and your stone will read "Edgar Allan Poe, Orphaned Son of heathen Strollers."

⸺ ⚮ ⸺

Sharing a room with my older cousin James, I confide in him one night: "I am going to run away."

"Where're you going to, Ned?"

"To find my Ma."

"Och, aye," he says, his tone dripping with disbelief and mirth.

"She's in London." I insist I know where that is.

"And how're ye going to get there?"

I do not know the details of my escape, but I reckon I can make it out alive. Ships with English destinations anchor in the harbor on any given day, and I'm quite the old hand at seafaring by now. If I get caught or stuck, I will call upon the name of John Allan, and he will make way for my rescue. I am not afraid of any old sea captain, even if he ties me to the mast or makes me sleep in the bilge.

If you're thrown overboard, locked in the brig, or sold as a slave, do you think Allan will give two shillings? It would be a tidy and inexpensive end to any obligation he feels to you.

The Voice must be wrong. John Allan is my father. He is dutiful and oft indulgent. He would not abandon me.

I divulge my schemes, but Cousin James is less than encouraging. "That sounds right dangerous, Ned. I think ye ought to quit your fussing and mind yourself before ye wind up in a world of trouble."

My ambitions succeed without my stowing away, however. James, I suspect, tells on me to Aunt Mary because she soon packs up my belongings and sends me to London, straight into the arms of my bonny mother, who languished without me.

Chapter Three
1816–20

"Edgar Allan was a quick and clever boy and would have been a very good boy if he had not been spoilt by his parents, but they spoilt him, and allowed him an extravagant amount of pocket-money, which enabled him to get into all manner of mischief—still I liked the boy. . . ." —Rev. John Bransby

"Edgar is in the Country at School, he is a verry [*sic*] fine Boy and a good scholar." —John Allan

John Allan Residence
Southampton Row, Russell Square
London, England

"Ma, what's he saying?"

"Who do you mean, Edgar?"

"That black bird." I point at the raven perched on the hanging sign of an inn.

"It's not saying anything. It's a wild bird, my darling." My foster mother speaks softly with a slight yet endearing lisp.

"'Rock, rock.' What could he mean by that?" The bird squawks again, fixing me with a beady eye.

It says "wrong," not "rock," Master Allan. Listen again.

The Voice is right.

"No, Ma, it's not *rock*. It's 'wrong, wrong.' That's what he says. Hear him? What did we do wrong that he scolds us so?"

I do not notice at the time that Ma looks disturbed. She grips my hand tighter and yanks. "My dear, there's nothing wrong. A raven cannot make any sense. It's not speaking, only making a clamor."

Yet it seems to be talking to me, and I resist her pulling. My tam-o'-shanter nearly slips off my curly head in the struggle. *Wrong, wrong.* This baffles! *What* is so wrong?

"He's laughing, Ma," I say, laughing myself. "He laughs because he thinks it's funny that he's upsetting us."

"I'm not upset," tumbles past her lips with a false laugh and then a shudder. I see a shadow fall over her face, the smile falling with it. "It sounds like shrieking to me," she mumbles.

"Well, I think he means to say that it's wrong to deny me a sweet from the shop when we get there," I say, finally allowing my feet to follow in the direction of her tugs. I beam up at her, trying to recover her better mood.

"Ah, Edgar, it will spoil your supper," she sighs, but I can already hear the yielding in her voice.

"That's a smart lad there, Mrs. Allan." A man with ruddy cheeks doffs his hat.

"Why, thank you, Mr. Wilson. This is my son, Edgar. Say hello, dear."

"Good evening, sir. Do you know why the raven says 'wrong'?"

When I reached London, I was pleased to find a letter from my little wife, Catherine, all the way from Richmond. I am happy she hasn't forgotten me (although I hadn't thought much of her):

Give my love to Edgar and tell him I want to see him very much.

I will ask Pa if I can write her back.

Pa. . . . My childish mind cannot abide this discrepancy in our relationship. Being intellectually mature for my age does not mean I can abstract, and although my imagination is vast, it is also cast-iron. This is the man who pays for my education, my clothing, my doctor bills. But this is also the man who sent me away, who separated me from my mother.

He meant to keep you away for good, Master Allan. He wants Ma all to himself.

This fear of being separated from her is not a new one. I expect it comes straight from the side of my mother's deathbed. My mother Eliza, I mean—the vague, dreamy actress, who died so young.

Sometimes I swear it's easier to love people who are dead. Thank you, Mother, for being such a saint.

I suppose you, dear Reader, ought to thank *me* for being
so agreeably, appealingly dead. Enchanting, isn't it? I tell
you secrets. I give you counsel. I cannot hurt you . . . because I am dead. See? Nothing to be afraid of here.

You are most welcome, dear Reader. Most welcome
indeed.

Manor House School
Stoke Newington

Frances, my foster mother—still alive and still my whole
reason for being—seems unhappy to me. She is often
ill and talks of going home to Richmond, although she
dreads the voyage. She says it is the chilly, damp weather
that ails her, but now that I think about it, she kept to
her bed a good deal in Virginia as well.

This is no time to worry about her, however. I am
to be enrolled at a new academy in Stoke Newington,
a suburb of London. The Manor House School is under
the tutelage of the Reverend Dr. Bransby. He resides in
the sprawling manor with his little family and flock of
pupils.

There is something altogether quaint and gloriously
forbidding about my new domain. The village of Stoke
Newington looks apt to host a ghost or a dozen, with its
dark, twisting alleys and soughing trees, tall and dense
hedges that might be hiding who knows what. The air is
cool and teeming with spirits, ancient and gentle. I will
never forget the deep, hourly clang of the church bell
that resounds from the steeple and strikes a calm, time-
less order over every roof, into every chest.

Keeping time, time, time...

And the school itself is Gothic and vast, with a warren of corridors and staircases that I never quite master in the three years I am there. Elizabethan paintings line the halls and medieval statuary guard dark alcoves, making candlelit wanders utterly terrifying.

One night, I awaken to use the chamber pot and find that I cannot open the apartment door. I wrench the knob, somewhat panicked. My noises rouse my roommates, who are none too patient.

"We're locked in," I cry, still pulling and pushing the door, which budges but little in its jamb.

What if there's a fire, Master Allan? How will you escape? To perish in a fire would be a most horrific end.

Drowning, burning . . . this imagination is ever recalling to me my brittle mortality.

As they awaken, the boys are drawn in by my hysteria. One, in his nightshirt, looks out the arched window with dismay. Even if it would open, our room is on the third story and overlooks a gravel courtyard. Beyond it are the great iron gates and stone walls. We are caged.

It is, I believe, mere minutes (although it feels like an eternity) until the door, with the help of an exasperated chambermaid on the other side, comes unstuck. After that, I never fall asleep without first checking the lock.

Despite its anomalies, this school provides the setting I crave, as learning and letters would become my escape from unhappy thoughts. One might question why I find this reversion to the Dark Ages such a comfort. Oh, but it is the ideal sanctuary for a boy starved for affection—a boy who requires tales of adventure and suspense to settle his nervous nature. Said boy can hide himself away with his books, locking his mind from such melancholy as gotten by a father who wants him out of the way and a mother who is too sick to take care of herself, much less her child.

Here, he can fancy himself Childe Harold, brooding and self-pitying. . . .

Now, I realize I have just alluded to Lord Byron, but I must not mislead you: his is not approved reading for lads of the Manor House School. And although I wouldn't meet the Byronic Hero until I return to America, somehow I know he exists. And somehow I know his is my part to play.

Dr. Bransby is the very opposite of the headmaster at the Old Grammar School in Irvine, who was old and likewise shirty. The reverend is a jolly chap in his early thirties, who is fond of nature and sports. Although he styles me *wayward* and *willful* in a letter to my father, I know he favors me. Naturally, I want to please him in exchange.

When I entered the Allan household at almost three years of age, I charmed my new parents by quoting Shakespeare and performing short musical acts. A neat parlor trick when guests joined us for dinner, I was readily set on a table to deliver a soliloquy from *Hamlet* or *Julius Caesar*, or to sing a song from my dead mother's repertoire. No doubt these acts were learned from untold nights backstage at my parents' company venues.

But until this point, my education has been inconsistent and limited. Here in London, I learn French and Latin, history and literature and arithmetic. This pleases John Allan, and he is proud of my learning. If he is at all disinclined to pay for my schooling, I do not hear about it.

As much as I read, I play hard too, wearing out many a pair of shoes during my three years at Stoke Newington.

"Keep an eye out, Bates. I'll go first, and when I say the way is clear, you lot follow."

I organize regular student breakouts, leading the charge over the school wall. It's all pretend, of course, and we never actually conquer the wall, but the object is to see how high we can climb. In this game, genial young Bransby is a severe elderly warden who keeps us imprisoned within the gates and makes us endure hard labor, boring lessons, and solidified porridge.

I issue commands over my shoulder. "Come on now, lads. Find the footholds. Follow me!"

Almost to the top, I cry out and flick a smarting hand away from the stone wall, almost losing my footing. Retreating with cautious progress and blinking back tears, I jump the rest of the way when I know I won't wrench my ankle. Once on stable ground, I hold out my hand for my mates to examine the wound, earning me several sympathetic *oohs*.

"What happened, Ned?"

"Bransby's stuck the top of the wall with shards of glass."

"Aw, the tyrant!" a ginger-haired boy says.

This becomes part of our make-believe play: pieces of cut glass atop the wall—a *cheval-de-frise*—to prevent young scholars from escaping intact.

All this tends to remind me that I suffer from a lively imagination—as a child and to the present day. Thus, I would do well to insert a statement of intent here. That is, I am attempting to present the truth as best I can in this account. I feel I owe you that, dearest Reader. But writers do embellish, and I would ask you to indulge me. Little embellishments do not affect the truthfulness of a tale. I would furthermore set forth the idea that writing it makes it so. We all invent our own mythologies, which in turn become our realities. These myths enable us to better endure our existence. What's the harm in that, hm?

You see, these made-up stories and games helped me as a boy relate to my twenty English schoolmates, who might have otherwise found it uncomfortable to chum about with an orphan from America. By nature, I am temperamental and competitive and, let's not forget, *spoilt*. Thus, I require, and avail myself of, little lies to serve as a friendly enticement. I'm sure you understand.

After five years abroad, financial decline requires us to leave England. I'm taken out of the Manor House School and sent to Scotland for a last farewell. Then, by the late summer of my eleventh year, I have crossed the sea for the final time. If not for my foster father's failing business, I would have been thoroughly Englishized, as the Virginians would say. I was romanticized enough as it was.

Chapter Four
1820–23

—ฆ ๏—

"No boy ever had a greater influence over me than he had. He was, indeed, a leader among boys; but my admiration for him scarcely knew bounds; the consequence was, he led me to do many things for which I was punished." —Tom Ellis

Charles Ellis Residence
Franklin & Second Streets

&

Belvidere Estate
Richmond, Virginia

Now, let us travel together to the city on the James River, where my first mother intrigued audiences and breathed her last in a boarding house bed.

(At this point in our narrative, I'm feeling a bit like a Dickens ghost, which is annoying, but what can be done? Ah, you are fond of Dickens? Well, you would be, I suppose. All the better then.)

My second mother fared the journey as well as one could hope, and she duly perks up being back in Virginia. She is the merry entertainer once again. If I am not the centerpiece of her social affairs, I am at least an outstanding accessory, and she schedules parties for me and my peers on special occasions.

Pa is taking an interest in me again, which is not always convenient. Allan is irascible, and I learn to watch out for his temper. Ma and Aunt Nancy and the servants shield me as much as possible, but I choose to go my own way, knowing I might be punished for it later. I cannot in truth say that I do not sometimes deserve his correction, nor that any other man of the times wouldn't do the same. My complaint would be that I never know if he will chuckle at my antics or send me outside to cut a switch. It is a gamble, and I do not always win.

Yet often you do.

Yes, often I do.

For a while, we live with his business partner, Mr. Ellis. His son, Tom, is my everyday playmate and holds me in high regard. This is generous, seeing as I drag him with me into hot water. On one Saturday, I lure him to the countryside, where we stay all day, roaming the fields and woods.

"Tie your laces, Tom."

"Where are we going, Eddie?"

"To the country. We are going to build a shelter and find our own food. Like Robinson Crusoe."

Tom twists his toe in the grass. "I have to tell my mother first."

"No, don't worry. No one will know we're gone."

"Oh . . . you think so? Hey, Eddie, is that a gun?"

"Of course. How are we going to hunt if we don't have a gun? We have to share, though. I only have the one."

"You got powder?"

"It's here," I say, patting the horn I wear on a leather strap.

Since no one in the house knows where we are, it is a great worry to the mothers when we do not return home for supper. Meanwhile in the wilderness, Tom and I are as contented as ever. I harvest turnips and shoot birds with Pa's gun. The birds, fat and flightless, happen to belong to a judge, who also happens to own the turnip patch, as well as the grounds on which we trespass.

But how are we to survive otherwise? I couldn't let wee Tom Ellis starve! I say all this to John Allan later, who with red face and flared nostrils lets the gunpowder strap make his reply. Despite being humiliated and insulted, I am only relieved the judge hasn't condemned me to the gibbet.

I'll never forget John Allan's saying, "You're unmanageable, Ned, but I suppose it is to be expected of a genius."

I am pleased to report that I not only taught Tom to survive in the wild, but I saved him from drowning. Since he cannot swim, but was keen to learn, I threw him into the falls to sort it out for himself. But soon, I saw that little Tom was not going to make it out alive, and I cut the swimming lessons short and fished him out of the white water. From that day on, I am his guardian angel and hero.

I teach Tom everything I know about being a boy. We fence and box and skate and play bandy. Although I am skilled at all sports, swimming is my finest, and I swim often with my chums—including Tom, who eventually learns to keep his head up—in the Shockoe Creek.

One day on a dare, I swim six miles against the tide of the James River, much to my peers' amazement and a great number of whom follow me by boat or on foot. Judge Stanard's little son, Rob, came home late that day, hot and covered in mud, giving his father the excuse that he was watching Edgar Allan swim to Warwick.

My athleticism produces a lean, muscular body that is growing manlike. I am not likely to shy away from a fight either, which I always win. I've learnt to suck in my breath, and then, when hit in the chest, exhale so that the brunt of the blow is deflected.

Ebenezer Burling and I keep a rowboat hidden in the weeds by the riverbank, for when we set out for castaway islands. With Tom, Rob, Jack Mackenzie, and other boy natives, we forage for chestnuts and fruit, steal from gardens and orchards, and catch fish to fry on the strand. When the river overflows and floods Shockoe Bottom, we row our little boat behind the Main Street businesses.

I am inclined to take risks, and I like to play pranks. Tom, as much as he loves me, still has not forgiven me for frightening his sister, Jane, with a toy snake. Strange, you might say, but for an overly sensitive child, I do not hesitate to nor weary of frightening others.

Staunton

Virginia

{1815}

Although I was very young at the time, I recall when my mother's cousin, Edward Valentine, takes me on horseback to pick up the post. On the way home, after

sunset, as we pass an old graveyard, I shriek and cling
to Edward, all but climbing over his back. He must stop
to keep me from falling off the horse, and he slides my
stringy, rigid self to the front of the saddle to quiet me.

"For God's sake, *what* is it, Ned?"

"They will run after us and drag me down," I cry.

"Who?"

"The dead people!"

"No. No, they will not. Dead people do not run, and
they cannot hurt us."

Panting and peeking around Edward for ghosts and
ghouls, I bleat, "At sunset the spirits come out to haunt,
and if you're out of doors after dark, they will take you
back with them."

"Look at me, Ned. Who told you that?"

I am often dumbfounded by this question. *Who else?*

Now, my Ma tends to tell variations of the same
lovely story: a young boy, a peasant orphan, who is very
poor but very well-behaved, is granted wishes and comes
to live in a grand castle as a rightful prince. Not a dead
body or spirit in sight, no graveyards or fog or mur-
ders—all terribly boring for a lad like me who resem-
bles this protagonist in form but is not always so well
behaved or as lucky. I much prefer the bedtime stories
of my nursemaid, Judith, a fearsome storyteller. In hers,
the graves open up and corpses come to life to chase the
unfortunate young master who did not come home before
sunset like his mammy advised.

Of course, I cannot tell Cousin Edward that my Ma
told me this story—he would never have believed it—
and it is suggested with firm, well-meant insistence that

I not be permitted in the kitchen with the servants after supper's been cleared away.

Mr. Poe, must you persist in calling these good folks "servants" and "nursemaids"? You are no longer a child, and you know now what they were.

This is a most regrettable penalty, for I prefer the buzzy, doting company of the servants. . . .

Oh, jolly good. We'll continue to call the slaves "servants" then.

I am trying to stay true to the setting and characters. Who is telling this story again?

It is you who has the way with words, Mr. Poe. My apologies. Please go on.

It should be noted here that it is this Edward from whom I acquire my appetite for terrorizing people. These capers include pulling the chair out from under a big boy as he is sitting. Although, in my immaturity, I do not discriminate between big boys and big women, much to John Allan's irritation. The bigger the boy the better, Edward told me, which translated in my mind to the bigger the *lady*—and perhaps the grander her position in society—the bigger the outcome. I only managed to pull this prank once before being reformed, in the Scottish manner, but it was a memorable occasion.

Washington Tavern

9th & Grace Streets

&

Old St. John's Burying Ground

Grace & 25th Streets

Richmond

{1811}

The best part about being back in Virginia is that I am
reunited with old friends, including my younger sister,
Rosalie. When I was taken in by the Allans as a wean,
the infant Rose was adopted by the Mackenzies, another prominent Scottish family in Richmond. Rose has a
Mackenzie brother named Jack, who is a lifelong friend
of mine. Their mother is mirthful and maternal, and I
call her "Ma" too.

There are days when I wish the Mackenzies had adopted me, as well as Rose.

My actress mother, in spite of her work ethic, was destitute. She barely scraped up enough to provide for herself
and her children. The stage was her only constant home,
and it was constantly changing cities. As a result, she
could not afford proper food or care. And thus weakened,
she succumbed to the wasting away of consumption.

Although I do not remember the scene, I imagine my
Ma and Jane Mackenzie attending my stricken mother
in her dingy rented room a few blocks from the theatre.
Thanks to an appeal for charity in the Richmond news-

paper, the ladies pitied the widowed English actress and her little children, relying on strangers' mercy in a Southern city.

"Oh, please, missus! Take pity on my babes. Let me die in peace, knowing Edgar and Rosalie will be cared for when I'm gone."

"Rest your soul, Mrs. Poe," Mrs. Mackenzie would have said, perhaps bouncing the bundled baby Rose against her bosom. "We won't let your wee bairns be lost."

I see Frances Allan wiping Eliza's fevered brow with a cool cloth, all the while fixing her tender gaze on me, who repeated, like the raven, "What's wrong, Mama? What's wrong?" Frances's empty womb ached with longing when I took the cloth and dabbed my mother's pale face. "Shh, Mama. Don't cry."

When she died, the Allans and the Mackenzies arranged to have my mother buried on the outskirts of the St. John's yard. The grave is as yet unmarked, as the Church was not approved to inter *strollers* in said holy ground.

It will not always be so, Master Allan. Although her gravesite is unknown, Elizabeth Arnold Poe will one day be memorialized in stone.

The Ellis Residence

My friends tease me for my way of speaking, which is more influenced by my years in England and the Scotch dialect heard in my house than the slow drawl of Richmond. When I was younger, I affected a colorful negro patois at will, but that only earned me disapproval. By contrast, I learned to amuse my foster father by speaking in broad Scotch.

Make of that what you will. I am a gifted impressionist—perhaps it is the actor in me, handed down from my parents with, I assume, my coloring and build. But let's keep that a secret, shall we? As much as John Allan dislikes my parents' profession, stagecraft is a valuable talent for an orphan in society.

Finances are precarious for my family these days, and yet appearances must be kept. The Allans host grand evening socials, at which I behave like the well-bred lad I pretend to be. If only I act like I belong here, perhaps I can fool myself as much as our neighbors.

At one of these parties, I make my appearance in a manner that did not meet my foster parents' approval. It was a gentlemen's whist party at the Ellises'. Always ready to make a scene, I throw a sheet over my head and drift into the room, using a cane because I cannot see from under the sheet.

At the entrance of a ghost upon their game of cards, the men startle. Some jump up.

"What the devil is that?"

"It is the ghost of Benedict Arnold! See the cane?"

General Scott, incapable of abiding a traitor or a ghost, comes at me as if to attack, but Dr. Thornton reaches me first. I whack at him with the cane, but the sheet twists around my legs and I stumble. Finally, the men catch and unmask the offending apparition. Those having been frightened laugh with me in relief, but perhaps do not laugh as hard as I.

It may be customary to dazzle my peers, but I do not always manage to impress John Allan, who is fine-tuned at correction and exact with a cutting remark. He likes to remind me, in front of my friends, that I am existing on his charity. He regularly threatens to turn me out, and I find it difficult to properly grovel after such declarations.

Monumental Church

{Pew No. 80}

1224 E. Broad Street

Sundays, we sit in our pew box. Well, not John Allan, who has no practical use for religion, but Ma expects me to go with her. Even though I am older—and now taller than she—and can refuse to go if I so set mind to it, I oblige her. I know all the responses by rote.

Ecclesiastical worship leads me to ponder life and death, which I suppose is its intent. Messages of eternal reward or eternal agony train my thoughts to my own fragile existence and the (dis)continuation of those I care for. It makes me think of my first mother, even as I share a hymn book with my foster mother.

Monumental Church, of the Episcopal denomination, is built on the site of the Richmond Theatre, where Eliza Poe spent many an evening on the stage. That theatre burned to the ground days after she passed away, killing seventy-two, many of whom were prominent townsfolk. It was considered a national tragedy, and this sanctuary was erected in their memory.

During sermons and prayers, I imagine that the

church altar stands at center stage, where Eliza made her audience laugh, weep, yearn . . . *feel*. Isn't that what church is—a collective feeling? Isn't that worth something more? The feeling may be fleeting, but the performance, the sacrifice she made . . . is *it* not eternal?

My mother is in heaven; I will not consider any other possibility. Unless there is no heaven. But it matters not because I am here, and this pew box is the closest I will ever get to her. Her remains—whatever is left of her—are buried somewhere near the eastern wall at St. John's, but *this* is where her memory lives on.

Let us not forget our second mother—this woman sitting beside you, who is chronically ailing. You will one day lose her to heaven too. Memorial stone lasts longer than the woman herself, and your first mother has none.

Oh, why must Death take the mothers? Why, God? We sons of men need our mothers! The fathers . . . these husbands . . . are cruelly fickle. They demand, they bully, they leave, they drink themselves into oblivion. But the death of the mother is a rejection I cannot rationalize or overcome.

Verily, verily I say unto you: it will haunt you 'til the day you die, Master Allan.

Perhaps that is so, but I am *not* Master Allan. My name is Poe. Edgar Poe. That is the name my mother gave me.

Chapter Five
1823

"When Eddie was unhappy at home (which was often the case), he went to [Mrs. Stanard] for sympathy, and she always consoled and comforted him."
—Maria Clemm

"His imaginative powers seemed to take precedence of all his other faculties, he gave proof of this, in his juvenile compositions addressed to his young female friends. He had a sensitive and tender heart, and would strain every nerve to oblige a friend."
—Joseph Clarke

Richmond

Such existential thoughts turn into verse when I escape to my room or the rose garden across the street. But it is not enough to keep these verses to myself. I crave an audience. It must be the Eliza in me.

My Ma is the first to see, and she is overawed. Easily impressed, you might say, but she shows my poetry to John Allan, and he thinks enough of it to share with his friends. In hindsight, I think Allan recognizes something nostalgically *Scottish* in my poetry, reminding him of Ayrshire and the Plowman Poet himself, Robert Burns. I ask him about printing the poems, and he seems inclined. But when he mentions it to the schoolmaster, they agree that it would do my pride more harm than good to have a published book at such a young age.

Is my poetry relegated to the subject of death? By no means. . . .

William Mackenzie Residence
Grace Street, between 5th & 6th Streets

"Jack and I are off to do manly things, Rose," I tell my sister. "I think you better go inside now." I am fond of Rosalie, but she more than anyone can make me forget my tact.

"There's nothing to do at home but needlework! I want to go with you."

"You'll ruin your frock, and Ma Mackenzie will be fit to go mad. Here, before you go. . ." I draw an envelope from my pocket, on which I've sketched a drawing. "I've got an undertaking for you. You know Elmira Royster?"

She raises her hands like I'm offering her typhus. "Buddy, I can't deliver your letters anymore." (Rose calls me Buddy to my dying day.)

"Why not?"

Jack chimes in with a smirk. "Because Miss Jane's had it up to her bonnet with schoolgirls moonstruck over your love ditties. She caught Rosalie giving one to Anne, and Ma was none too happy to hear about it."

Rosalie bites her lip and nods, her vacant blue eyes veiling some unfortunate memory playing behind them.

"They're not ditties. They're sonnets. I am sorry you got in trouble, Rose." I mean it too, but I am more anxious than sorry to sidestep this snag. "Who else can smuggle my notes into the girls' school?"

"Jane Ellis?" Jack suggests my father's business partner's daughter.

"Too young," I say.

"No, Buddy!" Rose shakes her head. "If Miss Jane finds any more letters from boys in the dormitory, she will have it out for me. Besides, the word going 'round is that every girl is getting the same poem."

I scoff. "Not so." I revise the poem each time I rewrite it.

As it is, these minor complications will not keep Don Juan from his lady admirers. I can climb the walls of Miss Jane's precious institution for Richmond's privileged belles as capably as any romantic hero. Time will tell whether I can do it and not get caught.

Judge Robert Stanard Residence
9th Street & Capitol Square

My greatest romance is not found at the Mackenzie School for Girls. These ingénues are mere wrens compared to the dove of beauty and sophistication who glides on the scene in my fifteenth year of life.

Remember young Rob Stanard, the judge's son, who followed me six miles along the James's muddy shore? He adores me, that little chap, and I feel an instinctual fondness for the boy. One day after school, he takes me home to see his pet rabbits and pigeons. I had promised to teach him to play cards afterwards, although in secret, as it is an unsuitable activity for well-bred lads.

"Very fine pets, Rob. I like that fat one there. What

do you feed that fella?"

"Scraps mostly."

"Do you ever let him in the house?"

"Oh, no. Mama's cat would make a meal of Roger. Let's go inside, and my mother'll give us something to feed him."

"Is that your mother in the window?" Having turned towards the house, I see a floaty figure draped in a sleek white gown and muted light. A moment later, she emerges with a plate of seeds for the birds.

"Edgar Poe," she gushes. "*The* Edgar Poe who swam all the way to Warwick Wharf?"

"Yes, ma'am. And walked back to town." I don't know how I manage this boast without getting tongue-tied. I am wonderstruck by this beguiling woman, whose speech is like delicate chimes. I will later claim to nearly lose consciousness at the sound of her voice.

"Thank you for letting Robbie tag along. You are not only *his* hero, but you are mine as well. The Sullys say you are a godsend, that you fend off the bigger boys who tease the weaker ones. . ."

I am only somewhat listening, but I quite like what I hear. Rob's mother is the very vision of Art and Wisdom and Virtue. The face, flawless and youthful, is like Helen's, whose beauty made men to kill and be killed. She is my Muse, and I will do anything she says, surviving on her adoration alone. No more will I scribble for silly girls. From here on, my pen belongs to Mrs. Jane Stith Stanard, whom I call Helen in my poetry—for classical reasons, you see, and because it sounds less common and bland than the undeserved *Jane*.

Of course, I do not let on that the verse is for her.

"Let me see what you're writing, Edgar," Mrs. Stanard says, her voice, her attentions like a sweet, intoxicating wine. Whenever I go home with Rob, she asks to see my latest work.

"Well, it's for—it's some verse I wrote for . . . a young lady."

"A young lady. Well! She will be so flattered. Edgar, this is immense! You will be a renowned American poet. Write *that* down, will you? I can see the future, you know." She winks at me.

"You really think so? That's what I want more than anything. I want to be a poet."

"You *are* a poet, Mr. Poe. The next Lord Byron, make no mistake."

My face reddens. This is the best compliment one could bestow upon young Edgar Poe.

"Please don't tell that to my father," I say, sheepish.

She smiles slightly, sadly, then pats my shoulder.

"Is he averse to poetry?" When I look down, she nods. "You mustn't cross him, Edgar. Mr. Allan's done much for you, and you owe him your respect. But do not forsake your talent. One day, you will make him proud, when the world knows your name. Edgar A. Poet, the Bard of Virginia."

This, I decide—spoken by the Oracle of Fortune herself—is destined.

Yes, yes, I know what you're thinking. This is all very love-sick and barmy. But I *am* in love with her. Romantic love, you ask? Yes . . . it is romantic, in the way that castles and princesses are romantic. Not romantic in that I love her like a lover. I love her like a mother rather. But I worship her like a goddess.

I am fourteen years old, and I have met the love of my life. The Stanards' house is my new church.

"And how are you getting on with the new schoolmaster?" Mrs. Stanard asks. "Rob tells me he is very stern."

"I cannot say that I don't miss Master Clarke awfully—"

"The ode you gave him at the farewell ceremony was exquisite. I saw tears in the old Irishman's eyes."

"Thank you," I say through a reluctant smile. "He was very good to me. I cannot say Master Burke is as fond, but I know how to appease him. He is well educated, and I am learning a great deal from him."

"I am sure you are, Edgar. But you will be careful, won't you? That man thinks he can beat the 'boy' out of his students."

"That's almost exactly what my mother said. Don't worry, Mrs. Stanard. I know how to avoid a beating."

She smiles, I think seeing the affection on my face. "How is your mother, Edgar?"

"She is unwell at present, complaining of a fever."

"Aw, that is too bad. Do give her my condolences. I have some flowers from the garden I'd like to send home with you. You don't mind?"

"Not at all. Ma will be delighted. Thank you."

Time to time, Jane Stanard and my Ma visit with one another. I'd like to think that I am the subject of their tête-à-têtes, but it makes me nervous not to know what they say about me. I adore my foster mother, but I find myself more open with Mrs. Stanard. Ma appreciates my company and accomplishments, and she spoils me when she can avoid the provocation of John Allan. These are her main ambitions: to keep me happy and to keep her husband in the dark. Unfortunately, these two ends do not always complement.

She consorts with the servants to hide my exploits from Pa. He disapproves of certain friendships and activities. He forbids me to go to Eben's house, and he doesn't like me spending so much time at the Mackenzies'. Under no circumstances will he tolerate my acting in plays. Which is fine, if truth be told; I crave a larger stage than any theatre can boast. I want the whole world's attention. But for now, I'll take Helen's.

That is Mrs. Stanard, who, on the other hand, admires performers. When she was a little girl, she saw my mother on stage. "Oh, your mother had the most enchanting voice, Edgar. I'll never forget it. When she was Ophelia, she left me in tears. . ."

When I am with Helen, the Voice fades away. The pressure, the fear—all seem to lift. And yet the Voice is not altogether gone. I am aware that it is paying attention, biding its time, waiting to catch up to me.

Sometimes, I go to Rob Stanard's house and his mother

is confined to her bed. I don't think much of this at first because the mistress of my house is often abed too. Then I hear that the Stanards' new baby died during the birth.

My visits become more sporadic. It's not that I want to stay away, but Rob tells me not to come. His mother is not well, he says, biting back worry.

One day Rob is not at school, and I walk to Capitol Square with his lessons. I meet his mother on my way up to the house and nearly drop my satchel. It is early spring, and it's been weeks since I last saw her.

Mrs. Stanard is in her night shift and robe, feeding Robbie's birds in the garden, like the first time I saw her. Back then I pictured her a classically sculpted statuette. Now she looks further diminished, almost like a phantom. Her movements are frenzied, her eyes wide. And when she sees me, I wonder if she in truth *sees me*.

"Oh, Mr. Poet, it's you. So good of you. . ." She seems to forget the proper greeting mid-sentence.

I am embarrassed to see her in her night clothes. I—I glimpse her breast through the flimsy fabric, where the robe has fallen off one shoulder, and I try to look away, but. . . .

"Miss—Mrs. Stanard. I'm sorry—I brought Rob his books. . ."

"The birds, Edgar—they don't make any sense, and I cannot sort it out. Listen. I do not know what they want, and their racket, it makes me—rather nervous! Why don't you write a poem about it? Their nonsense." She thrusts the plate of bird seed at me, but I don't catch it level and most of it spills on the ground.

Helen walks away, soullessly but swift, her robe billowing in the March wind.

Dazed, I run inside to find Rob, and we go to tell his father, who is in his chambers downtown. One of the servants catches Mrs. Stanard and steers her home and up to bed.

This is the last time I see her—fleeing down the road in her nightgown, so as not to hear the squabble of the birds. I'll never forget her gaze that day—glassy and troubled. Once, it was as though she saw my innermost soul. This time, it was like she looked right through me, like I wasn't there. It was as though *she* wasn't there.

I do not think she was, Mr. Poe.

Chapter Six
1824

⁓☙☙⁓

"He was a beautiful boy—not very talkative. When he did talk though, he was pleasant, but his general manner was sad." —Elmira Shelton

"Since the sad experience of my school-boy days to this present writing, I have seen little to sustain the notion held by some folks, that school boys are the happiest of all mortals." —Edgar

The Allan Residence
14th Street & Tobacco Alley
Richmond

"Edgar, come in here, dear." I hear Aunt Nancy call from Ma's sitting room as I pass by. She comes to drape an arm around my shoulders and guide me in.

"Yes, Aunt Nan?"

My mother is resting on a sofa, but she cries when she sees me. "Oh, Edgar!"

"What is it, Ma? Can I get you something?" *Why is she not smiling*, I wonder. She always smiles at me.

"No, darling. We need to talk. It's better you hear before you go to school tomorrow."

"Hear what?"

Aunt Nancy takes over. "Something awful happened

this evening." Her eyes fill with tears, and I see that Ma is already dabbing her wet face with a handkerchief.

"Mrs. Stanard. . ." Ma's voice staggers.

"Something happened to Mrs. Stanard?"

"She passed away, Edgar."

My eyesight turns murky around the edges. I'm unaware that Aunt Nancy is leading me to sit beside my mother, who is rubbing my hands. I have lost my voice and my balance.

It is that feeling of lying awake at night and trying to contemplate eternity. You try to remember your existence before being born, or imagine what it will be like after you die, and the feeling is so vast and dizzying; it overwhelms. It may be called disbelief, but I think it is in fact a belief so true we cannot absorb it. Hence, we call it denial.

But I know this truth: Mrs. Stanard was not meant for this world. She was too good for it.

"How did she die?" I ask Ma. She was young. Only just thirty, I think.

"She was not well, Edgar. You know how she has declined these last few months."

No one here will say what killed Jane Stanard, but I will not deceive you. Come, Mr. Poe. I will show you.

The Stanard Residence

That night, I sneak out of my quiet house and into the Stanards' quietly bustling house, where I grab Rob and crush him to my chest. We sob, convulsing in each other's arms. Sons—one grieving the woman who conceived his being and the other grieving the woman who conceived his *to be*.

To be. As long as Helen was alive, she was my Lady Fortune, my destiny. She saw who I was, apart from the Allans' charity. Helen was my Voice.

"My Ma—my mother, she—she—she's upstairs," Rob gasps.

We plod up the steps but find ourselves held off at the landing.

"Laws," a wide-eyed black man declares in a hushed tone. "You ain't going up there. No, sirs. No childrens ought to see that. Master Robbie, your momma done gone to glory. She in the arms of Jesus, with them angels. Miss Jane done gone to glory, but it ain't no pretty sight here. No, sirs."

When Mrs. Stanard's body is taken down, it is shrouded, like a sheeted deity.

I told you I would be truthful with you, Reader. I admit, it did not happen this way. Beauty is not always the truth, but beauty is of a higher existence. The truth is that I did not see Rob until some weeks later, and I was never in the house while the corpse was in it. But this is what I saw when I blacked out, while Ma and Aunt Nancy comforted me with sips of brandy on the sitting room sofa.

My soul traveled to the house on 9th Street, and I

saw Mrs. Stanard laid out on a bed in a white gown, like the one I'd first seen her in. I tried not to look at the dark slashes across her wrists, but they were her only glaring blemish. Her mouth opened in a silent wail.

"It is only your imagination," you say. You may be right, but it is more powerful than ever. The Voice—the To Be—is back, to fill the void Helen leaves. Only it is not telling tales this time. It is showing me images, scenes, playing back conversation. And I am helpless to turn away or close my eyes because it is *in my head.*

Try as he might, Mr. Poe, one cannot close his eyes and ears to the story inside him.

New Burying Ground
Shockoe Hill
Hospital & 4th Streets

I do not remember a funeral or a wake, and as far as I know her body was never displayed for viewing. Not for the public. But folks talk about it. Whispers you hear but cannot fathom. They need to talk about it, to unravel it for themselves, but they don't want the children to hear or the servants to know. So they murmur behind their hands and in private parlors, busy streets, thinking we cannot perceive them. This is how the upper castes of the city sort out an untimely death—a tragedy amongst their own.

And I should know about whispers. There have been those about me and my family, as much as there is now about Mrs. Stanard.

She is laid to rest in the new cemetery on Shockoe Hill, and this is where I devote my vigil. There is no stone for her yet, but I spend my nights, as late as I dare, sitting by the recently dug earth, conjuring romantic images of this site centuries later.

> *There the reedy grass doth wave*
> *Over the old forgotten grave—*

Well, I mean to say, I would have liked to spend nights on Helen's grave, but I am afraid of the dark. Remember my twilight ride with Cousin Edward past the churchyard? Although older, I am still afraid of the graves' occupants. My most fearsome nightmares feature ghosts and cemeteries. And as much as I miss Jane Stanard, the thought of her coming back from the dead to visit me is grossly unappealing.

But I envision myself, decades from now—an older, tortured poet—spending nights in the Shockoe Burying Ground, having never loved another woman as purely as I loved this one. The Voice, which I now call "To Be," suggests I slash my throat to spill my blood into the ground that covers her. Helen and I will turn to dirt, decomposing together to compose this little plot of earth.

I foresee being found by my unbelieving parents. Ma and Aunt Nancy hold each other, in agony and wailing. John Allan laments over how wrong he was about me—how sorry to be so unloving towards me. I see my schoolmates and headmaster mourning the most clever and attractive schoolboy in Richmond, now a famous poet.

No, now a *famous* dead poet. (The dead poets are *for aye* more famous.)

I should confess that I would never—even in the bleak future—be so bold as to mortally wound myself, no matter how romantic the notion. I am more of a Romeo and poison my would-be weapon of choice. The To Be should know this, and you, my dear Reader, should know this too.

I visit the cemetery if I happen by during the day. But it is in my room after school that I entertain myself at the gravesite: I feel the dirt, I see my tears and blood turning it to mud, and I know this clay will sprout literature, nourished by my grief.

By care of To Be, I see what happens to that fine body below me. I am shown the soft masses of hair that go brittle. The hands that touched me with such tenderness—served me food, held my poems, fed the birds— now food for the worm. That image dreadfully contradicts the Helen I knew—the lovely, doting woman whose affections I will never again feel.

And when the To Be speaks, it calls me Poe:

This is death's kindness, Mr. Poe. Helen will never grow old. Her tears will be replaced by ours. That is our sacrifice for her immortality. We must be happy for her.

But I am devastated for me. I feel like my heart is broken and pieces of it sunk into the ground with her. Helen was more than her body. She was a soul that touched mine, in ways her body could not. She was the foster mother of my heart, my dreams.

And Death has taken that mother away from me. Once more, I am abandoned, rejected by the dead.

That is not to say we cannot take our revenge, Mr. Poe. We can make Helen to live again.

How? I dare to ask, imagining a grotesque Dr. Frankenstein resurrection.

With the pen.

Indeed, I can defeat Death with paper and ink. And the result is neither as unsightly nor ungodly as Shelley's monster, and certainly not as perilous. It is scriptural. It is lovely. This is my power, my science, my art.

And so we write. *I write.* First in my head, where I listen to the Voice. And then, when I come home after dark, by my candle, where I make the thoughts into words and the words into verses, with rhythm and flowing and feeling . . . and life.

And Helen lives.

Chapter Seven
1825

"He has had little else to do for me; he does nothing
& seems quite miserable, sulky & ill-tempered to all
the Family. How we have acted to produce this is
beyond my conception—why I have put up so long
with his conduct is little less wonderful. The boy possesses not a Spark of affection for us, not a particle of
gratitude for all my care and kindness towards him."
—John Allan

William Burke's Seminary for Boys
Marshall & 10th Streets
Richmond

"Which Eddie Allan are you?" asks a boy with a sneer in
the schoolyard.

I stand from buckling my books. "Edgar. Edgar Poe."

"Oh, you're the Eddie Poe Allan."

"No, Edgar Allan Poe. . ." I know he knows my
name. He's the son of one of Richmond's elite, and I hear
he's been insulting me behind my back, calling me a
charity case.

"Not the Eddie Collier Allan then," he says, upper
lip curled in cruel amusement.

"Collier? Who's that?"

"John Allan's son."

"I *am* John Allan's son," I say, jutting out my chin in

a subconscious mimicry of Allan.

"No, you're the playactors' son. Edward Collier is Allan's bastard son."

I try to keep calm on the surface. "You must be mistaken."

"No, he goes to school here in Richmond. Allan pays his tuition. Mrs. Allan is barren, which is why she keeps you."

I glance at the schoolhouse and see Master Burke in the doorway, rapping his cane in his palm. I will figure out a more subtle way to humiliate this pompous ass than cuffing him here in the open. After all, it is not the first time I'm hearing such talk. Allan's got at least one illegitimate child out there, probably more, but this is the first I'm hearing a name.

A bastard would mean a mistress. And a mistress means my mother is not the sole recipient of John Allan's affection, as she ought to be. She and I do not talk about it, but I suspect she knows. Her health has so declined that she takes meals in her room, while John Allan, Aunt Nancy, and I dine at the table in awkward formality.

The Allan Residence

Moldavia

5th & Main Streets

My foster father's finances have more than recovered since a wealthy uncle died, leaving much of his vast fortune to his nephew. When the will is executed, Allan purchases Moldavia, a brick mansion with a two-story portico and grand ballroom. Here, we have more rooms and more servants, thus more parties and more reasons to be gossiped about.

Distractions are an advantage after the loss of Mrs. Stanard. At the new residence, I possess a magnificent view of the countryside and the river from my bedroom. A swing on the upstairs porch is where I like to sit with a book—but only if John Allan isn't in his room, from which he can oversee me.

With the inheritance, my foster parents purchase new furniture, wallpapers, draperies, and pieces of art. To my delight, a library is established; some books are given especially to me, and these I keep in my room. A telescope is another fantastic plaything that comes with the house, and stargazing is a regular hobby for me at Moldavia.

When we first move, I oft invite my friends over to take advantage of the space and good things to eat. But later, I reckon I'd rather go to the other boys' houses, like Jack's, where Mrs. Mackenzie dotes on me, or Eben's, where we sneak out the upstairs window without his mother knowing.

The Royster Residence
2nd & Main Streets

I already mentioned the scenic view from my room, but from Moldavia I can also see into the Royster residence across the street. The Royster family includes a daughter near my age, Sarah Elmira—another reason I am fond of the telescope.

From her staircase landing, Myra (my own term of

endearment for her) can see my bedroom window, and we establish a way of communicating with white handkerchiefs after dark. Before bedtime, we wave the kerchiefs in the windows to say goodnight.

Myra is a sweet and bonny girl with thick dark hair and big blue eyes. We spend hours together in her parlor or the rose-wreathed courtyard I call the Garden Enchanted, which is across from the Ellises'. She is accomplished at the pianoforte, and I either sing or accompany her on my flute.

One day, while she plunks out a tune on the piano, I sketch her likeness into my writing tablet. When the song ends, I tear out the page. "For you."

"Oh, Edgar! Who's she?" Myra asks with a lazy Virginia lilt.

"Why, it's you!"

"Me?" she squeals.

I want to kiss her dimples. Myra is somehow capable of revealing her dimples and her amusement without actually smiling. She is the Queen of Smirk, and I adore her wry humor.

"Don't you like it?" I ask.

"I do. And I like you too."

I know she likes other boys. And I like other girls, flirting being a favorite pastime, more so than swimming. But girl-next-door Myra is my constant sweetheart, and as time passes, we see more of one another exclusively. Even John Allan approves of the match.

Richmond Slave Market
Shockoe Bottom

Having been summoned to Ellis & Allan to perform an errand for Pa, I invite Myra to walk with me. As we leave the offices, mission accomplished, I turn to the right, towards home, expecting Myra to do the same, but she has stopped to stare across the intersection of Main and 15th.

"Do you know they sell the slaves here?" she asks, no dimple in sight. "On days when the red flags hang." Sure enough, I glimpse a red flag floating along the facade of a shop, with what looks like printed papers pinned to it.

"Those are hotels mostly. . ." I trail off, understanding as I say it that the slave traders would need somewhere to stay. Her face is highlights and shadows, displaying both curiosity and repulsion.

"Do you ever think about it, Edgar? That it's wrong?"

In all honesty, I *didn't* think about it at all. But her question causes an unpleasant roiling in my stomach. "I would run away," I say, as though I could ever be bought and sold at auction.

"Sometimes they do." Myra guts me with a pointed look. Even if we are not permitted to go there, all Richmond schoolchildren know about the Devil's Half Acre, the jail for slaves, where runaways are harshly punished, and the nearby gallows, where slaves are hanged for stealing, murder, or rebellion. "They have no means of survival, Edgar. No food. No money."

"Still, I'd rather die than be owned."

I hear the To Be make a noise of derision that sounds quite like John Allan.

The Enchanted Garden
2nd & Franklin Streets on Linden Square

"Sarah Elmira Royster, may I have your hand in marriage?" I ask her, on bended knee, in the Garden Enchanted.

"I thank you for the offer, sir, but I must decline." Her eyes dance, her dimple deepens.

"Perhaps I have not made clear my affection for you." She extends her hand, which I kiss.

"Miss Royster?" I look up and see her trying not to giggle.

"Yes?"

"Marry me."

She pretends to dither, tilting her head to the side. Finally, she nods. "I would like to marry you very much, Mr. Poe." This is the third time I've asked today, but the first time she's accepted. Myra does not want to be branded "fast" in our prim Southern town.

I stand and spin her in my arms. The roses and myrtle are silent witnesses to our impulsive promises, and we never tell of our engagement.

Nonetheless, we are deemed a genuine match among the townsfolk. Myra's father seeks my foster father for a word about my prospects. It is all well and good to play in the parlor with his daughter, but if the match is to be taken seriously, he must know my situation. I am the son of dead actors, but I am also living under the roof of the most prosperous man in Richmond.

I do not know what is said between them, but I can suspect that John Allan did not exactly commit to making me an heir of his newfound wealth. Since this is what matters most to James Royster, Allan's withholding my fortune shatters any chance I may have had with his daughter. That and the fact that I am not Presbyterian.

At the time, however, I am happily unaware and blissfully in love. Not even the To Be is emphatic enough to forewarn me of the impending heartbreak.

She is not our Helen, Mr. Poe. These young, living ladies have expectations and caprices ... and fathers.

Capitol Square

At fifteen, I am made a lieutenant in the Richmond Junior Volunteers, along with some of my school fellows. We wear real uniforms with trimmings and bear real weapons, mine being a saber. This display not only fortifies my selfhood, but fetches the collective attention— dare I say, admiration—of the fairer sex.

When the Marquis de Lafayette, hero of the Revolutionary War, makes a tour of the States, our city is one of his destinations. The Junior Volunteers are charged with the duty to escort and guard the French lieutenant general during his processions.

"General, may I present to you Lieutenant Edgar Poe."

I salute the marquis, who, although no longer the young man who fought with George Washington, impresses me all the same.

"Ah, Poe. I once knew a General David Poe." The old war hero's English is musically accented.

"General Poe is my late grandfather, sir." My father's father was a Revolutionary hero himself, well known in Maryland as General Poe, although he wasn't a general except by name.

"A great friend and a great patriot. I am sorry for this country to lose such a man, but I see his grandson will follow in his footsteps."

"Merci beaucoup, monsieur."

I recently received a nagging letter from my brother, Henry, who lives in my grandfather's house in Baltimore. My grandmother is still alive and persisting on a pension from the state, thanks to my grandfather's service in the war.

Henry is seventeen, but I do not remember him from early childhood. He was gone from my life before my mother died. My parents, fallen on hard times, left him with my father's family during a stint in Baltimore. Nowadays, my brother and I keep regular correspondence, although we will not meet again until the following year.

Henry received a letter from John Allan complaining of my sulky and spiteful behavior. I am ungrateful, he told Henry, for all that's been given to me—particularly the grand home and education, for which he paid. He said I show no affection for my foster parents and that I am idle.

Henry wrote me, asking why I behave so towards the people who took me in. He also asks why John Allan said that Rosalie is "half your sister."

Because, dear brother, John Allan has nothing but contempt for your parents—the strrolll-errrs—and this is one more way he can injure an already-dead woman: by accusing her of infidelity and inciting an argument among her surviving children.

How dare he so casually inflame such a scandal!

The man fathers bastards and emotionally abandons his wife and has the gall to make that kind of claim against your mother. It is he who is spiteful and ill-tempered!

Henry, however, did not have to tell me the contents of this letter. John Allan kindly left a copy where I would see it.

For our moral instruction, I am sure, Mr. Poe.

How very pious, Pa.
It is a very pious letter too.

Had I done my duty as faithfully to my God as I

ought to Edgar, then had Death, come when he will[,] have no terrors for me, but I must end this with a devout wish that God may yet bless him and you and that success may crown all your endeavors and between you, your poor Sister Rosalie may not suffer.

If only Death would do us this favor.

I will take this time to tell you, with heavy heart, that all is not well with Rosalie. She is feeble-minded and vacuous, having not mentally progressed past the age of a young child. But do not believe that I ever neglected dear, wretched Rose. Yes, I am grieving Mrs. Stanard, and I may seem more distant to my folks and friends for all that. But any sullenness and bad temper is because of John Allan!

He, who would have left us in Scotland with nary a regret if you hadn't raised the dickens about it. Idle? When we work in his warehouse and as a clerk in his shop?

"Rely on [God]," John Allan wrote Henry, "my Brave and excellent Boy[,] who is ready to save to the uttermost."

It is high time that his hypocrisy and wrongdoing is brought to light, Mr. Poe.

Ma will not like it, but it is for her also that I do so. For my two mothers, for he mistreats both.

I remember one morning when I was young, Ma came to breakfast with a blackened eye. At the time, I did not think much of it; after one of our recent friendly scuffles, Eben's eye had turned quite the same shade. It wasn't until I was older that I questioned it, knowing then that girls generally, and ladies especially, did not fight with fists.

But Allan cannot hurt me. He is lame, and he walks with a cane. The worst he can do is turn me out on my ear, which has been the threat for too many years.

You are sixteen years old. We can take care of ourselves now.

But I do not think he will throw me out. Because appearances matter. And how would it appear to turn out a lad of sixteen? A lad he himself raised from a wee bairn. Furthermore, the brightest, most accomplished lad in all of Richmond?

Chapter Eight
1825

"I have the greatest respect for his memory. He was very generous. . . . He had strong prejudices. Hated anything coarse and unrefined. Never spoke of his parents. He was kind to his sister as far as in his power. He was as warm and zealous in any cause he was interested in, very enthusiastic and impulsive. . . ."
—Elmira Shelton

The Royster Residence
Richmond

Soon after these stinging letters, my brother comes to stay at Moldavia for a spell, while his naval ship is docked in Richmond's wharf. This is only our second visit, but we get along splendidly. I introduce him to Myra, and she is impressed by his smart sailor uniform.

"The Brothers Poe," she drawls, opening her door to us.

"At your service, Miss Royster." Henry bows. He is slender and pale, just taller than me.

Myra invites us to stay for tea, and her mother allows her to serve it in the parlor. She makes chitchat while she pours, asking Henry about his travels with the navy.

"Hattie Mills says that sailors go months without seeing a female, and, as such, turn to buggery."

"Elmira!" I spit, sending biscuit crumbs across the

parlor. "You forget yourself."

With a mischievous grin, she hands me a napkin.

Thankfully, Henry is not one to be taken aback. "I couldn't say, Miss Royster. My captain would hang us up by our toes if anything improper transpired below decks. When our vessel makes port, the crew seeks romance on land. Whether it's proper or not, I'll leave to your judgement." He winks at her. "Now the marines may be another story."

"Hattie Mills is a vulgar girl," I say. "I'm shocked you would keep company with someone so unladylike. I can see she is a bad influence on you."

Myra has the decency to look ashamed, but then she smirks, teacup at her lips. "Well, Edgar, I keep company with you, don't I?"

Moldavia

"Sarah Elmira is a right spunky one, isn't she?" Henry chuckles, nudging me with an elbow.

"She never ceases to scandalize me."

"Aw, you ask for it, Eddie. You place her on a pedestal, I reckon the first thing she's sure to do is leap off of it."

Speaking of scandal, foremost on our minds to-night is John Allan's claim that our sister was born on the wrong side of the blanket. Henry is furious at the accusation, but I feel it's because he believes it. When Rosalie calls in on us, we coddle her. She is a big girl of fifteen, but she sits in Henry's lap. I wonder when was the last time we were all three together, if ever.

"We always must look out for her," Henry says when

she is gone home. He leans on the porch rail, trying to smoke a pipe, though a shallow cough nags him.

I fetch a great sigh. "Thank God the Mackenzies got her." I cringe at the thought of Rosalie in an orphan asylum . . . or taken in by the Allans.

"She looks well cared for. They don't mistreat her?"

"Oh, no. It's a good home. I wish the Mackenizies had taken me in."

"But what happens when she outlives Mr. and Mrs. Mackenzie? I do not think she can look out for herself. Something's not right—"

"Provisions will be made for her care. The Mackenzie siblings would make sure of it. If not, then yes, we would take her in." I lower my voice. "Henry, you don't think she's our half-sister, do you? Our father was with our mother at the time Rose was conceived. He left after."

He offers me the pipe. "Right, but did you ever wonder why?"

"Because he died in Norfolk," I say, cringing and blowing smoke.

Henry nods, eyes dark. "He died. But that was after—" Overtaken by a coughing fit, he is unable to finish.

"Master Eddie!" a negro woman calls from the window. "Supper's being served!"

I acknowledge her and give Henry back his pipe, inwardly bracing myself. The hostility between John Allan and myself is the worst it's ever been, and the mood at the dinner table is certain to be tense.

Allow me to stop for a moment, dear Reader, and put forth here in plain words—with mature reasoning and a perspective gleaned from the afterlife—what is happening at this point in my story.

You saw how John Allan indulged me as a child. I do believe he possessed a fondness for me as a boy; he was charmed by my precocity and, I think, amused by my naughtiness. After all, he had been a laddie once upon a time too.

He was my Pa, whom I worshiped and feared, and on whom I depended.

I remember the day I got caught at nursery school stealing vegetables out of the garden. I was four or five years old. When I came home wearing said radish around my neck, as the teacher required for all to know my crime, John Allan was furious. Not with me, mind you, but with that teacher. And he marched straightaway to the school to un-enroll his foster son, but not before giving that woman a piece of his dogmatic Scotch mind.

But by the time we come to my adolescence, our relationship is no longer father and son, but man and *almost*-man. And yet, we are two very different creatures. Adolescence brings with it its own natural conflicts and vexations—new sensitivities and insecurities and melancholies. And perhaps it is safe to say, as an orphan, I had an extra dose of what the normal young man can expect at this age. Add to that the discord at home. Add to that John Allan's affairs.

You guessed it, dear Reader: this is a prescription for disaster.

As I come of age, I discern more about this man who

raised me. I know he would have been less bothered had I stayed with his relatives in Scotland. (God bless Frances Allan and Nancy Valentine for coming to my rescue. Aunt Mary may add her own prayers of thanks here.) It would have saved him a lot of headache if I'd stayed in the Auld Country.

I know now that he is unfaithful to Ma, that he has illegitimate children, that he sends money to provide for those children, and that he continues to engage in extramarital affairs. I know he doesn't like that I know this, and he especially doesn't like that I refuse to keep quiet about it.

I know that I am not his son. Perhaps once, realizing that Mrs. Allan would not bear him any children, he thought of me as his heir. But once I choose to confront him, that is no longer the sentiment. To call him out for infidelity is to be ungrateful.

I can no longer pay homage to this man, and that is what he cannot tolerate. He did not ask for a foster son. It was Frances who deigned to take in a dead actress's precocious little boy. But her husband did what was right in the sight of God and the neighbors. He fed me, gave me a home, gave me learning, and gave me a place in society. How dare I disrespect him. How dare I take up a fight that is not mine.

Quite right, I did.

Stay close, Reader, for the confrontation is nigh.

Chapter Nine
1825

⁓ ✄ ⁓

"His natural and predominant passion seemed to me, to be an enthusiastic ardor in everything he undertook; in his difference of opinion with his fellow students, he was very tenacious, and would not yield till his judgment was convinced. As a scholar, he was ambitious to excel, and tho' not conspicuously studious always acquitted himself well in his classes."
—Joseph Clarke

Ellis & Allan Company
14th & Cary Streets
Richmond

"Come in, Edgar. Tot of whiskey?"

"No, thank you, sir."

John Allan is seated at his desk, surrounded by books and ledgers. This office at Ellis & Allan is smoky and cramped, especially with him in it. His face looks tired, but his eyes are keen, accented by spectacles that slip down his nose when he looks up from his papers.

I come before him dressed impeccably in waistcoat, jacket, and cravat.

"I can water it down for you, Ned. Nay? Well, what is it?"

I want out of his household is what, but I must apply diplomacy here as I still require his support. I sit, ramrod straight, across from his desk in a creaky Hitchcock chair. "I would like to discuss my education."

"Is it? Something wrong with Master Burke's?"

"No, sir. But in the past, you have spoken of sending me to college."

He takes a swallow of spirits, and his lips pucker then smack. "And you want me to *pay* for you to go to college?"

"Well, sir, I always thought it was your intention."

He considers this. "I do not know if you're fully prepared for university. We would have to see about hiring a tutor first. That, too, costs money."

"Yes, sir." I am prepared for this rambling on how much I cost. I endure it frequently.

"It wouldn't be sensible to pay school tuition *and* tutoring charges. We would have to take you out of Master Burke's for private instruction, in preparation for college. There would be books to purchase, not to mention the tutor. Then we would need to plan for your going away. Tuition, more books, living expenses, room and board. . ."

Ask him if he'd prefer to bend over so you can kiss his—

"Yes, sir."

"This is more than any young man in your position has a right to expect."

He means to say that this is more than any *orphan* should expect. But I can hardly say that for him.

"The College of William & Mary—" I halt. He rattles a drawer open, pulls out some folded papers, and the suggestion falls silent from my lips.

"Mrs. Allan and I have fed you, clothed you, and educated you for thirteen years, Edgar. Although William & Mary would be pleased to accept you, on our behalf"—he unfurls the papers and pushes one page across the desk, a meaty finger pointing to a section of text—"my uncle specified in his will that some of his estate be set aside for your education at the University of Virginia. Uncle William was sympathetic to those such as yourself."

I suppose that is so, since John Allan himself was an orphan, and he was given the whole of William Galt's inheritance.

"The University of Virginia," I repeat, nodding. If I had my choice, I would go north to Boston or New York—sophisticated cities with literary reputations. But beggars should be no choosers, my foster father might say if I should ask.

"And what do you intend to do with a college education, hm? If I'm to pay for it, I want to know it will not go to waste."

"I want to study the arts, language—"

"The arts." He steeples his fingers and pulls a face of disgust.

"Yes, sir. Modern and ancient languages."

"I hope you do not imagine yourself a man of letters or anything so absurd."

Because that would be a waste of money? My composure begins to fracture. "I fail to see how my continued education could be a misuse of Uncle William's fortune."

"That is not for you to see. It is my duty to see my

uncle's inheritance spent wisely, doing the most good. There is a limit to the handouts."

"My education is a handout? Since when do you consider me a beggar? I am your foster child!"

His hand pats the air, as though to settle me down. "Aye, but—"

"You're paying for Edward Collier to go to school and who knows who else. If you are worried about your pocketbook, you might subdue your inclination to create illegitimate sons."

Allan's face turns an almost purple color and his lips draw back as though chomping an invisible bit. He stands up like he's about to lunge at me, but he sways and falls back in his chair, which, I think, is fortunate for me. Thank God for the Scotsman's devotion to whiskey.

"You forget yourself, young man. Who do you think you're speaking to in this impertinent manner?"

Oh, stop it, I tell myself. Scrape and bow and do what you must to survive. Yet To Be urges me on, supplying words for my ire.

"I think I am speaking to my mother's husband, the man who raised me to be a gentleman. If I am to be so, I must be educated. You have the means. So let me go. Let me study and see what I can make of myself. It's more than I can be here, that is for certain."

John Allan coughs a bitter laugh. He stands again and staggers to the window, which looks out on Cary Street. Hands clasped behind his back, he frowns, peering down the street towards the canal, where the whores perform their unspeakable business.

"You think you're so blameless. Young man, you

have not yet known temptation. You've no need to be tempted, having not faced poverty and ruin. And that is thanks to my protection and provision. But I am looking at a lad, who thinks himself righteous, but who has no idea what the world is like outside of the life I have given him."

He turns away from the window, bitterness turning to conceit.

"Well, go and see for yourself then. I will arrange it. But you"—he chills me with a dark grin—"must tell your mother."

PART TWO:

The Student

Chapter Ten
1826

⁓ ᏻ ᏹ ⁓

". . . A lad of uncommon good appearance who attracted attention wherever he went, his manners were
cheerful and gay. . . . Although reserved at times,
nothing of a morose character was observed in him,
until after his return from college." —James Galt

Moldavia
Richmond

Allan didn't turn me out on my ear. Although regret was
expressed for not having done so, the rich dead uncle has,
in so dying rich, provided a neat way of getting rid of me.
I will be sent to Thomas Jefferson's new university.

Charlottesville is seventy-some miles away, a good
enough distance for John Allan. And since the old
uncle's will mentioned it, he thinks it's "no such a bad
idea" after all. If I am not destined for Ellis & Allan, at
least I can make a decent living as a lawyer. Why, perhaps the old founding father, Thomas Jefferson himself,
will recommend me to hold office.

*Then John Allan might claim
you—his ward, the congressman.*

"These women have coddled you long enough," he
says. "They're turning you into a good-for-nothing fop.

Time's come to go your own way, Edgar."

My Ma is shattered. It grieves me to see her like this. Yet, I must leave John Allan's house, and a university degree is an opportunity I cannot forgo.

After Henry's visit, I tease Ma with talk of joining the navy. I'm quite taken with the notions of seafaring—a ship and uncharted territory sound like the best sort of adventure for a sixteen-year-old schoolboy.

"Don't be irrational, son," she says. "I cannot bear the thought of you on some savage island. I want you here, where I can see you." Our conversation is polite and calm, but her breathing is shallow and quick, her voice raspy and low.

"I only wish I could earn my own living. Then I wouldn't have to depend on him. I could make enough to send you money to live on too. Then you could leave him."

"Hush, Edgar. You know very well I cannot leave him. What would people say? Where would I go? I would be shunned. And my sister? What about Nan? This is our home. We are comfortable here." She pauses to catch her breath.

"You tolerate too much, Ma."

"Oh, I do not. He is the one who suffers, knowing what he's done."

"He's an opinionated, domineering oaf, who ought to do us all a favor and drop dead."

"Edgar Allan, don't say such a thing!" Her scolding

is half-hearted, though; she is trying not to laugh.

He called our mother a moll.

I repeat what the To Be said, with a bit more tact, and her mirth fades.

"Listen to me, Edgar. That 'oaf' does not know what he's talking about. He is only trying to rankle you. Your mother was a lovely woman. Moral and God-fearing. And, oh, so talented. Like you. You are too good for swabbing decks, my darling."

I duck my head and smile. "So I am going to the university."

Ma lifts my chin in her palm. "How I rue the day."

And when the day comes, Ma insists on going with me to get me settled. But not before saying farewell to John Allan.

"Goodbye, sir."

"Goodbye, Ned. Don't look so miserable. Many a man would trade his mother for a chance to go to university."

My shoulders tense, but I see Ma subtly shake her head at me.

"I am grateful, sir," I mumble. Despite all the conflict between us, I still want to make this man proud.

"I am sure you are," he says, handing me an envelope, which I assume is holding enough money for my tuition, room and board, and supplies. "I want you to do your very best. Work hard. Behave yourself. I know you will. Remember that you represent Mrs. Allan and myself."

"Yes, sir. Thank you."

It's not the affectionate parting one would hope for, but he shakes my hand and pats my shoulder. "Good chap. We will have you back at Moldavia for Christmas."

Three Notch'd Road
Richmond to Charlottesville

Jim, the old black coachman, drives us in one of the new carriages. My Ma looks like her pet rabbit died. I jest and make up silly stories for her sake, but she is overcome by her memories.

"I know you probably won't remember, but I cannot keep from thinking of the day I brought you home with me. You were at the old Washington Tavern, where the innkeeper was looking after you. I hired a hack that day and wrapped you in a blanket and held you on my lap. You were so funny and sweet to me. You loved that horse and wanted me to love it too. You kept pointing and saying, 'Is it a horse, miss?' You took my face in your little hands to make me look. 'Yes, horse. That's right, sweetheart. Clip-clop, clip-clop.' I had to hold tightly to you, otherwise you were going up on the box with the driver, to do what, I don't know. Take the reins probably. Now look at us. You, a young man on his way to university."

Her voice is so faint, I strain to hear it. How do I say *au revoir* to this dear woman? What will I do without her? This feels like I'm moving to the Western settlements without any provisions. As frail as she is, she was my protection in a world so cruel to orphans.

Oh, here I am, thinking only of myself. *What will I do without her?* You must think me awfully self-centered, dear Reader. Well, I am at this age. I do not consider her feelings at all. Yet I am the one going away, and I am leaving her with that adulterous man. Except for the steadfast company of her sister and the ever-present society of the servants, she is alone, returning to a home in which she is resented and left to suffer, with an illness that wears on and on, with no sign of getting better.

The University of Virginia
Charlottesville

When we arrive at the university, we find my lodgings, and Jim helps me with my trunk.

My room, half the size of mine at home, is shared with one Miles George, who is two years older than me. There are two beds, two desks, a table with washbasin and ewer, and a fireplace. I stack my books on one side of the windowsill, and Ma makes up my bed with a quilt Judith and Aunt Nancy sewed. Jim finds flint and tinder, and makes a fire.

It is quite like a cell, cold and sparse.

Ma and Jim prepare to leave the next day.

"Will you please deliver this to Miss Royster." I hand the coachman an envelope, inside of which is a letter and a mother-of-pearl purse I bought with the pocket money Ma and Aunt Nancy gave me. The silver plate on the purse is engraved "E. A. P." and "S. P. R." for Sara Elmira Royster—the jeweler engraved a "p" instead of an "e," but there wasn't time to correct it.

"She won't mind the slip," Ma assures me, climbing into the carriage.

It is St. Valentine's Day, 1826, and I look on as Frances Keeling *Valentine* Allan, the greatest patron of my young life, is carried away from me, back to her loveless married home life, and I go back to my cell.

Chapter Eleven
1826

"He was very excitable & restless, at times wayward, melancholic & morose, but again—in his better moods frolicksome, full of fun & a most attractive & agreeable companion." —Miles George

The University of Virginia
Charlottesville

The "Oxford of the New World" is not the paragon of sophistication and culture it will one day strive to be. Most buildings are still under construction, including the grand Rotunda, where Mr. Jefferson's collected books will be housed. In the meantime, scaffolds are assembled, pillars erected, and trees planted.

Flanking a long park, called "the Lawn," colonnades house students in small rooms. At five-thirty each morning, the faculty secretary knocks on our doors to ensure we are up and dressed for class. I take breakfast and, by seven, attend lectures in the Pavilions: the modern languages of French, Spanish, and Italian, and the ancient Latin and Greek. Once a week, the colored women come 'round to do the washing—that is, if you can pay the fee.

But for all its busyness, the university, in its first year, exhibits a wildness. Our presidential founder instituted a democratic government for his "Academical

Village," in which its students manage themselves.

Only they do not, Mr. Poe.

I suppose for young men, so soon away from parental and academical authority, self-government is not likely to produce *self-control*. The younger well-to-do gentlemen readily adopt the recreational follies of their forefathers: namely shooting, drinking, and playing cards.

There are incredible fights here, even duels with pistols.

In fact, I start out my door one day to witness a brawl, in which one Wickliffe from Kentucky takes hold of another student and bites him. Not just one bite, mind you, but multiple attacks, tearing the skin from elbow to shoulder. On seeing the mangled arm afterwards, I think it looks like a rabid fox got it.

Another conflict lasts for days. When one student is hit in the head with a rock, he draws his pistol. Fortunately, the weapon misfires, but soon after, factions form, each student taking a side. I cannot go to classes or the dining hall without finding raucous arguments and posted threats amid the colonnades. It is the same unrest I imagine in the frontier territories, with feuds between settlers and Indians.

Gambling and drunkenness are also widespread. Peach and honey, or "honey-peach," is the drink of the day in Charlottesville. What can I say? It is a small town, and there is not much to occupy a young man.

When the faculty cannot stand the riot anymore and threaten resignation, the local sheriff is called. He and his deputies invade the college with a list of suspects and witnesses for the Albemarle County court grand jury hearing. Much of the student body flees to the surrounding woods, even those not on the list—

Because no one likes a tell-tale.

For two or three days, the slaves run back and forth from town to the student encampment, supplying food and provisions. And if the faculty thought it was wild on the Lawn, it cannot compare to the carousal in the hills around Charlottesville.

Eventually the worst of the offenders are caught and punished, and the unruliness dwindles.

Even I am not immune to violence, being in close quarters with an obstinate roommate. I haven't had to share a room since boarding school, and I find my patience growing thin.

"Miles, it was your turn to empty the ash bucket." I am on my hands and knees before the hearth. It needs rekindling, but I cannot build a proper fire because I cannot shovel out the ashes when the bucket is full.

"It's not my turn," he says from his bed, a forearm covering his head. "Yours."

"No, it is not. It's your turn. I've done it the last two times. And I seem to build all the fires too." I say this while furiously sweeping debris from the grate.

"Not my turn," he drones again. The way he slurs makes me realize he's been at the peaches and honey, or some other kind of toddy.

"Well, do me a favor and empty it, will you, so I can clean this fireplace. Do you want a fire this evening or not? Miles, get up!"

He groans. "I thought I'd left my mother at home."

I stand up and throw down the broom and shovel. "I am not your mother! And she's not here either, so you're going to have to do something for yourself."

"Or what?"

"Or I make you sorry."

"I'd like to see you try!"

"Fine!"

"On the Lawn then."

"After you," I say with mock gentility.

Neither of us "wins" this fight because I don't think Miles is in a fair state and I do not want to hurt him over fireplace ashes. But I cuff him before he can throw the first blow, and we tussle in the grass until dusty and sapped. Eventually we shake hands, back on friendly terms.

Although he acknowledges the fight, Miles will later refute the fact that we roomed together. I do not hold that against him. I can only be responsible for telling the truth as best I remember, and my roommate may have been too drunk to recall. (Do not tell him I said so.)

Be that as it may, I soon request a private room and move to No. 13, West Range, in the pavilion that stands by the name of "Rowdy Row."

Chapter Twelve
1826

—❧ ❧—

"Poe, as has been said, was fond of quoting poetic authors and reading poetic productions of his own, with which his friends were delighted & entertained, then suddenly a change would come over him & he would with a piece of charcoal evince his versatile genius by sketching upon the walls of his dormitory, whimsical, fanciful, & grotesque figures, with so much artistic skill, as to leave us in doubt whether Poe in future life would be Painter or Poet. . . ." —Miles George

"I call God to witness that I have never loved dissipation. . . ." —Edgar

No. 13
West Lawn ("Rowdy Row")
The University of Virginia
Charlottesville

University folk know me as the ward of John Allan, heir to the renowned Galt fortune. Nevertheless, here I feel like the orphan that I am.

The other students want for nothing. Furthermore, they come with horses, hunting dogs, and guns—"pistols are all the fashion here," I write in a letter home—and even slaves to do their bidding. I do not possess any of the aforementioned, which I can do without, but I discover that I do not have enough money to cover tuition, much less the other required necessities.

Using all the money from John Allan's envelope, I am still $39 short my bill for school. But I must also pay for laundry, firewood, rent, and meals, not to mention books and ink and other supplies. I expect that my Pa knows this and will be sending more soon, but as the session carries on, I grow anxious. I write to him, requesting funds, and I do so a second time, when the need arises. He sends me the money to cover my tuition, plus one dollar.

Although I try to keep to myself, and thus avoid conflict, most nights I entertain schoolmates in my new quarters at Rowdy Row, reciting stories and poems by candlelight. The lads are fond of my comedy, and I toss in a ghost story now and then when the mood calls for it. Some of the latter include bodachs and fairies, such tales I have nurtured since my days in Scotland.

Often I illustrate the stories I narrate, using a stick of charcoal on the plaster walls. I may draw caricatures of our professors, while imitating and exaggerating their voices and gestures with funny dialogue. I also sketch landscapes with castles and lochs and the obligatory damsel and foe.

One young man named Peter Pease interrupts me in the midst of a satire, tottering for a look at my pages. "'Gaffy spoke. Gaffy hopped. Gaffy wept.' What's his name again?"

Another student speaks up. "Is it Gaffy?" Laughter rings the room.

"Ha, Poe, we get it, eh? His name is Gaffy! What will Gaffy do next?"

Peter grasps at my paper, but I snatch it back and throw it in the fire. A shocked silence and brief swell of light illumine No. 13 as the story is consumed.

"Forgive me this *gaffe*," I say, stone-faced.

"Oi, we were only teasing you," he says, the derision drained from his voice. "You said 'Gaffy' again and again."

"So I hear. If you think it's rubbish, then it's fuel for the fire. I have written stacks of drivel to keep me warm at night."

"Aw, Poe, have some grog, will you? You're too tense."

Although I regret this rashness, my mates thereafter hesitate to tease. Still, the name Gaffy follows me for years. This rollicking audience may be my nightly company, yet I feel lonely and detached.

One must be capable of accepting good-natured jests if one is to be intimate. But do not be bothered, Mr. Poe, if they do not understand the sensitive nature of the genius mind. We mustn't expect special treatment.

You ask if I indulge in drink at the university. So you have heard the rumors? I am a drunkard—that's what they say, is it not?

I do take a drink on occasion. This was the custom at home. But no, I do not partake in more than the acceptable portion at social gatherings or elsewhere. When I can, I beg off altogether, for alcohol does not agree with me.

Eben and I once guzzled rum punch at a Mackenzie party. Did I regret it! I was sick for days. One glass lets loose an effect I do not care for—an out of control and unbalanced sensation. It makes me somber rather than merry, overly excited instead of mellow. Alcohol produces a reverse effect, so when I do imbibe, it is reluctantly, and I dare not swallow more than a little.

Most evenings, when the other lads take to the bottle, I take out my paper, pen, and ink. And as I throw the last log on the fire before succumbing to bed, I think of Myra. In particular, I recall one afternoon when we made more than music in her parlor.

The Royster Residence
Richmond
{1825}

I am tired of kissing this flute. I rest it atop the piano and walk to the parlor door to survey the hall. Not a chaperone in sight. I return to the bench beside Myra, nudging closer until our thighs touch and she giggles.

My mouth to her ear, I whisper, "Keep playing, Sarah Elmira. Miss not a note." Her curls tickle my lip.

She turns her head to meet my gaze, the music never stumbling. Still carrying the tune, she closes her eyes and our lips brush. We press together, and Myra's fingers slow for a moment. But then, pushing firmly, she catches the tempo again and carries up the song while we make love. I use my teeth to capture her pouty lip and—

BONGGGGG!

—the pianoforte rumbles. We pull away, stifling laughter. Myra's mother's head pops into the parlor.

"What happened? The music was so lovely."

"I am at fault, Mrs. Royster. I clumsily stepped on Elmira's toes."

"Oh, dear. Well, keep playing. You know I love that song. The flute was lovely too, Edgar."

"Yes, ma'am," I say, and she leaves us to snicker.

"It wasn't my toes you stepped on, mister," says Myra.

Albemarle County

Virginia

I write Myra as many letters as time allows.

Why do you think she never writes back, Mr. Poe?

I worry that she entertains another chap on her piano bench.

Let us leave behind these matters of the heart. I hear the anatomy students are digging up corpses for dissection tonight. That will make a ghoulish story for a dreary eve's soirée.

When free from lectures and study, I find myself drawn to the surrounding foothills, especially when milder weather emerges. I understand why Jefferson is so fond of his hilltop Monticello. In the late spring, the landscape blooms, green and lush, and the sun beams straight from heaven to light upon these knolls and valleys. The Blue Ridge Mountains become the playground that the James River and Enchanted Garden once were, and I escape with my worries into its pastures and forests and hollows.

The seclusion is a tonic to my soul, as any dreamer will tell you. I need these afternoons away from people, who tend to vex me. I am anxious about many things: one being Ma, another being John Allan. There is still silence from Elmira. Lastly, I worry about money and, consequently, that I am making enemies in Charlottesville.

Unlike the antagonists of my boyhood, these are enemies I cannot put off with a challenge to meet behind the schoolhouse. These are the ruthless, card-playing sort, who pour liquor down your throat and shove you into the dealer's lair.

Why do I gamble? It is an easy trap to fall into, but harder to admit when you are caught. For one, everyone here is a player. (Although everyone *else* is able to pay when they lose.) For another, my foster father sent me to college without enough money to cover my expenses.

Looking back on it now, I think I want to provide for myself. It pains me to ask John Allan for provision, especially knowing that he will begrudge me for it. I also have Myra to think of; I must find a way to make enough to afford her hand in marriage. If I could only win a prize. . . .

The sad fact is, I am miserable at cards. I lose almost every time. But I win enough to think that if I keep playing, I will eventually make good. And like any other man who falls victim to gambling, I am in too deep before I see that I need to stop.

Finally, I must beg for rescue. I owe $2,000 in gambling debts, and I am behind in payments to the university.

No. 13, "Rowdy Row"

In the fall of 1826, John Allan travels to Charlottesville. I offer him the only chair in this drab chamber, and I sit on my trunk, rigid and restless. When I tried to erase the drawings from the walls before this visit, I left gray streaks, which seem to steal his attention and affect his mood.

"I am not here to give you more money, Edgar. I do not believe it to be in your best interest to pay your losses in Loo. What sort of lesson would I be teaching you? I thought we raised you better than this. Gambling is a wicked habit."

"I understand if you refuse to pay for my wrongdoing—"

"Sin."

"Yes, but the shopkeepers in town let me buy on credit, and I took out loans from the Jews—"

He picks up a stack of notes from my desk and waves the bills at me. "Like this one, you mean? This one for seventeen coats? *Seventeen* coats, Edgar!"

"I was trying to pay my debts."

"With coats? Ah, I see, because how could I protest a wardrobe bill? A lad must be clothed for school, aye?" He speaks through gritted teeth.

If Mr. Poe is going to fail at school, then he is going to look dignified doing it.

I cannot look up from the floorboards. This is serious trouble, and if he will not help me out of it. . . .

Do not let him hoist all the blame on you. You did not come here seeking the den of iniquity.

"I did not have enough money to live on, sir."

"Have you ever heard of a job, Edgar? It is work you perform for pay."

"Where was I supposed to find a job here?" I raise my voice to match his. "When did I have time to 'perform work for pay'? Do you understand that I will be unable to return to this town if you do not help me?"

He sighs and thumps his cane, glowering at the smeared walls. "Then you are finished here. At the end of the session, you will come home, and we will sort out your future."

I must not panic, I tell myself. He will change his mind. During the December holiday, I will talk him into sending me back. It's my destiny. It's in the blessed will!

Do not rely on it, Mr. Poe. You may be a talented talker, but John Allan might be the most stingy man in the New World.

"I will work for you," I say. "For as long as it takes to pay off my debt. But, please, do not make me leave dishonorably. Please help me pay these bills."

"I will pay the loans and shops, but not the card dealers. According to the law, a student's gaming debts must be renounced."

I close my eyes and let my head fall against the wall. I want to tell my foster father that he is supposed to save me, but he is already hobbling out the door.

⎯ ∽ ❧ ⎯

With the advance of warrants for my charges, I feel very much like the Prodigal Son coming home from the pig sties.

> Father, I have sinned before heaven, and before thee, and am no more worthy to be called thy son: make me as one of thy hired servants.

Only there is no forgiveness for the lost son in the Allan house—not from the father anyway.

The maddening factor in this tragedy is that he has the money. It would not hurt him to pay off my debts—$2,000 would hardly be missed.

In conclusion, it is not bad grades or bad behavior that forces me to leave the University of Virginia. It is for lack of funds. I didn't have enough to begin with, and at Mr. Jefferson's college, a modicum of wealth is necessary to make a go of it. In theory, I should have been able to afford university. But without John Allan's endorsement, I am as good as any indigent without means.

This scene will set a precedent for the rest of my life. Debt, hunger, cold. Begging. For a boy from the Allan household, which even in lean times had been lavish, this is a harsh reality. I have written as many letters as my pride will allow, asking him to pay my creditors so I can at least walk away with some dignity. When I receive no reply, I resort to entreat other relatives. No luck there either.

As the year winds down, I am obliged to break up pieces of my table to keep the fire blazing. Eventually I run out of table and other pieces of furniture to burn, and I dare not abuse my books thus. When I run out of candles, I am finished. It is a cold, dark December, and I feel all the colder for my shame.

Chapter Thirteen
1826

"But I am not about to proclaim myself guilty of all that has been alleged against me, and which I have hitherto endured, simply because I was too proud to reply. I will boldly say that it was wholly and entirely your own mistaken parsimony that caused all the difficulties in which I was involved while at Charlottesville." —Edgar

Moldavia
Richmond

The night of my return home is one of my worst. As your solicitous narrator, I must warn you that my life's story is about to turn grim. If you cannot go on with me, I understand, and I'll allow you to rest this book until a time when you can better handle it. Or, should you be so inclined, you may skip ahead to a section of this memoir in which life is slightly steadier, if not happier.

If you do decide to carry on with me, I will give you a universal truth to keep in mind:

This does not hurt me anymore. It cannot hurt me, and it cannot hurt you, dear Reader. We are both unconditionally safe in the pages of this book.

When I look at these upcoming scenes, I view them with the benefit of perspective, and even humor (a practical resource available to me in the afterlife). If my first life had gone a different way, a more comfortable way, you would not have gotten from me what you did.

Now, this may be hard to reconcile; believe me, I understand. But it was for you, dear Reader, that I suffered. Perhaps I did not know it then, but I know it now. And I want to assure you that I do not suffer still. Neither should you.

When the coach bears me home from Charlottesville, Thomas, our old manservant, dodders out to the street to help me with my trunk. I glance over at the Roysters' house, but it is quiet.

"Welcome home, Master Eddie." Thomas lifts one side of the trunk and I take the other, and we carry it up the steps to the front door.

"Thank you, Thomas. It is good to see a friendly face."

"How was the journey, sir?"

"Long and damp. Now I need a wash, as do my clothes. Thomas, what is this?" I ask, stepping over a bundle of river birch branches on the porch.

"Master Allan told Dab to cut some switches, sir."

I would laugh aloud if I did not already feel beaten. "I see. You can tell Master Allan that if he tries to whip me with those, he'll find that I hit back."

Thomas looks askance. "Master Allan is hardly fit enough to lash anyone."

Ah. John Allan does not intend to use the birch— that would take too much time and effort. The order to cut the switches was meant to degrade me. John Allan knows that his servants, some of whom raised me, feel much too devoted to the boy he took in. But he is the master here, and we would all do well to remember it.

He's given the servants permission to flog you, Mr. Poe. How humiliating.

"And you've naught to fear from the likes of us," Thomas concludes. "You go on in now, Master Eddie. I'll take care of your belongings and laundry."

"Edgar! Why, a sight for sore eyes!"

Ma and her sister do not hold back their affections for the Prodigal Son. Aunt Nancy is the first to greet me, and she prods me towards the dining room, where I find my mother and one of the kitchen girls taking out the silver.

"I'm back, Ma." I curl my shoulders to fit better in her thin embrace. Her delicate hand reaches up to cup my face. "I am sorry."

She laughs. "Whatever are you apologizing for, my darling? I want you back!"

"Well, here I am," I say with a bow and a shrug. "At your service." My smile collapses almost as soon as it comes. I wonder why she is not in bed. She looks ready to swoon, despite the familiar twinkle in her eye.

"Let me look at you, Edgar."

"Look how thin he is, Franny." Aunt Nancy clucks her tongue. "Didn't they feed you at university?"

"Not so well as you do, Aunt Nan."

"We will fix that," Ma says, hooking an arm through mine for support. "Now, we already heard how well you did in your examinations, but what we want to know is—"

"Any great romances in Charlottesville?" Aunt Nancy interrupts.

I stifle an eye roll. "Er, no. I danced with a number of Charlottesville's young ladies, but I suppose I prefer the daughters of Richmond."

"Not one to inspire any sonnets?" she asks archly.

I must smile at that. "My inspiration remains here." Specifically at Second and Main.

"Well, that's fortunate," Ma says. "Did Nan tell you? We have invited your friends tonight for a party!"

"For me?"

"Yes, a Christmas party and a coming-home party all at once."

The Prodigal gets his welcome-home shindig after all.

"Is Elmira coming?"

She glances sidelong at her sister. "I do not think Miss Royster can come. But Jack and Rosalie and Robert and your other school mates, some of whom will bring their sisters. Now look, this port came in last week. . ."

John Allan catches me preening in the ballroom mirror.

"Ah, Edgar. You're back. I wish to have a word with

you in the library."

I run fingers through my side whiskers, the only facial hair I will wear until my late thirties. "Actually, sir, I was going to the Roysters', to invite Elmira to the party."

He glares at me, first in surprise, then rancor. "You can go later." He stomps away, expecting me to follow. I only hesitate a moment.

Once in the library, he shuffles papers on his desk, closes books, inspects drawers, not meeting my gaze. "We need to discuss what is expected of you now that you're here."

My heart sinks because I know he will not offer to pay for another university session. I cannot go back to Charlottesville anyway. Without money, I risk getting stabbed in the back there.

"Have you given any thought to your responsibilities? What you will do next?"

Marry Myra, I think. *I am going to marry Myra.*

But Myra is not yours.

I stammer. "I—should—I should like to enlist."

"In the army?" His eyes flick up.

"Yes." I mean, I suppose. I was in the Junior Volunteers, and I more recently participated in military drills on the Lawn, conducted by a West Point alumnus.

Army, navy ... does not matter, Mr. Poe. You must be away from here.

"Do not be rash," Allan says. "You cannot be an officer without a university degree. And one would question if you have the discipline required for the military."

Discipline? Need we remind him that you never made any trouble at school? That you excelled in Latin and French?

I nod, too weary to disagree with him. "Then what would you have me do? I'll take a post in the counting house, if it pleases you—"

"Nay. It does not please me. Although I would be happy to receive some compensation for what you owe me—"

What I owe him?

Bloody tyrant!

"—I do not have a position for you at Ellis & Allan. But something will need to be done about your creditors. They are writing to *me* now, demanding recompense."

"Sir, if you could put in a word for me to gain employment elsewhere—"

"I think a bright lad like yourself can make a go of reading law. That's something you can do here at home. We have the classical law books. And Mrs. Allan would be happy to keep you close by."

Since when does he care what makes Mrs. Allan happy?

She would be happier if he hadn't neglected to pay your tuition.

"Whatever you wish, Pa."

The old term of endearment visibly startles him, but he recovers and nods once. "That's settled then. Now, go up to your room and get ready for your party. You can ask Eleanor to draw you a bath."

"I am going to see Miss Royster first—"

"Leave the Roysters alone, Edgar. Her father and mother have sent the lass to stay with relatives in North Carolina. She will call on you, I'm sure, when she comes home."

From my bedroom I hear a visitor call, and I creep onto the staircase to listen. The house is decked with evergreen and holly, and the air is warm with the promise of savory dishes to come from the kitchen. Downstairs, servants bustle to set out punchbowls and light fires.

Allan invites the visitor into the sitting room, but he declines.

"I see you're expecting other guests. I'll come at another time."

"Nonsense, Bolling. Stay and join us," I hear John Allan bellow. It must be Tom Bolling; his parents own a plantation near the Allans' in Goochland County.

"But, sir, I am not properly dressed for a formal dinner."

"That is no problem at all. Go up to Edgar's room, and he'll give you a suit. He has suits to spare. Seventeen new coats to be exact. I've just paid the bill." Bolling cannot miss the implied irritation.

I dash back to my room so that, when he knocks, I am reclined on the sofa with a book in hand.

"Welcome home, Edgar! Happy Christmas."

Is it?

◦§◦

Bolling and I don appropriate suits for the festivity. My costume is in accord with the noble façade I so well enact, making this affair something of a masquerade. I engage in polite banter when the partygoers arrive, so that no one may guess what is amiss between me and John Allan, or that anything is wrong at all. I talk up the University of Virginia to be a grand venture of enlightenment, rather than admit to the misadventure it was for me.

"Were you well acquainted with Mr. Jefferson, Eddie?"

"Why, I did meet Mr. Jefferson, in the library on several occasions. I even dined at Monticello once. . . It was a sad day when he died, although we all knew it would be soon. The death shadowed the scheduled Independence celebrations, and we wore black crepe bands on our sleeves. . ."

Later I lean over to Bolling as the pudding is served. "How about we go out?"

"Whatever do you mean?"

"Leave. With me."

"Leave the house? Oh, no, we couldn't. What about your other guests? What about Mr. and Mrs. Allan?"

"I am old enough to come and go as I please."

"But it's your celebration!"

Yes, but it is also questions and false compliments and awkward silences. My disgrace has followed me home, that is plain, and I cannot abide it anymore.

"Let us go take the air."

Chapter Fourteen
1826

—ᔆᕂᕠ—

"He was known to drink wine and toddies at home, but no excessive appetite for liquor was noticed." —James Galt

". . . It was my crime to have no one on Earth who cared for me, or loved me." —Edgar

Mrs. E. C. Richardson's Inn
Main & 11th Streets
Richmond

My old mate Eben Burling also happens to be making merry at the tavern tonight. It's been almost a year since I've seen him, but I am not surprised to find him here. Ma would not have invited him to my party because of his reputation, but he is still my friend.

After two drinks, I am more talkative than usual. I tend to gulp my spirits straight . . . and the spirits tend to go straight to my head. I'd sipped wine at my parents' house already.

"Burling and Boiling—I mean, Burly and Broiling—no—"

"Let's leave it at Tom," says himself.

Tom bought the first round of drinks; I bought the second . . . on credit.

"Tom," I repeat. I attempt to say *Ebenezer*, but the

result sounds something like strangulation. "Ben. May I call you that? Ben rhymes with *gentlemen*. Me and Tom and Ben, three gentlemen. No. Tom and Ben and—how to shorten my name to three letters, one syllable?"

"Ed?" says Eben, lifting his head off the bar.

"That's *two* letters, Ben. Need one more."

"Ned?"

"Not Ned." I despise John Allan's nickname for me.

Poe.

"Poe! Now why didn't I think of that? Tom and Ben and Poe, three fellow—"

"I like it," Eben slurs.

I sit up straighter and raise my empty glass. "It's Christmas Eve, gentlemen. Let us toast the end of a wretchedly unlucky year. Unlucky in cards, unlucky in love. Or at least for me. I wish you lads better."

The Royster Residence

We must go back an hour or two, before my inebriation. Before coming to the tavern, I led Bolling to Second Street. As we came nearer the Royster home, I heard music and laughter. A Christmas party, I assumed.

Perhaps Myra has come home for this, I thought.

Bolling and I pushed into the crowded entrance hall, then weaved our way into the parlor, dodging dancing couples. It was not Myra at the piano, but an unfamiliar musician, accompanied by a fiddle player among others.

Finally I spotted her, dazzling in a new red tartan frock with her hair coiled up on top. She saw me too and approached with no smile.

The corner of my mouth turned up, and she looked at me through her lashes, much more shy than I ever remember her. Bolling discreetly occupied himself with the refreshments.

"May I have this dance?" I asked.

"Oh, Edgar," she said with queer disappointment and a shake of the head.

"My father said you were staying with relatives in North Carolina."

"I was. I've just come back. Edgar, what are you doing here?" Her accusation caught me off guard.

"I came to see you. I thought you'd be happy to see me after so long."

"Why didn't you write to me? I wrote you twice a week at least until last summer."

"What do you mean I didn't write to you? I wrote often. I never received one letter from you, Myra."

Lips parted, brow furrowed, she looked down at the rug, eyes roaming from corner to corner. Then she looked back at me. "My father. . . My father must have intercepted our letters. Someone must have." Her eyes filled with tears.

"Don't cry, dearest. We can make up for lost time."

Her voice broke. "Edgar, this is my engagement party."

At that, I felt all the blood drain from my head, and I swallowed a bitter cry.

"To whom are you engaged?" I managed to ask.

"Barrett Shelton."

I knew of Shelton, but I never took him as a rival.

"But he's old."

"He's only two years older than you, Edgar."

Was he? He seemed like a much older man, with a prominent shipping business and a sour affect worn by the aged.

"Myra, why?" Without knowing, I'd clutched her upper arms. Her tears spilled over, and as soon as I saw I'd hurt her, I dropped my hands to my sides.

"I thought you didn't write back," she rushed to say. "I thought you didn't like me anymore. My parents told me to accept Mr. Shelton's proposal and I did." Head back, Myra moaned, and I wanted to wrap my fingers around her lovely, white neck, to stroke her throat with my thumbs.

A feeling of helpless rejection washed over me, while grief and rage fought for dominance. The glass of wine I'd drunk at my party made the room spin.

This was not right. The To Be growled inside of me.

It was Allan. Your foster father did this to hurt you.

"Please, Edgar. You shouldn't be here. I am so sorry."

I clenched my teeth but unclenched my fists. I saw that Myra was also on the verge of breaking down, and I took pity. My mother would have expected me to exercise self-control. I could do that. I could behave honorably for Myra. For my mother.

I reached for Miss Royster's hand and bowed down to kiss it—extravagant and tragic. Not looking away from her wet eyes, I kissed those long, delicate fingers that made music while we made love. I straightened and backed away a step.

"You will marry *me*, Myra," I vowed.

If it's the last thing you do.

Mrs. Richardson's Inn

My heart threshes restlessly and weighs heavy in my chest. If it is the cause of these unhappy feelings, I think I would rather cut it out and not feel at all. I imagine even so it would continue to flop and flail outside my body, telling the tale of my anguish, beating the song of a young man's heartache. Uncut, still I bleed.

Tom, when he discovered I'd left the party, found me pacing outside, a boiling kettle on the point of screaming.

"Do you need to go home?" he asked.

I refused and instead walked to Mrs. Richardson's, where we found a sympathetic Eben. I told the lads what happened at Elmira's house. I told them what happened at university. I told them all about my miserly foster father—my maudlin lament.

And then, as though I'd summoned him, he stalks through the door of the tavern, just as I am giving another toast. I never even heard the advancing beat of his cane.

"May Barrett Shelton be hit by a carriage or suffer a heart failure at work," I say, lifting an empty glass.

"Aye-aye," Eben mumbles.

"There you are, you wee scapegrace." Allan raises me up by my collar. "Should've known I'd find you here with this no-good wretch." He points his chin at Eben, who lolls on his chair.

"Mr. Allan, I am sorry we left without excusing our-selves," says Tom.

"It wasn't his fault, Pa. I talked him into it."

Allan ignores me. "Bolling, no need to be sorry when he dragged you with him."

Now the old man turns to me, snarling. "Is this any way to treat your guests, Edgar? Or your mother, after all she did for you? And you're drunk. You left your own party to go among the Philistines."

Closing my eyes, I do my best to steady the swaying in my legs.

But the liquor makes me bold. "You were wrong about Elmira Royster, Pa. She's not in North Carolina. She's home."

He stares at me in silence for a long moment. "Go home, Edgar, and go to bed."

Mrs. Richardson, the proprietress, waddles over with one hand on her hip and the other palm up. "Happy Christmas, Mr. Allan. That'll be eighteen pence for the three beers."

Chapter Fifteen
1827

"I had no hope of returning to Charlottesville, and I waited in vain in expectation that you would, at least, obtain me some employment. I saw no prospect of this—and I could endure it no longer. Everyday threatened with a warrant." —Edgar

The Lower Byrd Plantation
Goochland County
Virginia

After Christmas, I convince John Allan to give me an errand that will take me to his plantation west of the city, near Tom Bolling's farm. But I do not hasten back to Richmond. Instead, I stay in the country for some weeks. I do not see when all the university lads leave on the coach for Charlottesville—nor must I make excuses for why I have not paid them back. I pass my eighteenth birthday at the Lower Byrd.

Warrants for my loans still float around in the post, and I know I must help myself if John Allan will not. I am studying to read law as he would have me do. But I must somehow earn money . . . and I must start anew, somewhere not in Virginia, where John Allan is too big an entity. I consider Philadelphia, it being an acclaimed "literary" city. If I could find employment there, I might meet the right connections to see my work published.

On one of his trips to the plantation, John Allan finds me scribbling verses by the fire.

Last night, with many cares & toils oppres'd,
Weary, I laid me on a couch to rest—

"How many times have I told you not to lean back?" He pushes the back of my chair, in which I am leaning precariously, so that I am thrown forwards.

Hands out for balance, I brace my feet against the floor. "Perhaps a hundred times," I say when I am steadied.

"At least. So here you are. I thought you may have run away with the gypsies."

"No, sir. I'm no good at tinkering."

"But I bet you could read a pretty fortune." He peers over my shoulder at my paper. An enormous sigh almost lifts it into the air. "I've had about enough of this, Edgar."

"Enough of what, sir?"

"This—this dandying about with words."

Did he mean to call you a dandy? I resent that.

Or did he mean *bandy*, as in "to bandy words"?

"That is not a word," I say feebly.

"What?"

"*Dandy* is a noun, not a verb. One may be a dandy, but he may not dandy about."

Allan's eyes narrow. "Do not *bandy* words with me, lad."

It would seem he knows that turn of phrase after all. A genuine Shakespeare of our time.

"Sorry, sir." I say, crumpling my paper. "I won't dan-dy *or* bandy the words anymore."

"This is idleness, Edgar. I've given you more than enough time to straighten up and do right."

"I am studying! Like you told me to. I spend hours reading the classics."

He pokes me with the end of his cane. "You are read-ing novels. I told you to study mathematics. *Don Quixote* is not going to help you achieve a legal career. You are dallying, Edgar."

Tired of being prodded, I stand up. "Then send me back to the university."

"So you can squander your time and my money? Nay, I do not think so."

"You said you would provide me a college education. You are breaking your promise."

"And *you* are going behind my back, young man. A letter came, returned from Mills Nursery in Philadelphia, about your potential employment."

I go still. I sent an application for a position there. "That letter was mine. Did you open it?"

"You used my name as a reference, did you? You think that should not be my business?"

"That was a private letter, addressed to me. You should not have opened it."

"It's a good thing I did. Now I can write to Mills to say they do well to keep you out of their business and I do not lend my endorsement to your employment there."

"Why, you are undermining me on purpose! I need a job to make my own living."

"What do you want me to do—be your literary patron? Ridiculous. How do you suppose to support a wife as a poet?"

A wife? I hadn't thought—

If do you take a wife, Mr. Poe, you will treat her far better than he has treated his, I daresay.

"You dream childish dreams, Edgar. Ye think you're all grown up, wearing a gentleman's suit, but a man would know better. A man must care for his family first, like I have cared for you—"

"You don't care about me! You never cared for me. I hear you say so when you think I'm listening. Otherwise, you would help me get a job so I can hold my head high again. But no, you don't want me to have anything I can feel proud of."

"I have tried to humble you, lad. Pride cometh before the fall."

"Do not quote scripture to me, *sir*. You know you do not believe it any more than you believe in decency and kindness. You have not humbled me. You have ruined my chances of making a life for myself. You have sabotaged me at every opportunity because you do not like what I know about you. You do not like when I tell stories about you."

I know I should stop, but I do not. He is turning red to the tips of his ears, and I instinctively step back. But my mouth is incapable of censor.

"You want the neighbors to think that you are goodhearted—a moral, charitable man, who took in an orphan, the child of strollers"—which, of course, I say in a mocking Scottish accent—"when in fact, you are an adulterous quack and the father of unfortunate bastards."

His cane clatters to the floor, the hand that held it raised to strike. But I catch his wrist before his hand can fall, and I tighten my grip. He needs to know how strong I am now.

We will not cringe before you, Johnny Allan, you miserable old bully.

When I feel his arm slacken, I let go. "We will not be doing any more of that. I know you gave the servants authority over me, and I hope that gave you some amusement. But I will not be belittled anymore."

One eye squints as he processes my declaration. Then a smug expression comes over his features, as he perhaps remembers my first night home from university. "How are things with wee Sarah Elmira?" he asks with a grunt. "Are we feeling, perhaps, a bit heartbroken?"

The smile gloats, the eyes glint, and that is when I know: he had a hand in that too. The To Be was right. I landed myself in financial trouble, even if he had refused to give me enough money. But he also, by conspiring with her father, stole Myra away from me.

"You!"

"Me? I did nothing, Edgar, except discuss your future

with Mr. Royster, who was none too pleased with what I told him. The lassie cried her eyes out, so I hear, when you didn't write, and her parents told her you had lost interest."

I think my heart might stop beating here. And if it doesn't, then my eyes may pop right out of my head. "I *did* write to her."

"Oh? Then how is it that she never received your letters? No money enough for stamps? How sad. Fortunately for her, another suitor came 'round."

You ought to burn his house down tonight.

"You are a hateful old hound with no scruples, no compassion. Why Ma married you, I will never know."

"She should have married *you*, Edgar. She loves you more, and I cannot see how that would be any more scandalous than what is said about us already."

"That is all that matters to you."

"What? Gossip?"

"That she loves you. That people speak well of you. So I ask, what shall I ever do to please you? I will never be good enough."

He presses his lips into a stern line and fidgets with his pocket watch.

"Fetch your coat, Edgar. We ride back to Richmond tonight. I will give you until the morning to make a choice. You may remain under my roof if you accept my authority and do as I say. That means no more arguments, no more idle pursuits. You will work towards a profession in law, which will give you some standing in the world. Lastly, you will cease asking me to pay your gambling debts."

His chin juts, as do the cords in his neck.

"You must decide by tomorrow if you will do these things. And if not, I leave you to your own destruction. You will no longer be welcome here or at Moldavia. You can write letters to your foster mother, but you will find another roof under which to live and another way to support yourself. Mark me."

"Sir." I nod. I feel some relief for having the power to choose, even if I do not like the alternatives.

"Gather your belongings for the carriage. We will leave at once."

He frowns at his cane on the floor. I bend to pick it up, but I do not hand it over right away. Without his walking stick, he is impotent. Deliberately I offer it with a slight bow of my head. He takes it and exits, which is when I hear the nervous scattering of the servants from behind doors.

He is going to be sorry for this. When the world comes to know Edgar A. Poe, they will also know the villain of your story. Mark me.

Chapter Sixteen
1827

"You have moreover ordered me to quit your house, and are continually upbraiding me with eating the bread of idleness, when you yourself were the only person to remedy the evil. . . ." —Edgar

Let us rest here and reflect. You have just witnessed a rather thorny argument with no intermission.

At this time, the things I want do not align with the things John Allan wants. Furthermore, I hold on to other desires that do not align with the realms of possibility.

I want to be Myra's husband, but this is no longer conceivable, despite my swagger. What if I revise to say, "I want to be *a* husband to *a* wife"? Do I want a wife, or was it only Myra I wanted? Let's say I do desire a wife, even if she is not Myra. Then I would want to make a comfortable home for her. With John Allan's suggestion to study law, I can achieve this kind of traditional home life.

But I also want to be known. *Renowned* is more like it. I want my poetry to be read the world over. The mad idea—and perhaps we can blame Mrs. Stanard for it— is that I think I can be. It is far-fetched, yes, but not impossible. I have studied Byron, Shelley, Coleridge, and Moore, and I can pen a poem almost as good, and I am getting consistently better.

I suspect that to pursue a literary calling may mean giving up that former want: domesticity. The life of a poet may bring fame, but I cannot expect fortune. I cannot rely on the financial support, much less moral support, of John Allan. I cannot expect an inheritance to live on, and I must find a way to support myself. These setbacks are not likely to intrigue any eligible society ladies.

I find, after considering the possibilities, that I do not care. Myra was my true love, and she is now out of reach. There is a strangely sad freedom in this new understanding.

I do not presume happiness or love from this point on. Heaven is locked and barred; its angels mock me.

There are always the poor lassies, Mr. Poe, whose fathers do not care who they marry and want only one less mouth to feed. These make the best poet's wives, in my humble opinion, as they live on very little bread and more warm kisses.

Moldavia
Richmond

I spend the night on the road to Moldavia, unable to sleep, and not because of the carriage's jolts and judders or John Allan's sonorous snores.

My mind is made up. Yet. . . . Choosing to leave means leaving Ma, and she is so fragile that I wonder if

I may never see her again. If I study law like my foster father insists, I will sacrifice my life of renown. But to choose a literary path means I sacrifice the comfort I know in the Allan household.

We reach Moldavia in the wee hours, and I spend what is left of the night dithering in my apartment. When the house begins to stir, I dress and go down to breakfast. I wait at the table alone, sipping coffee and chewing toast, until a surprised Aunt Nancy comes down and greets me. This morning Ma will have her breakfast served to her in bed.

The servants seem jumpy. No doubt my row with John Allan last night at the Byrd has been carried here by way of our coachman.

When John Allan comes to the table, the meal is being set out. He sits and glares at me. "What is your decision, Edgar?"

Nancy looks from me to him and back to me. I grab another piece of toast and mumble, "I am leaving."

"What was that?"

I swallow my nerves and determine to be bold. "I do not want to study law," I say, louder.

His nostrils flare. "Then go!" he thunders, slamming his fists on the table.

The bread falls from my fingers. "Now?"

"Yes, now. Go! You made your choice."

"I haven't finished breakfast."

"This was the choice put before you and you chose to not eat here again. I will not have you sit at my table and disrespect me."

Aunt Nancy interjects. "Mr. Allan, what is this about?"

"Do not fash, Miss Valentine. Edgar and I have an agreement."

"I haven't said goodbye to Ma," I say.

"With all due respect," Aunt Nan offers, "I do think Franny will be vexed—"

"Then say goodbye, Edgar. You have one minute before I toss you out." He pulls out his pocket watch.

I dart up the stairs and barge into my mother's room. She looks as frightened as a trapped hare under her canopy. I kiss her face, which is wet.

"I will make you proud, Ma."

John Allan is yelling from downstairs. "Edgar!"

"I am proud of you, my son," Ma says, tears flowing freely now.

My last backwards glance shows my mother wrapped in her bed silks, arms pitifully outstretched towards me.

"Enough, you wee upstart. Time to go." He is at the foot of the stairs.

"But what about my things?" I call down. "I have nothing."

"Get out! Get out now!" The cane stamps the floor with his shouts. In the dining room, a servant nearly drops a platter of bacon.

I descend the stairs in a gallop as he stalks towards me, cane rapping and catching my toes. "Ah!"

"Go!" With his hand under my arm, he hauls me towards the door.

"I'm going!" I say, grabbing one of my coats from the tree in the foyer, nearly tipping it over as I am pushed past it. I leave Moldavia with only what I have on, and I have not eaten more than a piece of toast. I suppose these are the consequences of my choice, and there is no time to adjust.

And this, dear Reader, is how poetry ruined my life.

Chapter Seventeen
1827

"I have not one cent in the world to provide any food." —Edgar

Court House Tavern
Richmond

I pray the same never happens to you, my friend. Let this serve as your tale of caution. When faced with the choice of poetry or breakfast, choose the bacon. You can always write in secret.

By ordering me out of the house before breakfast, John Allan deprived me my turn to speak, and that will not do. I beg paper and pen from a tavern proprietress and dash off the most reckless letter of my life. It is more passionate than all my adolescent love letters. The To Be rants, calm but cursory, and I write down what it says.

Address the letter, "Dear Sir," not Pa.

After my treatment of yesterday and what passed between us this morning, I can hardly think you will be surprised at the contents of this letter. My determination is at length taken—to leave your house and [e]ndeavor to find some place in this wide world, where I will be treated—not as *you* have treated me. . . .

*Now tell him how our disappoint-
ment and disgrace are all thanks to
him.*

. . . But in a moment of caprice—you have blasted my
hope because forsooth I have disagreed with you in an
opinion, which opinion I was forced to express. . . .

I request my trunk and belongings, as well as—I
know you cringe to hear it—money.

If you fail to comply with my request—I tremble for
the consequences.

*We must be gone, Mr. Poe. John
Allan's influence is too great here.*

Boston will be my new home, I decide. It was my
first home in this unloving world. The one memento
from my mother Eliza is a little watercolor painting of
Boston Harbor, on the back of which she wrote:

For my little son Edgar, who should ever love Boston,
the place of his birth, and where his mother found her
best, and most sympathetic friends.

I failed to mention it before, but I was born in Boston on January 19, 1809. Perhaps this memoir should
have begun there. Or, like *Tristram Shandy*, some months
before. But since I do not remember the unfortunate
circumstances of my birth, nor Boston, and certainly not
my conception, then we must go back to Boston at the

age of eighteen.

My mother says she found sympathetic friends here. If I cannot have a family, I could surely use friends. It feels prophetic, destined, that I go back from whence I came—to come full circle, as it were.

I send word to John Allan that I need $12. I sail on Saturday.

I have not had any decent food since that deplorable breakfast on Monday morning. The $12 should be enough—enough for food, enough for transportation, and enough to establish myself in Boston until I find employment. He can *lend* it to me if he is not keen to give it.

Threaten him, Mr. Poe.

It depends upon yourself if hereafter you see or hear from me.

My letters may sound melodramatic to the Reader's ear, but I am hungry. Have you gone without food for more than a day? I wouldn't wish it upon you, but take my word for it: an empty stomach makes one's letters most fraught with self-pity.

My underlying hope is that my mother will see the letter and come to my aid.

"Does she save you?" How kind of you to ask. I see that you care deeply for me, Reader, and I appreciate that. But no. I receive no reply from Allan either. No trunk and no money.

And so I write again, asking would Dear Sir please be so good as to send me my clothes, for God's sake. I know he is trying to teach me a lesson, and I have learnt it. One may not disagree with John Allan and eat at his table.

Forget the money then. I only want my possessions, particularly my manuscripts. Those, I believe, are my bread ticket. If I have to starve to death to show him that I mean to do what I say, then so be it. I will not go back to Moldavia.

Mrs. Richardson's Inn

My first note, which John Allan labels a "Pretty Letter," did reach Moldavia. After a second communication, I receive an unemotional, almost official return letter, in which Allan answers my original accusations.

He agrees that he taught me to aspire to a higher position in society, but he argues that novels will not get me there. He has done his duty as a father figure by correcting and guiding me, and he does not apologize, but he fears for me. Lastly, he says that I already owe him for the education and rearing, and he points out the irony of my defying him, thereby refusing his support, and then directly asking him for money.

Obviously, we will not be getting anything from him, and it seems Franny knows naught of these letters. We must go through the Blacks. They do not love John Allan, but they do love you.

I persuade a serving woman to pass a message for me to the help at Moldavia. Tell them, I say, that Master Eddie needs his things brought to Mrs. Richardson's Inn.

Dabney Danbridge, one of the Allans' slaves, delivers a letter from my mother and a few of my belongings. When I open the envelope, I am relieved to see that she and Aunt Nancy sent me some money to live on.

"Dab, can you bring me some more things from my room? I need my papers."

"Master Allan don't know I'm doing you favors."

"It is very important, otherwise I wouldn't ask. I leave on Saturday."

"Leave? Where to?"

"Europe."

Eben and I think it best to invent a rumor about my whereabouts. That is why I am lurking in Mrs. Richardson's Inn during the day while spending nights at the Court House Tavern. With warrants chasing me, imprisonment is an alarming possibility. If I escape to a northern city under an assumed name, my creditors will think Edgar A. Poe in London or Paris.

"Don't you go that far, Master Eddie. I have half a mind to tell Miz Allan."

"Do what you must, Dab. It will break her heart, and she'll try to stop me, but—listen: I cannot tell you where I'm going, but I need them to think it's Europe."

He looks at me for a long time, then nods. "I'll be back tomorrow."

And that, ladies and gentlemen, is how the legend and legacy of Edgar Allan Poe can be partially credited to a sympathetic enslaved black man. Dabney Danbridge, bless his soul, spreads the report of my sailing to Europe, *and* he saves my poems.

Richmond City Dock

Meanwhile, I walk to the docks to arrange for my passage on a merchant vessel. But it seems John Allan got here first.

"May I speak to your captain?" I inquire at every outbound ship. I know all the captains, they having oft dined at Moldavia or the Ellises'. Thanks to Ma and Aunt Nan, a little money pads my pocket, and I offer to work in exchange for the fare.

"Edgar Allan, I am sorry, but I cannot allow you on my ship."

"Why ever not?"

"Your guardian has said so, and I cannot risk a quarrel with Ellis & Allan."

I cannot reconcile this. Not for one irrational moment do I believe John Allan gives a fig about where I go or how I get there.

It's your mother, Mr. Poe.

My exasperation and fear melt at the thought of it. *She stood up to him.* I know from experience how much plucking up that requires, and the To Be recounts for me the confrontation, my mother feeble but determined:

"Mr. Allan, my son is plotting to sail to Europe. If he succeeds, I will surely die. You will speak to the captains and insist that they not permit him on board."

"My dear, if he wishes to seek his fortune in the world, we cannot hold him back."

"We can. We are his caretakers. You will see to it that he cannot leave on any ship Saturday. Because you forced him to quit the house, he is out on the streets doing heaven knows what. But you will not let him go so far from me."

"I'll send word to the ships' captains. Do not fash."

"Oh, John. I am so afraid I will never see him again."

"He will be back, Franny. He cannot abide an empty belly. He'll go hungry for a spell, spend some cold nights out of doors, and then come to his senses. He's been too spoiled for his own good. Let him see how fine he had it here, and then he will sidle home like any wayward goat."

"I want him home now, John. . ."

Albeit I would never see her again.

Norfolk Harbor
Norfolk, Virginia

Eben and I finally find a foreign crew, who lets us on board their boat bound for Norfolk. I am using a French name: Henri le Rennét, for my brother, Henry Leonard.

Eben walks with a list, like he's been at sea for months, before we even cross the gangplank. He is thoroughly pickled, and it is my aim to sober him up. This is the boyhood friend with whom I sailed the James, when we fancied ourselves island castaways. It will be like playing instead of fleeing, and far less terrifying with a playmate.

On the water, however, he is not so jolly and bold as

in the tavern. When we reach Norfolk, he is nauseous and fretful about going forth.

The boat returns to Richmond, and I watch it sail back the way it came with Eben on it. Although I'm conflicted to see him go (he was turning out to be more of a nuisance than a mate), his new task is to further obscure my destination.

Let John Allan think you in Scotland to acquaint his countrymen with his hypocrisy and betrayal.

PART THREE:

The Soldier

Chapter Eighteen
1827

"I'm thinking Edgar has gone to sea to seek his own fortunes." —John Allan

Boston
Massachusetts

My mother is so convinced I am in Europe that she addresses her letters there. She uses my French alias, Henri le Rennét, for delivery, making me wonder if Eben divulged this secret as well. In the letters, which I would receive much later, she absolves me of all blame for the conflict in our house. I am a victim, she says, of her and Mr. Allan's marital strife.

Despite the legends that place me in far-flung corners of the world, I am working on a coal ship, which delivers me to Boston in April 1827. But Boston society is not all I hoped it to be. I do not find work; I do not find those best and most sympathetic friends of my mother's.

In the eighteen years since she was last here, the city of our birth has forgotten all about the Arnolds and the Poes. And Henri le Rennét est un étranger.

One day when I am near the wharf seeking a job in a mercantile warehouse, I come out of doors and meet the impish eyes of Peter Pease, my schoolmate from Charlottesville—the one who provoked me to set my story ablaze. But before he can "Hallo!" me, I duck and round the next corner into an alley. When Peter passes, I snatch his sleeve and pull him in after me, where his jocularity turns to curiosity.

"Do not speak my name, Peter," I beg straightaway, and I am frank about my situation. He nods and says, "I never saw you, Gaffy," and I do not see him again—at least not in Boston.

Calvin F. S. Thomas, Printer
70 Washington Street

But a ray of sunshine flares amid my Boston gloom. Fate would put me in touch with Calvin Thomas, nineteen years old, a printer's apprentice. Calvin has bought a print shop across from the State House and is now a printer in his own right.

If I do not find more permanent employment, I am soon to run out of money. But I think that if I can print my poetry, I can sell it and make enough to live on awhile longer. Thanks to Dabney, I have my manuscripts, and Calvin is keen to help me prepare and print the poems for publication—as long as I can pay for their production.

The result is *Tamerlane and Other Poems*, by "a Bostonian." On the run from creditors, I cannot afford to use my real name. But neither do I want New Englanders to deride my work on the basis of my being a Virginian. (The Northern literary society, or *literati*, generally rejects the value of Southern writing.) Of course, I am Bostonian by birth, so this is no lie.

I acknowledge in a preface that most of the poems were first penned when I was thirteen years old. The front jacket includes a quote from Cowper:

Young heads are giddy, and young hearts are warm,
And make mistakes for manhood to reform.

Except for "Tamerlane," which is Myra-inspired and somewhat recent, the poems have been refined over the past five or so years. Calvin prints forty-some copies in all. I must pay for my own books, and I purchase as many as I can, reserving two copies to send to reviewers and one for my brother, Henry.

A copy of this little book—which is really no more than a pamphlet—is today worth hundreds of thousands of dollars. Interesting, seeing that you cannot *pay* people of this century to read poetry. I think only a dozen surviving books are known to be in existence. You, my dear Reader, might do well to find a first edition, perhaps buried in a trunk in the attic or hidden in the walls. Better than buried treasure, I'd say. I do hope you are lucky enough to find it.

This is all the more ironic given that, in 1827, *Tamerlane* exhausts all my funds, and I am forced to enlist in the United States Army if I am going to live to write more books.

Henri, my alias, is too well known in this city—and perhaps beyond, if my foster parents have heard of him. So, at the army recruiting office, I transform into one Edgar A. Perry. My age is twenty-two years, born in Boston. My occupation, clerk. Hair: brown. Eyes: grey. Height: five feet, eight inches.

Little lies protected by little truths.

"I understand the name change, but why lie about your age?"

Well, four more years lend me more credibility. I can hear your dispute: "But wouldn't the *truth* give you more credibility?" Yes, but have you not ever needed to be someone better? Perhaps a little older or a little younger? Edgar Perry wants some edge over Edgar Poe. We require new selves sometimes . . . especially when we owe gambling debts. You see, I need not be Edgar A. Poe until that time when I can reintroduce myself to John Allan with my head held high. But moreover, and more truthfully, I am a writer, and writers lie. Take note of that, Reader. Take note.

Chapter Nineteen
1827–28

"He at once performed the duties of company clerk and assistant in the Subsistent Department, both of which duties were promptly and faithfully done. His habits are good and intirely [*sic*] free from drinking."
—Lieutenant Howard

Before I carry on with this narrative, I want to share with you an idea: An artist ought to be allowed to create art that sustains him.

In my day, one did not make a living as a poet. Well, now that I think about it, it would be ridiculous today too. Imagine meeting one who introduces himself or herself as a poet or a novelist. Absurd! Unless you are the poet laureate, it would be unthinkable—pretentious at the very least.

But I profoundly hope to see a time when one can do what it is he or she is meant to do and not suffer to do it. Perhaps such an age is dawning, when education is democratic and art is worthy.

I suppose there will always be those content with the job that pays the bills. I do not begrudge them. I have shoveled coal and kept records. These jobs are inescapable. But I do not either disrespect the teacher who is an aspiring musician, the postman who writes plays, or the soldier who paints.

And what about the man or woman who is called to dream? May God make a way for them to achieve their calling and hold their heads high. For our worth is more than the dollars we earn.

Fort Independence
Castle Island, Boston
&
Fort Moultrie
Sullivan's Island
Charleston, South Carolina

You might say that a fort is a fort, each featuring the same monotone rock walls, arched gates, and sharp angles. During the next two years, Private Perry will live at three different (but same) forts. He would be the first to tell you that soldiering, outside of wartime, is not conducive to verse.

First, I am posted as an artilleryman at Fort Independence in Boston Harbor. My experience at Ellis & Allan enables me to gain access to the quartermaster's office, keeping records of rations and supplies (like my grandfather Poe, the quartermaster general of Baltimore). It being peacetime, I endure training with no real implementation, and I spend hours in the barracks in between duties. I am never quite alone, which is hard on me, but it is a game of survival. For the time being, I have a roof over my head and food to eat and clothes to wear.

Eventually, my unit, Battery H, is ordered south to Fort Moultrie in Charleston Harbor. The South Carolina coastline offers exotic palm trees and sand dunes, and I wander the beaches during my off-hours of a mild winter. This region was once haunted by the fearsome Captain Black Beard, and its landscape piques my fascination for pirates and treasure hunts.

Perhaps you wonder whether any romance is sought during my military stint. Where is the impassioned lad who wooed boarding school girls with his pen? One of my friends said he did not remember a time when Edgar Poe was not in love with some girl or another. While I am ever inclined to escort a young lady to a dance or party, I am not forgetting Myra. It is she I think of when I hold the gloved hand of a Southern belle at the holiday balls.

But I can see the subject will not be so soon dismissed by you, my dear Reader.

You are correct. Naturally, wherever a port, there are ladies of ill repute. Do I take my broken heart to the brothel, you ask? I do not, I assure you. That is unacceptable behavior for he who answers to a higher calling, which I believe I do. True, after a strong drink, one's judgment is not what it ought to be, but I am on the whole sober and still a gentleman. I would not disrespect Myra or my mother so flagrantly.

But on lonely nights, you picture a disheveled Mrs. Stanard feeding birds in her night shift. If I may be so bold, I think you recollect a breast peeking through the cloth, do you not? Oh, what one can do with an imagination!

Known for my tidy appearance and well-spoken manners, I win across-the-board approval from the superior officers. I move upwards in rank with several promotions over two years, leading to higher pay (from $5 a month to $10).

I am favored by a particular lieutenant, to whom I am truthful about my situation and aspirations, including my real name and age. He agrees to discharge me from my enlistment, of which I have three more years to serve, if I can reconcile with John Allan. I suppose he is reluctant to turn me loose without any support, otherwise I wind up on the streets again without any bread.

This lieutenant sends a letter to John Allan, but my foster father is content to let me stay where I am. This is another supposition, but I think he cannot abide an enlisted soldier in house, especially one who is a foster son from that house. Such rank would be an indignity.

Why, you do not even have the decency to be a proper officer, Mr. Poe.

The To Be says my foster father can better practice his infidelities while I'm in the army.

Perhaps he is disappointed that you did not starve to death like he said you would.

I write to him personally with enough flattering remarks to, I hope, persuade him to give my superior the discharge approval—but also with enough criticism to perhaps persuade him to do the right thing.

> . . . I could not help thinking that you believed me degraded & disgraced, and that any thing were preferable to my returning home & entailing on yourself a portion of my infamy.

> In vain I told [Lieutenant Howard] that your wishes for me (as your letter assured me) were, and had always been those of a father & that you were ready to forgive even the worst offences. . . .

> [Howard] has always been kind to me, and, in many respects, reminds me forcibly of yourself. . . .

> Write me once more if you do really forgive me…

He ought to be proud, I think, of how quickly I have risen in the ranks. I am proud of myself. I am not asking for money this time. I am capable of making my own way and earning the favor of my fellow man.

Lest you forget, Mr. Poe, this is not how your story plays out. You are a good soldier, but a soldier is not who you are.

The To Be is right. A life in uniform is not the life I seek, and John Allan must not be mistaken in that. I do not intend to keep this up. Having not graduated West Point, I cannot earn a commission, and I have achieved the highest rung on the ladder without one. No, my destiny lies elsewhere, and if he will not give the lieutenant permission to discharge me, I will find another way to leave the army.

Chapter Twenty
1828–29

"He left me in consequence of some gambling at the
University at Charlottesville, because (I presume) I
refused to sanction a rule that the shopkeepers and
others had adopted there, making Debts of Honour of
all indiscretions. I have much pleasure in asserting that
he stood his examination at the close of the year with
great credit to himself. His history is short. He is the
grandson of Quartermaster-General Poe, of Maryland.
. . . Frankly, Sir, do I declare that he is no relation to
me whatever; that I have many whom I have taken an
active interest to promote theirs; with no other feeling
than that, every man is my care, if he be in distress. For
myself I ask nothing, but I do request your kindness to
aid this youth in the promotion of his future prospects.
And it will afford me great pleasure to reciprocate any
kindness you can show him." —John Allan

Fortress Monroe
Old Point Comfort
Hampton, Virginia

Before my twentieth birthday, I am appointed sergeant
major of regimental headquarters at Fortress Monroe in
Hampton Roads. And I thereby find myself back in my
home state.

There is more activity here than at my previous post-
ings—more soldiers, more drills. Yet, outside the moat

that surrounds us, is not much to entertain me. I am ordered to carry out as company clerk in the commissarial department.

You prepare for a war that will not come in your lifetime, when your very life will be a battle, the likes of which no armed force could anticipate or reckon.

It has been almost two years since I have had any direct contact with my mother, and I feel optimistic about her knowing my whereabouts. Some of Frances Allan's relatives live on the Virginia peninsula, and I make myself known to them, asking them to post a letter to my Ma, disclosing my station.

I had written to Pa in an earlier letter:

My dearest love to Ma . . . I hope she will not let my wayward disposition wear away the love she used to have for me.

John Allan makes no answer to my letter requesting discharge approval. I can only imagine his showing it to my mother, scoffing at my boldness, and saying, "We produced a poet, Mrs. Allan. Christ in his heaven. Perhaps it is a blessing we did not have children of our own. They might have grown up to be ballerinas or philosophers or some god-awful nonsense."

Wounded by his silence, I write to him again. The To Be urges me on, its voice both wheedling and sharp.

It must have been a matter of regret to me, that when those who were strangers took such deep interest in my welfare, you who called me your son should refuse me even the common civility of answering a letter.

You may be most affected when you read my final plea and threatening determination:

My father[,] do not throw me aside as *degraded*. I will be an honor to your name. . . .

If you determine to abandon me—here take I my farewell, neglected—I will be doubly ambitious, & the world shall hear of the son whom you have thought unworthy of your notice. But if you let the love you bear me, outweigh the offence which I have given— then write me my father, quickly.

I sign the letter "Your affectionate son."

I spend yet another Christmas away from home in a rough army barracks. The damp air leaves me with a persistent cough, and these stone walls do little to keep out the harsh sea winds.

Colonel House, who knew my father's father, General David Poe, is convinced that I can be admitted to West Point. This makes me reconsider leaving the army. West Point provides, if not a liberal education, an education nonetheless, which I still desire. I need John Allan's help, however, for if I am to leave my enlistment, a substitute must be found to fulfill my service, and if I am to become a cadet, I need someone with clout to recommend me.

At this time, I can only wonder about my mother. Surely she wishes to see me, and I am not far from Richmond. The silence from Moldavia is hurtful and worrisome. How can I move forward when John Allan is still holding me back?

Sometime around my birthday, I contract a fever and must be treated in the hospital at Fortress Monroe. Dr. Robert Archer, who is related to our family friends in Richmond, attends me, offering not only medicinal care but pleasant company as well. Trusting this man on the condition of his friendly name, I tell him who I am, with the hope that he can enlist his Archer relations to intercede on my behalf with the Allans.

Finally, I hear word from home. But it is not what I had hoped to hear. Ma is dying, and she wants to see me.

When the note reaches me, I am shaken—all the more agitated for having to suppress my feelings. First, I must follow orders before I can apply for leave from the army. Once granted, I travel to Norfolk to catch the coach.

If only these horses had wings! It takes one whole day, including an overnight, to make Richmond by carriage. I feel sick all the way, not knowing what awaits me at home. The To Be rehearses deathbed scenes, while I pray for the opportunity to kiss her face, to ask her forgiveness, to tell her how much she means to me.

Chapter Twenty-One
1829

"If it were not for the late occurrences, [I] should feel much happier than I have for a long time, I have had a fearful warning & have hardly ever known before what distress was." —Edgar

Moldavia
&
Shockoe Hill Burying Ground
Richmond

When I enter the house, I know I am too late for apologies and farewells. The servants drift about sluggishly, as though exhausted and overweight, and Aunt Nancy is clad in black mourning dress.

"She so wanted to see you, Edgar. That was her dying wish. If only she could have seen you! You look dashing in that uniform. . ."

Aunt Nan's sensitivity is expected, but John Allan stuns me with his tenderness. This rare show of paternal feeling deepens the shock of my loss. He may have neglected her emotionally, but Ma was his constant caretaker and companion, and her passing has pummeled him—his rough edges, for the time being, blunted by sorrow and vulnerability.

I have missed the funeral and burial, which was earlier

in the day.

"Come along, Edgar. Let us go visit your mother." In an unfamiliar display of gentleness, Allan orders a carriage to take us to Shockoe Hill, where Ma has been interred, not far from Jane Stanard, my *other* mother.

Here, I am utterly undone. The one person in the world devoted to me alone lies still in the ground. No more will that rosebud mouth part with peals of laughter, or those dark doe eyes reflect my face in liquid duplicate. The grave has swallowed my last hope.

Now I know this sounds hackneyed to your modern ear, Reader, but I am so bereaved that my prose and poetry suffer likewise. She leaves me defenseless and without a guiding light. Wounded as such, I cannot stand. Dabney and old Jim prop me up between them, and we three stagger back to the carriage.

I am aware that John Allan watched over this exhibition of my grief. He speaks softly, not consolations but intentions. "I am going to have you a suit ordered. You will need proper mourning clothes."

"Thank you, sir. I have only my uniform." My voice is little more than a mumble.

"I am sorry I didn't call for you before. She had been asking to hold her 'wee laddie' again. I think she was entertaining fantasies there at the end, imagining you still a bairn."

He bites his lip and feebly pounds his knee. "When one is ailing for so long, you expect her to go on ailing. I knew she would die of her illness, but I didn't believe it. I am almost angry with her." He smothers a small sob.

"You mustn't be angry with her, Pa. She was an angel. It is God who took her from us. But you can hardly blame him. What kind of paradise is a heaven without her."

Then it is my turn to stifle a moan and wipe away another cascade of tears.

"I suppose you're right," he says. "Her last breath was used on you. 'Take care of my dear boy.' She made me promise."

I release a great sigh. "I would have come before if you had answered any of my letters."

"The letters. Aye. Well, we were managing your mother's decline. I didn't write because I thought it was best you carry on at Fortress Monroe. I didn't want to upset her, and I didn't want to worry you, Ned."

This is the first time in a long time he's used that childish endearment. I want to trust him. I want to hope for reconciliation. But I hear the To Be grumble warnings.

"My leave is for ten days. I would like it very much if we can talk about my becoming a cadet and reach an agreement between us."

"I think we can do that." Pa turns his face to the window of the carriage, and I leave him to his thoughts.

The Royster Residence

During my stay in Richmond, I visit the Roysters', inquiring of Elmira. I have not given up, and I want to see her, no matter the outcome. Her parents receive me, but it is not a cordial reunion.

"We are so very sorry about Mrs. Allan. She was a virtuous, Christian woman. . ." I politely accept their condolences before I ask after Myra.

"But, Edgar," her mother says, "Sarah Elmira is married."

This may be boring old news to you, but when I left for Boston, Elmira was merely *engaged*. I half expected their marriage to founder. Why couldn't Barrett Shelton have died of consumption? Or typhoid. Or plague. Or a broken neck.

Once again, I am suffering heartbreak upon heartbreak. I think I cried all the tears I owned over Ma because, instead of giving in to weeping, I explode with rage. It is always one or the other with me.

"You tricked her, sir!" I point a finger in Mr. Royster's moustache. "You tricked her, and you tricked me so that she would marry the other man. You wouldn't even let me see her to tell her that I never forgot her, that I never stopped writing her."

Royster delicately pushes my finger out from under his nose. "Now, son, she wasn't even here when you were in Charlottesville."

"Because you sent her away."

"That was for your good and hers."

"For *my* good? Ha! That is funny, because I do not feel good about it at all. Damn your good intentions. And damn you, sir. I am going to find Myra—"

"Now, now, Edgar," Mrs. Royster condescends. "She is a married woman. Think what your appearance at her door would do to her marriage. Think of her interests. Think of propriety. Think of our dear Mrs. Allan, God rest her soul. . ."

I damn God and propriety—among other useless

conventions and objects—before I quit the house. I do not seek after Elmira, but at least I caused commotion enough to provide the help with a good chinwag.

Moldavia

I have learnt my lesson with John Allan. To be in his good graces is in my best interest.

We discuss the Military Academy and who he might petition for my acceptance there. I figure that if I can carry out his wishes in becoming an officer in the United States Army, West Point educated, I am more likely to receive an inheritance from him. As a man of the world, I can appreciate that a man of letters needs money to afford the time to write. If my Ma did indeed implore him to help me, this would satisfy that bargain.

On the morning of my departure, I enter my foster father's bedroom to say goodbye, but I find him still asleep. I do not wake him.

The next letter I send John Allan, upon my return to Fortress Monroe, I address "My dear Pa."

Chapter Twenty-Two
1829

"Since the arrival of his company at this place, he has made his situation known to his Patron, at whose request, the young man has been permitted to visit him; the result is, an entire reconciliation on the part of Mr. Allan, who reinstates him into his family and favor—and who in a letter I have received from him requests that his son may be discharged on procuring a substitute." —Colonel House

Fortress Monroe
Hampton

I prepare for my discharge, arranging letters of recommendation for the War Department and finding a fellow to carry out the remaining three years of my enlistment.

Colonel House writes a letter to the general in charge that gives my real name, but misleading biographical information. This is my fault *and* my prerogative. It is better for me to say that my parents died in the Richmond Theatre fire. The implication being that I come from a respectable, upper-class family, who patronized the theatre, not acted in it.

I may have also implied that John Allan adopted me. After my mother's death, I was christened Edgar *Allan* Poe, but Allan is not my adoptive father. (Adoption was not in fashion at the time.)

But had the big boor legally adopted you, the son of well-bred theatre-goers tragically perished in a fire, all the better for your recommendation to West Point.

Having an enlistment substitute in place, I depart Fortress Monroe with three letters from officers singing my praises. John Allan acquires other letters of influence for me; he even writes one himself and gives me money to live on in the interval. (Although, I use half the amount to pay my substitute in the army, since that is the contract. And still I owe more, but I will ask Allan for the rest in due time.)

As one would expect, I read John Allan's letter of recommendation before I deliver it. I am dismayed to find no affection in it whatsoever. He explicitly states that I am no relation of his and that he takes it upon himself to help any and all who are in need.

With a heavy heart, I make my way to Washington and hand my documents to the secretary of war for filing. Then I wait. I know better than to go home to Moldavia, but I do ask John Allan for another $50; he sends me a hundred for room and board and travel, with the charge to "be careful."

The Poe Residence
Mechanics Row, Wilks Street
Baltimore, Maryland

While awaiting my appointment to West Point, I jour-

ney to Baltimore to meet my father's family. My grandmother, Elizabeth Cairnes Poe, whose husband was
General Poe, lives on his pension in a small house in Mechanics Row. She is old and paralytic, and time is of the
essence. Knowing that the War Department gives pri-
ority to the descendants of Revolutionary War soldiers,
I come to find out what I can about my grandfather's
service during the war. I am not disappointed.

Not only was the quartermaster general a local hero
during the Revolution, providing rations and funding
to Lafayette's men *(which is never repaid,
I might add)*, but he also aided our country's
cause during the War of 1812. In Baltimore, anyone who
learns I am General Poe's grandson treats me with high
regard.

"I sewed five hundred pairs of trousers for the
troops," Grandmother Poe tells me with a weak smile,
which I return. My grandmother tends to exaggerate, I
think, but I also think she likes me.

In the meantime, I am advised to seek publication
for my second volume of poetry in Philadelphia. The
publisher's hesitance prompts me to ask John Allan to
guarantee Carey, Lea & Carey any loss in the printing.
It would only be a one-hundred-dollar loss if they do
not sell a single copy, but I assure him that is unlikely. I
receive a scolding letter in response.

*What did you think he would do?
Your poetry and expenditure of money
are two reasons for his long-held grudge
against us. I refuse to allow you to*

stoop and grovel, Mr. Poe. Our future is with our <u>real</u> family.

Then, I make matters worse. Upon learning my mother's maiden name—Arnold—I tell Allan that I am a grandson of the traitor Benedict Arnold. It is an innocent lie, more of a joke really, intended to lend me some celebrity. Instead, it makes him moreover suspicious.

Perhaps you inherited your talent for tales from Grandmother Poe.

Beltzhoover Hotel
Hanover & Baltimore Streets

While rooming with me at a Baltimore hotel, my cousin Edward steals what is left of John Allan's money. When I find $10 in Edward's pocket, he admits to the thievery but asks me not to expose his crime for his wife's sake. Now I must write home for money again, but Allan thinks I am lying.

Well, you would be a natural liar, descended from the great turncoat, as you say.

I admit, trifling with the truth is a foolish practice when an appointment to West Point Academy is on the line. If the War Department thought the descendent of Benedict Arnold were applying for the army's prestigious military school, it would end in a whopping refusal, if not public humiliation.

With no money for a coach, I walk to Washington, only to learn that there are ten extra cadets on roll at West Point. I am told to wait for resignations to trickle in. The secretary of war reassures me that I am not too old and that I will receive my appointment in due time.

I do not quite know what to do with myself during the delay, as John Allan has said he is not "especially anxious" to see me. I ask for my manuscript to be returned from the publishing house in Philadelphia. Money is running out, and I know not where to turn.

Allan sends me $50, but not without resentment. It is enough for me to live on for a few months, and I am taken into my grandmother's house, which is full to bursting.

The Poe Residence

Under this one roof lives not only my grandmother, but also my aunt Maria Clemm; her seven-year-old daughter, Virginia; her good-for-nothing son, Henry; and my brother, Henry—all existing on Grandfather Poe's meager pension and little more. The remittance from John Allan helps some. My cousin works as a stone cutter, and Aunt Maria takes in sewing.

Maria, my father's younger sister, is a godsend to her orphan nephews. To some comfort, I see a bit of Rosalie about her pale-blue eyes, and I wonder if she looks anything like my father. Her little daughter Virginia says "mudder" for "mother," and thus I take to calling my aunt "Muddy," as she is a mother to us all. I am immediately drawn in and willing to please. In Muddy I find a

long-lost maternal figure, who shares with me a mutual
care and attachment.

But with dread, I forthwith recognize my brother's
dire condition: pale, underweight, feverish, wheezy. The
familiar affliction of our mother and my foster mother. We share our aunt's attic room, in which Henry is
wasting away. As if consumption is not killing him fast
enough, he seems likely to drink himself into the grave.
But when he is able—if not sober—he tells such fantastic stories about deployments to exotic lands and
encounters with native peoples. Friend, you know these
tales are not wasted on me.

The house is crowded even without me, and so, when
I can afford it, I lodge elsewhere. I cannot very well
apply for work when I may, at any moment, be called
for West Point. So I nurse Henry and I help my young
cousin Virginia, whom I call Sissy, with her schoolwork.
She seems keen to spend time with her newfound cousin
and tutor but reluctant to open any books, preferring
instead to let me read to her. When I am not helping in
the house, I make a bid for my poetry with critics and
editors. I need the distraction.

When the summer is out, John Allan accuses me
again of lying. Why have I not received my call to West
Point? Had I not said that the secretary of war confirmed
my appointment for the beginning of the next fall session? I try to explain that I was not promised this, and I
tell him I will go to Washington to sort it all out. But I
do not. I ache, and I am out of money.

Soon I am obligated to ask for more. Rent is due, my
clothes are threadbare, and my bed linens need cleaning.

Dear Pa:

I sometimes am afraid that you are angry. . . .

Meeting my extended family proves fortuitous. My Aunt Eliza's husband and another relation, George Poe, know a newspaper editor: John Neal of the *Yankee and Boston Literary Gazette* out of Portland, Maine. Upon asking their acquaintance to give *Al Aaraaf* a look, he publishes a positive criticism in his paper. He is quite enchanted with what I call "exquisite nonsense," and he says I "might make a beautiful and perhaps a magnificent poem." This is the first ever encouragement I receive from an official literary source.

He publishes in the December issue some of my selections, and I submit a little biography to go with them:

I am and have been from childhood, an idler. It cannot therefore be said that

I left a calling for this idea trade,
A duty broke—a father disobeyed.

for I have no father—nor mother.

I do not know how John Allan hears the news of my praise (for John Neal is very flattering), but he soon after sends me more money and permission to return home. Furthermore, having the approval of a New England critic, I am able to secure publication for this volume of poetry.

In it, "Tamerlane" has been revised since its Boston publication, and the new "Al Aaraaf," about the afterlife, explores my love affair with Myra and subsequent heartbreak. I genuinely think that some of the best lines of verse, American or otherwise, are found within the volume. I still think so, although I would like to make some minor corrections, if I were permitted. I never can leave my verse well alone.

Before going home, I supervise the printing of my book, send copies off for review, and write letters. Then I say farewell to all the Poes and depart for Richmond with my remaining copies of books.

Now, I think, John Allan will take me as a serious poet with an acclaimed book of poetry. Despite the To Be's ever-constant cynicism, hope is restored. You will even see my real name on the title page: Edgar A. Poe.

Chapter Twenty-Three
1829

⸻ ☙❧ ⸻

"I am not so anxious of obtaining money from your
good nature as of preserving your good will—I am
extremely anxious that you should believe that I have
not attempted to impose upon you—I will in the
meantime (if you wish it) write you often, but pledge
myself to apply for no other assistance than what you
shall think proper to allow—" —Edgar

R. D. Sanxey's Book Shop
Main Street
Richmond

"Poe! How serendipitous. What are you up to, old boy?"

At Sanxey's Book Shop in Richmond, I cross paths
with Tom Bolling, the Goochland fellow who toasted
Christmas with me in the tavern.

"Tom, good to see you! Home for the holidays, are
you?"

"That's right. It's been—well, what—two years,
hasn't it? I'd heard you'd gone abroad. The Russian Em-
pire and such far-flung lands. Some say you got yourself
arrested in St. Petersburg?"

I nod with all the gravity I can muster and shake my
head at the nuisance of it all. I divulge incredible details
of my pretend exploits and legal troubles, borrowing
most from my brother Henry's international capers.

Whether or not his tales ring true, I do not know. He is a storyteller himself and often in his cups. But Tom seems to accept the story, and it amuses me to know that my fictitious travels make it into the history books.

"Are you sticking around for good?" he asks.

"Until I enter West Point in the fall. But, look here. I have had a book of poetry just published in Baltimore. Sanxey's is selling them, but you can have this copy for yourself. I'll sign it for you."

Following my far-fetched Slavic escapades, a published book does not astonish Tom, but he is nonetheless delighted. Soon, my hometown is well aware of my literary accomplishment.

Moldavia

&

Ellis & Allan Company

15th & Main Streets

My room is as I left it years ago, but my mother's, of course, is empty. The drastic conditions of my wardrobe are seen to and new clothing ordered.

Gout is getting the better of John Allan, and he is back and forth to the Springs. To manage his pain, he is taken to drink. Whereas, he always looked forward to an evening toddy after work or with dinner, that one or two was the extent of his drinking. Now, the indulgence begins early in the day and carries on throughout. Intoxication makes him more disagreeable, if that is even possible.

He is often away for days on end. If not to the

Springs, then finding comfort where he should not. He spends nights with a former mistress, who bore him a daughter some years ago. More illegitimate children are to come, as the woman is again expecting—twins, it is said.

One afternoon at his office, I interrupt his paperwork to confront him about this infidelity. Of course, I didn't come for this precise aim, but we got there soon enough.

"My wife is dead," he says, his discourtesy shocking me. I detect the lingering fumes of alcohol on him as he feigns busyness and indifference.

"But you insult her memory by philandering with this woman—the very one with whom you cheated on Ma when she was alive!"

"First take the plank out of your own eye, Edgar. Your own mother gave birth to a bastard."

That is her fault, is it? Her no-good husband had up and left, and she had to eat, didn't she? Her child had to eat. I'd say that makes her more righteous than that trollop who takes you to bed for free!

"I daresay, it is the tomcat who breeds the kittens."

"Oho, Edgar! Who do you think you are talking to? I can do as I please. And you do as you please, obviously. I have never seen one so lazy. You have some nerve scolding me about my behavior."

Do not stop now, Mr. Poe. Any

other foster son would have killed him in his sleep.

I can hardly tell him that. It is no use quarreling with him anyway. He always turns the argument back on me.

And like a bad dream that oft repeats, my lenders, this time from Fortress Monroe, submit inquiries regarding the repayment of my loans. I am required to tell them that Mr. Allan is not often sober and they ought not to expect compensation soon.

I wonder if John Allan takes my words to heart because, soon after, I catch him flirting with Aunt Nancy. Our uncomfortable table scenes do not make for easy digestion. I hope you have already dined, dear Reader.

"Miss Valentine, that is a very smart frock," he says, sounding unusually intimate.

"Thank you, Mr. Allan. I am grateful for the means you provide to allow for a new frock." Nancy is a plain, forbearing woman, the sort who can tolerate being John Allan's sister-in-law, but who has neglected marriage and family of her own.

The bulk of John Allan is leaning in her direction. I think he might slip out of his chair. "My means are at your disposal. I must say, you are very capably running the household since your dear sister departed. Perhaps Moldavia has found her new mistress?"

Nan looks down at the tablecloth, stammering for an

answer. John Allan's attention is deflected, and he raises his empty wine glass to one of the servants standing at the wall.

I pull my chair closer to Aunt Nancy and speak in a low voice as another servant clears the dishes away. "Miss Nancy, need I remind you how unfaithful he was to your sister. If you marry him, he is only going to prance about with this other woman—or women—behind your back."

I do not think he heard me, nevertheless he catches me interfering. "Edgar, keep your nose out of it. You interrupt my household with your self-righteous, unsought opinions. Miss Valentine has been with me for twenty years and some. Certainly before you came along."

"It is nothing against Miss Nancy. But you, sir, have you no shame? You are trying to fill Ma's place, with her not in her grave a year yet."

"Why do you care? Do you object to every woman who might be made my wife?" He taps his refilled goblet with his wedding ring. "I know what it is. By God, I know! You do not want me to create a true heir that would overtake your place. Ha! How very like you. Spiteful and selfish."

Is that true?

No. You tell the truth, Mr. Poe. He besmirches our foster mother's honor, replacing her so easily, so soon.

"That is ridiculous," I say. "I do not care how many children, legitimate or otherwise, you sire. Good luck to them all." I drain my glass in one swallow and leave the table unexcused.

After this bit of meddling, John Allan goes out of his way to have me admitted to West Point, and away I go. This makes me question why he did not do so before. When I have been waiting nearly a year, he could have hastened my application? It baffles.

John Allan shakes my hand, stoic and ceremonial, for the final time before I board a gangplank at the wharf. He does not linger to see the boat launch or fare me well as I sail into my new life.

My dear Reader, are you worried for me yet?

You should be.

Chapter Twenty-Four
1830–31

"As regards Sergt. Graves—I *did* write him that letter. As to the truth of its contents, I leave it to God, and your own conscience. —The time in which I wrote it was within a half hour after you had embittered every feeling of my heart against you by your abuse of my *family*, and myself, under your own roof—and at a time when you knew that my heart was almost breaking."
—Edgar

"You sent me to W. Point like a beggar. The same difficulties are threatening me as before at Charlottesville—and I must resign. . . . I have no more to say—except that my future life (which thank God will not endure long) must be passed in indigence and sickness—I have no energy left, nor health[.]" —Edgar

The United States Military Academy
West Point, New York

While camping by the Hudson River with some 250 West Point cadets, I receive a letter from John Allan containing $20 and an accusation of theft. I brought with me some books and belongings from my room at Moldavia, assuming they were mine to take. It seems not.

Despite the $20, I am ill-suited to secure essentials for my academical-military career, including such things needed to take care of one's body—soap, razors, socks—

as well as the things one needs for his room and comfort—fuel, furniture, candles. The curse of Charlottesville revisits me here. I borrow to make up for any lack.

As a result of my old age (twenty-one, but some cadets are as young as fourteen), I escape most of the hazing that befits new cadets, or "plebes." A rumor is born that I secured an appointment at West Point for my son, but that the son died and I came to take his place. I use such speculation to deepen my personal mythology, and I further regale my classmates with tales of Arabia and the Mediterranean.

Upon the entrance examination, I state my age as nineteen. Having decreased in age three years, I am still older than most. I look older too, wearing a new haggard, disgruntled face.

28 South Barracks

"Poe? I heard some talk going 'round the barracks."

"What about?"

"About you, in fact. Are you really descended from Benedict Arnold?"

I make time for a long, silent stare out the window, impressively Byronesque.

"I am an orphan, Henderson. I do not know my parentage. There are those who say so, but my mother, who was an Arnold, is not saying one way or the other. She's dead. As is my father."

"Oh, I am terribly sorry, Poe—"

"It matters not. The United States is my father now."

Yes, better to be cryptic, Mr. Poe. The reconstruction of your history undeniably beats the reality. Anything to skirt the fact that our actress mother was buried in an unmarked grave, having been abandoned with her children, one of whom may or may not be legitimate. Anything to forget that you belong to a miserly Lowland Scot who despises us, and his wife, the only good thing to have ever happened to you—besides myself, that is—is now dead too.

Rumors aside, I do not take well to the corporal rigors of cadet life. In my younger years, I could swim miles upriver and box with the best of them. Perhaps I still can, but I am not made to endure long periods of physical training. I tire early.

When we move to winter quarters in the South Barracks, I share Number 28 with two other cadets. We three are subject to numerous causes for discipline, there being 304 "thou shalt nots" to transgress. Consider Regulation No. 173: "No Cadet shall keep in his room any novel, poem or other book, not relating to his studies, without permission from the superintendent."

Lieutenant Locke is the dreaded disciplinarian I immortalize for the amusement of my comrades:

As for Locke, he is all in my eye,
May the devil right soon for his soul call,
He never was known to lie—
In be at a reveillé "roll call."
John Locke was a notable name;
Joe Locke is a greater; in short,
The former was well known to fame,
But the latter's well know "to report."

One evening, after lights out, Number 28 is devoid of brandy. Since the weather is so god-awful cold and damp, we draw straws to decide which of us is to fetch more. Gibson draws the unlucky lot, and we put together some articles he can use for the barter. He knows well the way to Old Benny's Haven, the unsanctioned market where we cadets can trade for such goods not stocked at the commissary. Off he stumbles into the murky night with as many candles we can spare, as well as my last blanket.

After a while, I become somewhat worried for the chap, and so I venture out on the path to see he did not meet with a fiend, an upperclassman, or Lieutenant Locke. When I see him lurching back, he is drenched and soaked in blood.

"Gibson! What the devil happened to you?"

Straightaway, I take the brandy, of which he has already partaken, and I notice the bloody feathers in his hand.

"Old Benny was crotchety tonight. He wanted money, not your ratty blanket."

"But I see you got what you wanted."

"He finally found me a bottle."

"Did you leave any for Pickering and me? What is that mangled mess? Do not tell me it was an animal in its former life?"

"The loudest, ugliest gander you ever saw. Old Benny dispatched it for me since I couldn't have very well walked into the barracks with him honking his head off."

"Ah, is that how he lost his head? I'd never have known that was a gander. . . Say, Gibson, I have an idea," I say, grimacing at the carcass.

I explain the ruse to him as I prepare the goose, tying its wings and neck down. When I am finished and we have rehearsed the scene, I go back to our room, where our unfortunate third roommate is studying and a guest from the North Barracks is lounging, hoping to share our bounty from Benny's.

Gibson staggers in minutes later.

"My God! What has happened?" I cry.

Gibson slashes at his throat with his hand. "Old Locke," he mumbles. "Old Locke—"

"What of him?" I ask. "Did he catch you?"

"Ha! He won't stop *me* on the road anymore."

"What do you mean?"

Then he draws from his coat a knife, which we had decorated with goose blood. "I killed him!"

"Nonsense," I say. "You are only playing one of your tricks."

"I thought you wouldn't believe me. So I brought his head back to prove it!" At this he launches the goose, flinging it at our only lit candle, which is snuffed out, leaving the room in pitch dark.

Our visitor leaps out the window, sadly landing in

the slop bucket and screaming that Lieutenant Locke
has been murdered and his head is in Number 28, South
Barracks.

"Who did it?"

"One of those in the room with Benedict Arnold's grandson!"

Our other roommate, Pickering, is stunned into a
trance, sitting vaguely in the corner until we revive him
with sips of brandy.

Do not think that I am only drinking and not writing. I
am writing my best poems thus far, up at night by candlelight while my roommates sleep. And, happily (perhaps the only happiness of this interlude), I have brought
my poems to Colonel Thayer, who is very commending.
We work out a subscription plan for the corps of cadets, in which a book of poems may be preordered with
seventy-five cents taken from their pay. Nearly the entire
corps orders a book, no doubt thanks to my bizarre and
sordid stories, not to mention my questionable lineage.

The cadets assume they will be getting more of the
satirical poems I am known for, which circulate and
feature West Point faculty and characters of notoriety.
By the time the book is in the hands of the corps and the
true nature of the poetry is revealed, I am gone.

Thanks to the subscription plan, I can guarantee the
sale of hundreds of copies. Thus, I am able to convince a
New York publisher to come to West Point to arrange for
the publication of my third volume of poems.

Gibson would later say that I "utterly ignored" my

studies at the Academy. I thought I would be finished with the courses in six months, but the organization of the school makes this impossible. The regimen is hard and fast, with hardly any time to study, much less write poetry. I am overcome with anxiety and exhaustion, and I am worried about my standing with my perpetually offended foster father.

John Allan is moving on after the loss of his wife, for he is taking a second Mrs. Allan. It gets back to him that I blamed his drinking for my unpaid debts from Fortress Monroe. My enlistment substitute, whom I call "Bully," has told Allan as much and, I am bound to imagine, uses this family secret to blackmail. Allan pays Bully off and sends a letter to West Point to say he wants no more contact with me.

I cannot help but answer his letter in my own defense. It is a long letter, and it takes me two days to finish. "Did I, when an infant, solicit your charity and protection?" I ask. I tell him that my grandfather in Baltimore wanted me—I was his favorite grandchild (in all probability)—and he had the means to provide for me. But that Allan said he could do better, that he could provide for me *and* offer me a superior education. And did he fulfill this promise?

Why, no! You have been unable to complete your education—not once, but twice!

I list all his wrongs against me. How in Charlottesville he sent me mathematics books when I needed texts for my classes, which had nothing to do with mathematics! How he left me with one dollar on which to survive, forcing me to buy my books on loan, to borrow servants from other students, to gamble to pay all my debts for firewood and the washing and "a thousand other necessaries." I call on God as my witness to declare that I do not love dissipation, but that he has made me to live this way.

And, as it happened at the University of Virginia, I cannot any longer continue at West Point with nothing.

Need I remind you, the two years without contact or support from John Allan were the two years that we managed on our own, without extravagance and without debt?

I can leave West Point honorably if John Allan will write and give his permission for me to leave. If he will not, however, I will cease to be present at roll call and parades and lectures. In anticipation of his rejection, I resolve almost at once to follow through with the latter plan. Indeed, John Allan makes this note upon my letter:

> I do not think the Boy has one good quality. He may
> do or act as he pleases tho' I would have saved him
> but on his own terms and conditions since I cannot
> believe a word he writes.

I do not even attend church. It is not hard to disobey orders, for I am quite sick and can scarcely leave my bed. I am eventually court-martialed for gross neglect of duty and disobedience of orders, to which I plead guilty. The

Academy dismisses me some weeks later, to allow my pay to catch up with what I owe.

I do not think I will live much longer. This is fine with me because what more time I have left will surely be times of poverty and infirmity.

You are not dying, Mr. Poe, for all that it feels like it. What will eventually kill you is heartbreak. Your heart cannot take much more abuse without giving up for good.

I cannot go home. I know I am no longer welcome at Moldavia with a new Mrs. Allan there. I have lost my parents and my home.

But home, I learn, is where my family is. And I still have a family.

The Poes. They are poor and ailing and alcoholic, but they are yours.

I haul my trunk down to the bitter Hudson and board a boat, wearing an old suit of mourning, a cadet's overcoat, and a tattered beaver hat, which I traded for at Old Benny's.

PART FOUR:

The Critic

Chapter Twenty-Five
1831

—❦❧—

". . . And when I think of the long twenty-one years that I have called you father, and you have called me son, I could cry like a child to think that it should all end in this. . . . When I look back upon the past and think of everything—of how much you tried to do for me—of your forbearance and your generosity, in spite of the most flagrant ingratitude on my part, I can not [*sic*] help thinking myself the greatest fool in existence, —I am ready to curse the day when I was born." —Edgar

Elam Bliss, Publisher
208 Broadway
New York, New York

Since the boat first stops in New York City, the heart of the literary world, I determine to find work in a publishing house or at a magazine or newspaper. I will deign to sweep the floors, if I must, for I have nothing. The boat fare took my last cent.

Though the trouble with sweeping floors is that I can barely stand on my own two feet. The river journey left me with a severe cold and an infection in my ear, which is draining blood and other discharge.

Although I want nothing more than to cut ties with the father who is not a father, upon finding lodging in the city, I must write him for money, or else die.

It will however be the last time that I ever trouble any human being—I feel that I am on [a] sick bed from *which* I never shall get up. . . .

Please send me a little money—quickly—and forget what I said about you—

If you do die, may the guilt of your demise be on his hands.

Be that as it may, I recover, and I land a job with the publisher of my forthcoming book of poems for the West Point cadets. Elam Bliss, probably for reasons of charity, offers me a job reading proofs at the office on Broadway.

Do you recall Peter Pease, the classmate who gave me the name Gaffy and whom I last saw at the wharf in Boston? I cross his path again in New York, and we dine one evening in Madison Square. I am in good spirits after rising off my deathbed, and I cover the bill, hailing my soon-to-be-published book.

"I have at last struck it hard, old friend."

You must be buoyant in the presence of your peers, Mr. Poe. If you allow yourself to think about where you've come from and how uncertain your future, you will descend into despair.

But how recklessly Fortune spins her wheel. My mood

plunges upon realizing that my book is not likely to make me any money, and I am finding it hard to survive in New York on my wages from the publisher. *Poems* by Edgar A. Poe, second edition, is printed and distributed to the U.S. Corps of Cadets, who do not comprehend the content that is dedicated to them.

When I depart New York on a steamer, I know I look like a tramp in my army-issued boots and tatty clothing. I possess only a little money from the sale of *Poems*. For this reason, I do not call on any editors when we make port in Philadelphia. I only want to go home.

The Poe Residence
Baltimore

Aunt Maria Clemm's house has a trick of drawing one in—for good. My grandmother is confined to her bed, and it looks like Henry ought to be. He is not long for this world, I am afraid.

Still and all, it is pleasant to see my merry little cousin Virginia, who is much grown since I saw her last year. And Aunt Maria—Muddy, as I call her—welcomes me. Her own son has gone to sea, and Henry is dying. I think she styles me a potential "man of the house," who is making a timely entrance. And because she admires me, the To Be takes to her.

Muddy thinks you are the next Coleridge!

I attempt to find employment in the city. I seek a position at the *Federal Gazette*, since my cousin Neilson has recently left a job there. When I was last in Baltimore, I argued with its editor, William Gwynn, about *Al Aaraaf*, and although I apologize for my past disagreement, he seems not keen to hire me. Teaching, I think, might supply a salary and time enough for writing, so I inquire about a position as an assistant at a boys' school in another town.

But my brother, ever the romantic, has other ideas to distract me. Weak and wheezing, Henry introduces me to the eligible daughters of Baltimore.

"Come on, Eddie. You can charm the stockings off any girl. Wear your West Point regalia and be mysterious and flattering."

I do like the ladies, and they like me, and I tend to do my brother's bidding. But my heart's not all in it, although I do write them some little poems—the least I can do. Perhaps once I land on my feet again I can better pursue a love interest.

Failing at that, Henry flaps a paper at me.

"What is this?" I ask, scanning the page.

"Short story contest," he says. "You can win it."

"Why should I?"

"There's more money in prose. Come on, brother. You may read me what you write, and I will teach you how to rewrite it."

My story, in fact, does not win the prize, but it is chosen for publication in the *Philadelphia Saturday Courier*, giving me some much-needed encouragement and a little money from the sale.

But then, my brother's condition worsens. Nights in our hot, confined bedroom terrorize me, as I keep awake to Henry's labored breathing. I seek medical treatment, but with no money for doctors or medicine, I must rely on those who will accept credit. And I pray that God will hasten to take him instead of leaving him to deteriorate before my eyes.

One of those nights, my prayer is answered and his breathing ceases altogether. How can I relay to you, dear Reader, without frightening you away, what it is like to watch someone strangle to death in the bed you share? It is unspeakable horror. He was twenty-four years old— my brother, William Henry Leonard Poe—a sailor, an idealist, and a generational drunk, who taught me to write a good story. The obituary mistook our last name to be "Hope." A cruel irony.

To be terribly honest, his death and burial grant me little respite from writing. It doesn't seem possible that Henry is gone—I still *feel* him here, or perhaps it is his void that I feel—and it causes me to wonder if we were too quick to bury him in the family plot at Westminster Hall. These thoughts lead to stories of the same sort. Death and dying, I have come to learn, stimulate the To Be and create the inspiration for future tales of the macabre.

After Henry's death, I resort to one of my favorite pastimes, which is writing to my foster father who does not want to hear from me. I send the letter by care of a relative at Ellis & Allan, knowing that he will make John Allan read it.

It is a long time since I have written to you unless with an application for money or assistance. I am sorry that it is so seldom that I hear from you or even *of* you—

Will you not write one word to me?

I am dreadfully homesick . . . and poor. Poes and poverty seem to go hand in glove. Grandmother Poe's house is not in the well-to-do section of town. This is no mistake. Although we keep busy, we lack income.

I am both sorry and amused to say that Muddy is an expert at her trade, and her trade is begging. She bustles from door to door with her big, empty wicker basket, asking for clothes or food. The begging commences at the relatives', but her solicitation is by no means limited to family. She always comes by what is needed, even when the potential donor is John Allan, whom she also beseeches by post.

Poor Henry was past-due his loans, having been too sick to work. As his next of kin, I will be arrested for this unpaid debt, for which he cannot be held responsible. Muddy collects $20 from our merciful family and neighbors, but more is needed to keep me out of debtors' prison. I am terrified at the prospect of incarceration, especially being that my own health is poor. Is it pauperdom that kills us Poes?

Consumption knows no class or caste. But you __will__ die if you go to jail, Mr. Poe, when there is still so much you must do.

I know it. I entreat John Allan. Aunt Maria joins in. No answer. Ten days later, I write to him again, this time supplied with desperation, not mockery, from To Be.

> . . . For the sake of Christ, do not let me perish for a sum of money which you would never miss. . . . If you wish me to humble myself before you I am humble. . . .

I threaten and I agonize, not knowing he had already answered Muddy's distress call, dispatching by letter an Ellis & Allan Baltimore agent to secure my freedom from debtors' prison and to give me $20 "to keep me out of further difficulties." Only—he forgot to post the letter.

I am saved from my predicament when the Poe family rises to my rescue. At nearly the same time, John Allan's agent turns up to act in my behalf, which is both flattering and bewildering. The man has a heart after all, and I do not feel so foolish for writing thus:

> [F]or the sake of the love you bore me when I sat upon your knee and called you father[,] do not forsake me.

Chapter Twenty-Six
1831–32

"I would sooner live on a crust of bread with [Edgar
Poe] than in a palace with any other man."
—Mary Starr

"He had the way and the power to draw any one to
him. He was very fascinating, and any young girl
would have fallen in love with him." —Mary Starr

The Poe Residence
Baltimore

I spend the next few years in my grandmother's garret,
writing stories, tutoring Virginia, fighting illness and
starvation, keeping out of debt.

When I am not at home, I frequent the bookshop on
Calvert Street or the Baltimore library, where I can read
without purchasing the book. Widow Meagle's Oyster
Parlor on Pratt Street offers a humble stage to recite my
poetry. The widow herself introduces me as "The Bard"
to the revolving audience of sailors who visit the tavern.

I am also known as "Captain" or "Major," the patron
saint of street urchins. I organize the young orphan strays
of the Baltimore gutters to execute drills in the street, and
I, still in my military coat, cannot shake them whenever I
leave the house. It is the Imp leading the imps.

One day, sitting at my writing desk by the attic window, I see through the clotheslines a young woman with pretty auburn hair sitting in the rear of one of the Essex Street houses. Now I may be beaten down, but I am not too frail to flirt. I wave my white handkerchief in the window to attract her attention. She sees and, I think, smiles, waving her own handkerchief back at me.

"Sissy!" I call down. Straightaway, I hear the clop-clop of my cousin's lace-ups on the stairs. "Young lady, how would you like to carry a message for me? You can be my very own messenger pigeon."

She whistles a coo and waves her arms. "I'll do it, Eddie."

"You see that house there?"

"That's the Devereaux house."

"Right. I want you to fly down there and ask for Miss Devereaux."

"Do you mean Mary? Mary Starr? Devereaux is the uncle."

"Miss Starr then. Tell her that your cousin, Mr. Edgar Poe, saw her sitting in the window and says she has the most beautiful head of hair he ever saw. Tell her that Mr. Poe is recently returned from the United States Military Academy at West Point and that he writes poetry. Say that he requests a lock of her hair to inspire an ode. Catch all that?"

She nods with a mischievous grin and scampers down the stairs.

The Newman Residence
Essex Street

Another day, as I am walking back to Aunt Maria's, I see Mary Starr sitting on Mary Newman's front stoop. The two Marys whisper and giggle.

"Do you know Edgar Poe?" I hear Miss Newman ask. Miss Starr shakes her head, although she did give Virginia a lock of her hair for me.

"Poe? Is he the brother who wooed Kate Blakely at the Armstead Hotel?"

"The very one! Kate still shows off the poems he wrote her."

"How do you do, Miss Newman?" I say as I approach. She introduces me to the other Mary, whose bonnet only partially hides her blush. But do not let this show of shyness fool you, Reader; Miss Starr proves to be one of the feistiest women I ever meet.

"Mary!" calls a voice from inside.

"What, Mama?" says Mary Newman, who disappears into the house.

I leap over the railing and take the now-empty seat next to Mary Starr. "I believe I have a lock of your hair."

And so sparks our romance, which is as fiery as Miss Starr's head of hair.

It begins gently enough. We conduct a handkerchief signaling routine from our windows, much like my practice with Myra in Richmond, and I call on her each evening. Virginia, just like a trained pigeon, dutifully passes our love notes back and forth, as once did Rosalie for me at the Mackenzie School for Girls.

I would have married Miss Starr, except that I
have no business being anyone's husband. Mary's uncle
expressly forbade our union on the grounds of my un-
employment. Muddy advises me to bide my time. "You
mustn't give up your writing, Eddie, not even for a pretty girl." I think it is mutually lucky that I did not marry
her. I am not easy to live with, as John Allan would
attest, and she, as tradition would say of those of her
coloring, is prone to provoke my temper. I admit I am no
match for hers.

James Devereaux Residence
Essex Street

One evening, her uncle is home with his friend Mr. Morris. This Mr. Morris stands next to the piano and thumbs
through the leaves of music on the rack.

"Mary, will you sing this for me?" he asks. It happens
to be my favorite song that she commonly sings to *me*:
"Come Rest in This Bosom."

She obliges Mr. Morris, sweeping her skirts under the
piano bench and he turning the leaves for her. Pacing the
length of the parlor, I bite my nails until I cannot stand
the man leering over *this bosom*—*my* bosom—anymore.
I stomp to the piano and throw the music sheets on the
floor.

"I can play the song without the music, Eddie," she
says, lifting her chin. She sings along, louder now.

"It's out of tune," I retort.

After the other fellow takes his leave, we have it out.
"Mary, why would you tease me? You know how jealous

I am."

"I wasn't teasing you," she says, with disingenuous wide eyes.

"You know you did. And I think Mr. Morris was in on it. Perhaps your uncle too."

"Eddie! You are making too much of it. It was only a song."

"*Our* song, Mary. Did you not see him making eyes at you?"

"What do you have against Mr. Morris?"

"Nothing, I am sure," I say with eye-rolling sarcasm. "He called you Mary and not Miss Starr. That's not proper."

"He knows me well enough to call me Mary. *You* call me Mary."

"Perhaps I should not call on you at all."

"Oh, Eddie. . ."

Our first lovers' spat, Reader, but far from the last.

Omitting those that come in between, the final quarrel happens the night I meet some old West Point acquaintances at Barnum's Hotel. I drink a little champagne, but by now you know that a little is all it takes to alter me. Afterwards I go to Mary's house, as is my custom every evening, but I find the door locked. It is well near eleven o'clock.

I go 'round to her bedroom window and open the shutters, waking her and telling her to unlock the front door. She does, going toe to toe with me on the stoop in nary a decent dressing gown.

"I waited all evening for you in the parlor, when I could have gone out with the girls. I could have gone out with a *gentleman*, for all that! Mr. Morris doesn't stay out all night drinking with his army chums. I should have accepted his offer instead. He, at least, goes to church!"

"Is that so? The righteous Mr. Morris, who wants to rest in your bosom?"

"Mr. Morris gives me the attention I deserve."

"I ought to give you to him then, you fickle, ginger-headed. . ."

Could it be, dear Reader, that my demeanor intimidates her? I must have been a fearsome sight because, instead of sparring words, she runs past me, down the alley between the houses, and around back. I chase her through the back door and into her mother's room.

"Mary! What's amiss?" Mrs. Starr exclaims. "Go upstairs," she tells her daughter when she sees me. Mary obeys her mother, and the door slams behind her.

"Tell her to come back," I say. "I want to talk to her."

"No, Edgar, you will go home now."

"If you do not tell her to come down, I am going up there. I have a right to speak to her."

"No, you do not."

My memory of that night is blurry, but I cannot forget that woman in her night shift shielding the door to the staircase with her body. I am ashamed to think that she expected me to bully my way into her upstairs.

"She is practically my wife, and I will see her," I say in rough fits and starts.

"Go to bed, Edgar. You can call tomorrow after you

sleep it off."

But she never lets me back in the house after that.

The Poe Residence

"Sissy!" I say, thundering down the stairs from my garret with a sealed envelope. Virginia rises from the table. "Take this to the Devereauxs, will you?"

"Yes, Eddie."

"That's a good girl."

But Virginia comes back with the letter unopened. "She wouldn't take it," she says.

My letter was apologetic and self-deprecating. I shred it to bits and write a new letter, one most uncomplimentary of Miss Starr. Virginia, obedient little bird that she is, delivers this letter with instructions not to leave until she has seen the recipient open and read it.

Well, Miss Mary is so outraged by my accusations that, I suppose, she passes the letter to her whole family. The next day I receive a scathing reply from the girl's uncle. He calls me a drunk and a ne'er-do-well, whose mother was a prostitute, and that the Allans did well to disown me. His niece will never stoop so low as to be wed with me.

You can imagine, Reader, how well I take this abuse.

In my fury, I acquire a cowhide whip (I borrow money to do so), which I take to the man's shop for a violent retort to his insults. But when I attempt to thrash him, his sons haul me off and throw me out. In the melee, my overcoat is torn from tails to collar.

Strips of said coat flying from my shoulders like

banners, I march myself, my dignity, and my whip out of the shop and down to Essex Street, where I demand to see Mary's father. I give him this letter, and he calls Mary to come down and answer for it.

I will never forget how lovely and contrite Miss Starr looks as she creeps down the stairs, nowhere to hide. One would think her almost innocent, lacking her typical temper or conceit. Still, this romance ends as all my romances do—in a fit of melodrama. I pull the cowhide out of my sleeve and throw it down at her feet. "There. I make you a present of that!" She blushes, and I leave for good.

Chapter Twenty-Seven
1832–34

"I am perishing—absolutely perishing for want of aid.
And yet I am not idle—nor addicted to any vice—nor
have I committed any offence against society which
would render me deserving of so hard a fate. For
God's sake pity me, and save me from destruction."
—Edgar

"I must say, in justice, I never influenced Mr. Allan
against him in the slightest degree; indeed, I would
not have presumed to have interfered or advised con-
cerning him. Poe was never spoken of between us."
—Louisa Allan

"Whatever came over you?"

I know what you are thinking.

"Violence seems quite out of character."

Well, you are a clever, clever Reader. I am sure you
can come to reason how I might succumb to brutali-
ty, after enduring insults from my foster father on the
same theme. But if you must know, this is the result of
repressed desire and diminished circumstances. Think
about it, Reader.

I grew up as an orphan in a prosperous household, in
which I was given every comfort, but no affection. I did
not belong there. My mothers are all gone, and Myra is
married to another man. I have nothing. So when a man

slanders me and my family, all because of a silly, obstinate girl, of course, it will come to blows.

That is, if you believe this story of Edgar Poe and "Baltimore Mary," as she is known to biographers. She is not the only woman to come forward after my death and claim a love affair with the Bard of Baltimore's Oyster Parlor. Some have even produced letters. Forgeries perhaps. I suppose it gives one meaning and import in her old age to have once been lovely and loved by a dead poet.

Whether it be true or not, I will leave that determination to you.

But I, your beloved narrator, am quite fond of the cowhide in that story.

About this same time, Mr. Poe, you learn that the editor of The Baltimore Saturday Visiter submitted a piece to his own paper's contest under a false name and <u>won</u>. When you confront him for his deceit, he retaliates with fists, and you fight back—do you not, Mr. Poe?—until the staff pull you apart. Now <u>that</u> is a true story.

Moldavia
Richmond

I learn that my foster father, who is suffering from dropsy, has drawn up a will. At twenty-three years old and without employment, I am compelled to go home again, for the hope of an inheritance.

Old Dabney opens the door to Moldavia, forgetting to step aside to let me in.

"Master Eddie! Lord a'mercy! What's it—*two years* since I last seen you?" His golden smile could have paid for my fare.

I smile almost as wide. "Very good to see you too, Dab. You can take my case up to my room, and please tell Aunt Nan—er, Miss Valentine I am here."

Dabney shuffles his feet as I nudge my way in. "Master Eddie, that ole room is for guests now."

"But I *am* your guest. My things are still in it, are they not? If you do not have other guests, I'd prefer to stay in my room."

Dabney looks uncertain. "Miz Valentine is out right now."

Not a good omen, Mr. Poe. Tread carefully.

I swallow the lump in my throat. "Then I shall see Mrs. Allan."

"Go on in the parlor then, and I'll tell Miz Allan you is here."

I notice that my baggage still sits by the door. As I wait in the parlor, I can hear a baby crying in another room.

Finally, a woman enters, and I stand. With an expression of disgust, her face is all nose and jowls. Please excuse the expression, dear Reader, but she looks as if she has opened the door to find excrement on her chaise lounge. Despite having latterly given birth, her dress falls off her shoulders, revealing sharp bones.

"I am Mr. Edgar Allan Poe," I say, giving a slight bow.

Louisa Allan remains in the doorway. Her eyes blink incessantly when she speaks, as though she cannot bear to look at me.

"I know who you are, and you are not welcome in my house. I will have you turn right around and go."

I tense, feeling the blood rush to my hands and feet. "Madam, wait. This is the house I grew up in. My mother was the first Mrs. Allan—"

"She was not your mother."

I feel my necktie tighten, as though a garrote. Was she not my mother?

"I believe your mother was an actress." She says the last word like it tastes foul, her tongue flitting between her teeth like a snake's. The baby is still screaming in its nursery, and I hear To Be wonder if it is a boy.

In spite of the hostile reception, I determine to remain civil and straightforward. "Frances Allan was in every other sense of the word my mother. And this is my home."

"From which my husband banished you."

Did he *banish* me?

Upstairs I hear a small child scampering and whinging, while someone hurries after him. "Master John, you come back here now," a young woman scolds. "You gone tear your new clothes." Then, more tussling, and she cries out. "Ah, he bit me! He done broke the skin!"

The woman in the parlor door seems not to notice. I sit back down and take a deep breath. "My room is upstairs, with my things in it—my books and clothes, my desk—"

"Those things were removed some time ago."

Never mind that. I wouldn't go up there if I were you. There's a wild animal on the prowl.

"I am not leaving without first talking to Pa—"

"If you mean Mr. Allan, that is all well and good because I've sent for him to come straightaway from the office. I want you gone, and he knows how to handle you."

"Good God, woman! What did I ever do to you?"

"Don't you swear in my house, Mr. Poe. You are not welcome here. You encroach on my husband's goodwill and charity, when you are ungrateful and undeserving."

"He doesn't give me anything! He doesn't send me money. He doesn't even send me letters!"

"Well, then, I would think a young man of your intelligence would take that to mean that he doesn't want you in his house."

The To Be sneers in my head. *Ha! John Allan has married the devil's wife and created demonic children with her. Run away, Mr. Poe! The infant cries for fresh blood!*

I am sitting on the chaise with my arms crossed, like

a stubborn child myself, when I hear a foreboding sound
from my youth: the rhythmic clack of a cane on the walk
up to the side entrance. In a panic, I lose my nerve and
make for the front door, where I pick up my case and flee
the house.

The Mackenzie Residence
Duncan Lodge
W. Broad Street Extended

Since I do not fancy a vicious run-in with John Allan, I
hustle down Main Street, thinking that since I have come
all this way, I ought to see my sister.

Rosalie, the perpetual little girl of twenty-two years,
still lives with the Mackenzies at Duncan Lodge, beyond
Shockoe Hill. My old friend Jack lets me in, and I tell
him and Mr. and Mrs. Mackenzie what happened.

"They took all my things out of my room," I say—
this for some reason, feels like the grossest insult. When
Aunt Nancy—you'll remember my foster mother's dear
sister—learns that I visited Moldavia, she finds me at
Duncan Lodge and gives me some money.

Although I cannot be sure who spins the Richmond
gossip wheel, I think it is Mrs. Louisa Allan herself. The
story goes that I, stark-raving mad and drunk, push
past the butler and storm upstairs to Mrs. Allan's room,
where she lay with a newborn in arms. Shouting and
flailing, I curse her and the child, an argument which
might have escalated had not Mr. Allan come home and
driven me out of the house with his cane, beating me
about the head and shoulders. This version of events,

among other rumors, lingers in the city of my youth until after my death.

The Poe Residence
3 Amity Street
Baltimore

Needless to say, it is back to Baltimore for me, where I
carry on miserably: writing, visiting, ailing, languish-
ing. I write John Allan one more letter in an attempt to
interest him in my welfare. I am, I say, "without friends,
without any means."

> It has now been more than two years since you have
> assisted me, and more than three since you have
> spoken to me. I feel little hope that you will pay
> any regard to this letter, but still I cannot refrain
> from making one more attempt to interest you in my
> behalf—

A knock at the door.
"Eddie?"
I turn to find Virginia at my doorstep, biting her lip.
"Ah, it's Little Sparrow. Hop in, Little Sparrow, I was
hoping you would hop by to see me today."
She giggles and looks less flustered. "I was wonder-
ing if you could help me? I can't figure these." She holds
out an algebra book.
"Of course, come here and we'll figure equations
together." I smile at her.
Coming closer, she inspects my smile, which I have
trouble maintaining in the face of such intense scruti-

ny. "Your teeth are so small and lovely and white. And perfectly spaced. Like baby teeth. It's no wonder all the neighbor girls fall in love with you."

I clear my throat and try to sound undisturbed. "Well, I say it's no wonder you can't do sums. There is no sense whatsoever in your pretty little head. Muddy!" I mock-call down the stairs. "We must find a convent that will let Sissy polish its silver. She's hopelessly dull and will never amount to anything. 'Get thee to a nunnery, go!'"

"We're not Catholic, Eddie!" Virginia laughs.

"Oh, you're right. Let's see that book then. Maybe we can make something of you."

At the time of the decline of John Allan, my literary efforts are rewarded. The *Baltimore Saturday Visiter* bestows my short story "MS. Found in a Bottle" with the fifty-dollar prize. Aunt Maria is thankful for the unexpected bounty, which I share with the household.

Furthermore, this recognition changes my life. Muddy engages Virginia in mending and cleaning my suit of clothes and prepares me to call upon the gentlemen who awarded me the prize. The publisher of the paper is so impressed that he in turn introduces me to John P. Kennedy Esquire, a local author of renown. Kennedy will be one of my greatest connections, a literary patron and true friend.

The To Be would like me to note here that such is achieved without the help of John Allan, who is on his deathbed.

Moldavia
Richmond

Knowing this to be the last opportunity for reconciliation, I once more make my way to Richmond. When John Allan dies, so will my chance of being anything more than an orphan.

If that shrew Mrs. Allan sees you first, there will be no reaching Allan's bedside. Hide me, Mr. Poe! She frightens me so!

It takes all the nerve I can muster, but as soon as the door opens to me, I dash up the stairs to John Allan's room. I think that if he can but see me, he might remember how he loved me once. Perhaps, in dying, he will be soft and tolerant, as he had when Ma died.

But no.

I approach him more noisily than I'd intended, taking great gulps of air, saying nothing but "Pa?"

He sits in a chair by the canopy bed, reading a newspaper. When he sees me, a look of fury—I daresay, *fear* comes over his features. He clutches for his cane, which leans beside his chair, and he wields it like a spear, as though I would attack him.

"Get out!" he bellows. "I'll wallop you if you don't leave at once!"

He cannot sit up properly, and yet he is going to beat me for coming to visit? I am stunned, my feet frozen beneath me. It isn't until the servants come rushing in to remove me from the house that I realize the harshness of what happened and what it means.

There will be no more Pa ... and no inheritance.

Chapter Twenty-Eight
1835

—☙ ❧—

"His figure was remarkably good, and he carried himself erect and well, as one who had been trained to it. He was dressed in black, and his frock coat was buttoned to the throat, where it met the black stock; then almost universally worn. Not a particle of white was visible. Coat, hat, boots, and gloves had very evidently seen their best days, but so far as mending and brushing go, everything had been done, apparently, to make them presentable. On most men his clothes would have looked shabby and seedy, but there was something about this man that prevented one from criticising his garments, and the details I have mentioned were only recalled afterwards." —John Latrobe

"I found him in Baltimore in a state of starvation. I gave him clothing, free access to my table, and the use of a horse for exercise whenever he chose; in fact brought him up from the very verge of despair."
—John Kennedy

John P. Kennedy Residence
Baltimore

Without a foster father to petition, I write to my new benefactor, Mr. Kennedy:

Since the day you first saw me, my situation in life has altered materially. At that time I looked for-

ward to the inheritance of a large fortune. . . . This
was allowed to me by a gentleman of Virginia (Mr.
Allan) who adopted me at the age of two years (both
my parents being dead) and who, until lately, always
treated me with the affection of a father. But a second
marriage on his part, and I dare say many follies on
my own at length, ended in a quarrel between us. He
is now dead and has left me nothing. . . . Worse than
all this, I am at length penniless.

At least I can use this betrayal as a point of pleading.
Kennedy, God bless him, appeals for the sale of my stories, fetching for me $15. When I entreat him to help me
obtain a position as a public-school teacher, he invites
me to discuss my prospects over dinner. I send Virginia
to deliver my regrets:

I cannot come—and for reasons of the most humiliating nature in my personal appearance.

This admission wounds my pride, but Kennedy is a
merciful man. He, having never wanted, never imagined
my predicament. Without fuss on his part and embar-
rassment on my own, I am outfitted with clothes and
invited to supper, from which my deprived body benefits.

Mrs. Kennedy hands me a hefty basket at the front
door at the end of the evening. "Mr. Poe, I am overrun
with leftovers. Would you do me the service of taking
these home with you?"

"Gratefully. My aunt will be very pleased. Thank
you, Mrs. Kennedy."

I am gazing up at the massive chandelier in the ves-
tibule when Mr. Kennedy clears his throat. "Er, do you

ride, Poe?"

"Why, I did often in Virginia."

"I only ask because I do not ride as much as I should, and my own mount suffers for it. I wonder, if you ever feel the desire, if you wouldn't take her out for some exercise? Any time you like."

Of course, I accept, my pride resurrecting with a slight smile. Spotting some apples in the leftovers basket, I suddenly feel like a gentleman again.

The Poe Residence

As I climb the hall steps of our humble dwelling, Muddy ushers me to the kitchen table, where she has been chopping onions. She looks careworn but resolved.

"Hallo, Granny," I say to the diminished mound in bed by the hearth. A thought passes: *What if we mistook her for dead? What if we buried her while she was yet comatose?*

"Where is Virginia?" I ask my aunt.

"Ginny's gone to fetch some mending. I need to discuss a matter with you, Eddie. Before she comes back."

"Of course. What is it?" I am worried that she is going to say we have nothing to eat for breakfast.

"Virginia is almost a grown woman."

Hardly, I think. Full grown, perhaps, but she still giggles and romps like a little girl. She is a bright, quick girl with an obliging disposition, but she is baby-faced and coltish.

Were you not playing tea party

with her and her dolly, not half a year ago?

"I see that you notice her."

Do you indeed, Mr. Poe?

"And Ginny is fond of you too."

"She is twelve," I whisper, feeling conspicuous with Grandmother Poe lumped on the other side of the room. She seems to be sleeping this evening, but how can one tell? When awake, she seems not to recognize us, much less understand us. Still, I glance her way.

"She will not always be twelve, Eddie." Muddy follows my gaze to Granny's cot, then picks up the knife and resumes her cutting. She speaks softly, "When Mamma goes to her grave, her pension goes with her. We are very poor, as you know, and female. If you would take my daughter as your wife, then I could be your mother in title as well as in affection."

I sigh. I want nothing more than a mother, but. . . . "I don't have any means to provide for you and Virginia."

"Not yet. But you are going to be a man of renown. I know it to be so. And when you are, you and your household will need taking care of. It would be my one desire to do that in return for your bond."

Aunt Maria looks at me with red, runny eyes. I do not know if it is the onions or the sentiment, but tears prick my eyes as well.

She acts as if I would be doing her a great favor, and yet I know the sacrifice she is offering. She is presenting me her only daughter, and her service, for the rest of her life.

I nod at first, but then I shake my head. "I cannot marry a child."

"I am not asking you to marry her now. Perhaps we could make you her guardian. But, you wouldn't be disinclined to marriage? A bit later, I mean. She is a lovely girl. . ."

"Oh, she is, Muddy. I am not disagreeing with you. I love Virginia. It would be a blessed honor to one day take her as my wife."

Although I say it with conviction, as I mean to keep my vow, To Be points out the shame and discomfort that thereafter overtake me.

What have you done?

———⁂———

Your situation is about to change, Mr. Poe, and much for the better.

To Be is not speaking of marriage, although I promise to marry Virginia when she comes of age. All the while I listen to Muddy's schemes, I recall a recent visit from a Miss Winfree, who I knew in Richmond and who is a close friend of Elmira Shelton, née Royster.

She tells me astonishing news from home. Myra is unhappy with Shelton. She uncovered in her parents' house one of the letters I wrote her from the university, and she is livid. She squabbled with her mother and father *and* her husband, accusing them of subterfuge to arrange her marriage, when she was engaged all along to Edgar Poe.

Miss Winfree brings with her a parlor album—a common scrapbook of my day—in which Myra has written about a lost love. This sign of regret is vindicatory, but utterly heartbreaking. Myra is off the market, forbidden fruit, while Virginia is offered, but not yet ripe for the taking.

Then, true to the To Be's word, John Kennedy, to whom I owe my turn of fate, connects me with Thomas W. White, the editor of *The Southern Literary Messenger*, who publishes some of my work. I correspond with White, who offers me a job at *The Messenger*, which will require a change of address. Lo and behold, the editorial offices are in Richmond, Virginia.

We know another in Richmond, and her name is Mrs. John Allan. She sullies your good name.

Forget that crow. I am thinking of Myra.

Myra is Mrs. Alexander Barrett Shelton. Do not forget that, Mr. Poe.

My women trouble must wait for me, as Mr. White is not yet prepared to move me into the office. I write for *The Messenger* in the meantime from my confined garret room in Baltimore. How vexing it is to stretch resources until I can occupy my paying job.

—⚬⚬—

"Mr. Poe, you have a weak heart and bad nerves," says Dr. Buckler, using a wooden cylinder to listen to my chest as my head lolls on the pillow. The pounding in my temples keeps time with my heartbeat.

"What can be done for him, Doctor?" Muddy asks.

"Only a sea voyage will make him well again."

A sea voyage? You are not paying for this quack, are you?

"Dear me, we cannot afford a sea voyage." Muddy wrings her hands over my bed.

"Perhaps let's start with some proper nutrition. He looks like he's wasting away."

"Well, sir, I do my best with what we have. The garden's gone mostly dormant, but I have onions and leeks and herbs."

"Those are good, but he needs meat, madam."

"Doctor, do you know of anyone who might be willing to donate some?"

No need, Mrs. Clemm. There are plenty of rats in the cellar. I hear them scratching up through the walls at night.

I would laugh if it did not hurt so.

Chapter Twenty-Nine
1835

—⁂—

"There was never a more perfect gentleman than Mr. Poe when he was sober, [but at other times,] he would just as soon lie down in the gutter as anywhere else."
—J. W. Fergusson

"My bitterest enemy would pity me could he now read my heart. My last[,] my last[,] my only hold on life is cruelly torn away—I have no desire to live and *will not*. But let my duty be done. I love, *you know* I love Virginia passionately, devotedly. I cannot express in words the fervent devotion I feel towards my dear little cousin—my own darling." —Edgar

The Southern Literary Messenger
Main & 15th Streets
Richmond

"Look, it's Edgar Poe."
"There goes Edgar Allan Poe!"
"He's the orphan—taken in by the Allans."
I am somewhat gratified and somewhat horrified to hear Richmond folks murmur as I go by. Most sound friendly, their whispers curious and deferential, but I am wary of rumors that run rampant in my hometown, perhaps even old resentments from my university days.
"Oh, yes, but he did not inherit the Allan fortune, I hear."

"There were too many illegitimate brats in the will, as it was."

One of the first orders of business is to read John Allan's will for myself. I want to be certain that there is no mention or allusion to the foster son whom he raised from two years of age. There is not, but I am amused to learn that the second Mrs. Allan is disputing the will and its many provisions for several bastard children. I cannot say that I am not pleased to hear of her discomfort.

Strolling to the offices of *The Southern Literary Messenger*, which is across the way from Ellis & Allan, is like traveling through time. I pass the Enchanted Garden, where I once made love to Myra. I see servants from Moldavia, who halloo me most amiably. Often I catch a Scotch dialect on the wind, and I am transported to a past that is both nostalgic and bitter.

My main responsibility at the magazine is to review all the books and submissions. I am making $10 a week, while making myself known as a formidable critic. We have several hundred subscribers when I start, but I will, during my time there, increase that number into the thousands—

When you have not gotten yourself fired, that is.

I am welcomed into many a Richmond parlor for a bite to eat and a cordial colloquy. The only thing that would make my situation happier would be to have Muddy and Virginia with me. I miss my aunt's steady guidance, and it makes me accept more drink than I ought to.

One of the first pieces I write for *The Messenger* is a poem, "To Sarah" by "Silvio." These are unobscured pseudonyms for Elmira and myself, as intended. Indeed, if all the city knows it, her husband knows it too.

> *. . . The stars above*
> *Witnessed thy vows to me—*

Manchester Estate
South Bank of James River

A new but known man about town, I am invited to an extravagant party at an estate across the river. I hear beforehand that Elmira Shelton will be in attendance, which, I imagine, is the reason for my inclusion. The Richmond aristocrats seek to cross Silvio with Sarah.

Now is your chance, Mr. Poe. You can make her sigh and make her sorry all at the same time.

I arrive early for the event and find myself holding a glass, the contents of which I take in sips and swallows, by degrees girding myself with confidence. Lingering in a window alcove across from the grand staircase, I grip my drink and wait for Mrs. Shelton, my once adolescent sweetheart.

And she comes, gliding upstairs, in a striking blue and green gown with white gloves. First I see her hair, plaited and pinned. Then her eyes, more serious and sophisticated than last I saw. A servant waits to take her shawl, but she feels my eyes on her and stands fixed at the top of the staircase, caught in the intensity of my gaze, which is full of both desire and castigation. The ballroom falls silent, as the partygoers, who all know our ill-fated history, witness this very intimate moment in public. This was precisely the opportunity I had hoped for.

Then, seconds after it is begun, the spell is broken. Shelton, who has followed his wife up the stairs, sees her locked in a torrid stare with me and snatches her arm. Myra must look away as an irate husband hurries her down the steps and away.

Mr. Shelton afterwards sees to it that his threats of violence if I further pursue his wife reach my ear and thus dissuade me from any such behavior.

Mrs. Poore's Boarding House
Bank Street

Muddy sends word that my grandmother died during one of her long naps. With our grandfather's pension nevermore too, my cousin Neilson Poe has offered to take in Virginia to help alleviate Aunt Maria's impoverishment. Muddy is stalling, but she also mentions all the accomplishments and comforts Neilson might provide her daughter. She asks me to act now. If Virginia goes away, then so too our arranged family.

This confusion, as well as having seen the unattainable Myra, sends me into a deep depression. For the first time, I have a literary job that pays, my name is becoming known, and I am well respected by the Richmond upper classes. And yet, I feel impotent.

I write to John Kennedy in Baltimore, implying that I am on the verge of suicide. Alarmed, he writes back, telling me to rise early, give generously, and write humorously—comedies being quite popular in France these days. Now, this may sound like unhelpful advice for a miserable man, but, honestly, what would you do if your protégé threatened to end his own life? You would tell him to *do* something, of course! Take exercise. Do those things which make him happy. But when one is so low, he cannot take pleasure even in those things. If I am not so brazen as to murder myself, I am thoroughly inclined to self-destruct.

You raise a good question, Reader. Why, yes, I still blame my suffering on my foster father, despite his being dead. If he had included me in the will, then I would have some provision to send Muddy and ward off Neilson.

Most days, I cannot rise from my bed. When I do make it into the office, I suppose it looks like I am suffering the excesses of alcohol. Mr. White, who has hitherto been patient and fatherly, finally throws me out in spite of my protests. "No man is safe who drinks before breakfast," he says.

The Poe Residence
Baltimore

Sick, depressed, and out of options, I flee to Baltimore, where I elope with Virginia.

Now, Reader, please. Must I defend myself to you? I hear your judgements, convicting me of wrongdoing, lechery—a base nature. "Thirteen? And your *cousin*!"

I know, I know. It is uncomfortable for you to ponder. But I would ask you, slip off your modern spectacles for a moment. The man I relate to you lived nearly two centuries ago. Please do not forget that. I was born into a world that operates on systems of ownership. Consequence of her sex, Virginia Clemm was a possession to be had. But God forbid I let Neilson, who I call my bitterest enemy, take her. I made a vow.

As for the relation, the marriage of cousins was a tradition from our English forebears, you see. In my day, marrying your first cousin was unusual, but not unheard of. It still happened. Sissy's age is more of a problem, but I want you to consider my motives.

I need Muddy. My sanity depends upon her, and I cannot do what I must without her guardianship. And so I marry her thirteen-year-old daughter, at her urging.

See, Aunt Maria? You can trust us, you old dear. We would do anything for you, and he (despite my warnings) has legally bound himself to your Virginia.

Don't you see he needs you, Maria? Abandon not your dead brother's child for he will perish without your motherly attention.

We lie about her age—nothing new for this seasoned storyteller. It is a secret wedding, and Virginia is disappointed. Not with me, mind you. She is, as Muddy said, fond of me—as a sister would be a brother. She may be much too young to marry, but she still wants what any young woman would: a pretty dress and a ring and a party. I cannot give those to her, as it would not be proper to make a show of our marriage. Certainly the Poes, who know her real age, would be scandalized, and so we teach Virginia to keep our secret, and she obliges. Only if Neilson insists on taking her away will we proclaim, "Stop right there!" and reveal the official church document.

Feeling better now that it is done, I write to Mr. White asking forgiveness, issuing promises, if only I may have my job back, *please, sir*. Good man that he is, he agrees, as long as I promise not to drink. I can hear the skepticism in his stipulation. He knows that, on my own, I will succumb to temptation.

I return to Richmond straightaway and let him know that my aunt and cousin are coming at my heels to help me behave myself. White grins and welcomes me back with a clap on the shoulder. "Your desk remains just as you left it, with the stack of submissions still up to the rafters."

PART FIVE:

The Husband

Chapter Thirty
1836

"Now it appears to me that he showed his affection in the right way, by endeavoring to make his companion happy. According to the opportunities he possessed, he supplied her with the comforts and luxuries of life. He kept a piano to gratify her taste for music, at a time when his income could scarcely afford such an indulgence. I never knew him to give her an unkind word, and doubt if they ever had any disagreement. That Virginia loved him, I am quite certain, for she was by far too artless to assume the appearance of an affection which she did not feel." —Lambert Wilmer

Duncan Lodge
Richmond

Virginia is a fast friend with my sister Rosalie. It is a sweet sight—*I'd call it disturbing*—to watch them play together. My twenty-five-year-old sister and thirteen-year-old wife—cousins, sisters-in-law, play-mates.

Children, Mr. Poe....

Sissy spends much of the day at the Mackenzies', skipping rope and swinging from trees with Rose.

"How do you do, Ma?" I call the benevolent Mrs.

Mackenzie by the name I used as a boy. And she calls me by Rose's nickname: "Buddy, there you are!"

I kiss her cheek, which is flush and damp with the late-afternoon humidity. She sits on her back porch, rocking and fanning herself. "Can I have Marianne make you a drink, Buddy?"

"No, thank you. I am here to fetch Virginia. Aunt Maria wants her home for supper."

"Aye, of course. Dear, dear girl. Rose is quite smitten." Mrs. Mackenzie asks her maid to summon Virginia. "Tell Rosalie Mr. Poe is here to take their cousin home." To me, she says, "How is it at *The Messenger?*"

"Excellent. My reputation is increasing."

She cackles. "I understand your notoriety is too."

"Some say so," I admit, eyes cast down but nonetheless glinting.

Virginia comes skipping in from the garden, out of breath and perspiring, and yet her cheeks are still as pale as ever. She wraps her arms around me.

"Eddie!" she says, looking up at me with unabashed adoration. I cannot help but smile back at her.

Mrs. Mackenzie is embarrassed by Virginia's demonstration of devotion. Look at the poor woman.

I see Ma Mackenzie frowning down at the lawn. I undo Virginia's clasp and push my girl-wife away, my chuckle nervous. "Come along, Sissy, before Muddy sends us to bed without supper. Say goodbye to Rose and Mrs. Mackenzie."

Along the way home I must reiterate to Virginia to

show restraint, otherwise our affection seems immodest. She is my first cousin, and she is much too young. Even if we do not speak of the marriage, we can still betray our secret if there is unseemly exhibition in public.

"Yes, Eddie," she chirps, wedging her arm inside my elbow.

Mrs. Yarrington's Boarding House
Eleventh & Bank Streets
Capitol Square

When I am at home, I teach Virginia to speak a little French and play a little harp. Muddy, ever occupied with her thread and needle, remarks that Virginia sings like a robin.

Ours is an odd but quaint domicile. It is a mutual dependence. At least I think so. Muddy seems content in her role of "Mother," and the three of us maintain more flesh on our bones these days. I see to it that the ladies are adequately fed and sheltered, and they in turn give me more reason to stay on task.

At this time, I am healthy and employed, making $800 per annum, which will soon increase to $1,000. I am writing a novel, which is serialized in *The Messenger*. My literary criticism is a national sensation when I accuse some very famous writers of plagiarism. Threats of lawsuit and libel only fuel our readership, therefore Mr. White enables me to proceed unbridled.

With my present life fine and my future looking even better, I decide it is time to publicly announce my marriage to Virginia. The simplest way to do this without suspicion is to organize a second wedding. We arrange for a small ceremony in Mrs. Yarrington's parlor, and Virginia gets her new dress, as well as a hat, a cake made by Muddy, and a party. We say she is twenty-one, and our dozen or so guests remark, "Yet she looks so young!" She looks especially childish standing next to her twenty-seven-year-old groom, to which I can attest, as the great mirror above the mantle is tilted down at an angle, showing me a reflection of myself and Virginia standing before the reverend to recite our vows.

We spend our honeymoon in nearby Petersburg, but I want to assure the Reader now: I do not improperly touch the girl. I have no desire to, and I told Muddy as much. Neither can we risk creating a child when the bride is a child herself. We do not have to explain this to Virginia, for there is nothing further from her tender mind. It is not a romantic match in that sense, but I mean what I say when I vow to cherish and protect.

The Reader is perhaps not understanding. Permit me to shed light?

For me, females tend to fall into age-based categories. Older women, like Muddy and Mrs. Mackenzie, may be motherly and fond. Women my own age, like Myra and Mary, may be old enough to be wives but cruel enough to break hearts. And it is the fathers and uncles and brothers of such women that I butt heads with.

Then there is Virginia: innocent, playful, smitten . . . untouched. Not a wicked or selfish bone in her body. I think if I keep her with me, she will remain this way always. Virginia is my Sissy (sister), and I am her Brother Eddie. Muddy is our mother, and this represents our peculiar family to a fare-thee-well.

Quaint, yes, but is this fair to Miss Clemm? She admires you; that is no lie. But at thirteen, how can she know what she consents to? She is doing what Mother tells her to do, like an obedient child. Furthermore, she thinks it all roses because she and Cousin Eddie can play house. She is the means by which you and I may have a mother, but you mustn't let Mrs. Poe be forsaken.

I wouldn't dare. This is what is best for Virginia, and we all know it. She will be known for posterity as the Poet's Wife.

The Poet's <u>child</u>-wife. Perhaps you are being a bit selfish?

I swear to you, it is my aunt and cousin I am thinking of only.

We three Poes idly occupy the parlor in which Virginia and I were married. It is a rare occasion when we are the only guests in it, and we relish this private time when I can read the paper while mother and daughter sip tea and prattle before supper.

"How do you like Richmond?" I ask Sissy.

"I like it very much. It's more civilized than I expected, and folks are friendlier here than in Baltimore."

"I would agree. I prefer Southern manners to the busy impassivity of Northern cities."

Muddy chimes in, "Mrs. Mackenzie is a kindly woman. I appreciate her hospitality to us, and she is very good to your sister, Rosalie."

"You will not find a bigger heart in all of Richmond than Mrs. Mackenzie's."

Virginia grins with a secret to divulge. "Yet Rose is wicked behind her back."

"Is she?" I ask with feigned indifference.

"Mm-hmm."

"How so?"

"She steals sweets when the black woman in the kitchen isn't looking. I told her that was naughty, but Rose told me to hush and mind my own. She said that if she didn't eat the cakes Mrs. Mackenzie would, and she eats too many as it is."

I bite back a laugh. Mrs. Mackenzie maintains her ample figure with a good deal of sitting and being waited upon by her talented kitchen staff.

"And so you demanded the plunder returned to the pantry," I suggest, winking.

"No, I helped her dispose of the evidence. Mrs. Mackenzie may have a big heart, but she also has the biggest bottom I've ever seen!"

Now, I cannot stifle my laughter.

"Virginia Eliza Clemm!" Muddy reprimands.

"That is not my name anymore, Mother. It is Mrs.

Edgar Allan Poe." Even with her nose in the air, she can carry off neither snobbery nor rebellion.

"My word," Muddy swears, "Mrs. Edgar Poe ought not to ruin her appetite with sweets, nor say such a thing about dear Mrs. Mackenzie. And Mr. Poe ought not to encourage her either. Do something, Eddie."

Sissy snorts and smothers her giggles in her apron. I throw the newspaper aside and stalk towards her, rattling the silver in the curio cabinet.

"And what shall I do with Mrs. Poe, hm, Muddy?"

Sissy shrieks and tries to run, but I catch her by the arm. I spin her and tickle her until she is doubled over with unruly giggles.

"I—can't—breathe—Ed—*stop*—*sorry*—I'm—"

We both fall to the floor, Sissy gasping. I jab and twist my fingers into her sides, which Virginia protects by slapping at my hands. She fights me until her titters turn to violent coughs.

Muddy nearly drops her teacup. "Stop it, Eddie," she says in a voice tight with fear, but I've already propped her up.

"Breathe, Sissy," I say, rubbing her back until the fit subsides.

"S—sorry."

"Do not be sorry, darling." I pause until my heartbeat slows. "The breadth of Mrs. Mackenzie's backside is known to leave one breathless."

"Oh, don't make—me laugh—Mr. Poe—it hurts—too much."

The Richmond gossip machine is vigilant and far-reaching.

"*Mr. Poe is having an affair with Mr. White's daughter, Eliza!*"

"*Mr. Poe is harassing Mrs. Shelton!*"

"*Mr. Poe's new wife looks like a child!*"

Yet I am the most wanted guest at every party, if only for the sake of scuttlebutt.

Wherever I go, the spirit of the South is offered. I partake. How else am I to take the pressure? But when I do, it makes me ill, and I begin missing days at the office again until Mr. White reaches the end of his vast patience, and I am unemployed again.

Chapter Thirty-One
1838–41

"I never saw him the least affected with liquor, nor
even descend to any known vice, while he was one
of the most courteous, gentlemanly, and intelligent
companions I have met with . . . besides, he had an
extra inducement to be a good man as well as a good
husband, for he had a wife of matchless beauty and
loveliness . . . she seemed as much devoted to him
and his every interest as a young mother is to her
first born. . . . Poe had a remarkably pleasing and
prepossessing countenance, what the ladies would call
decidedly handsome." —William Gowans

Burton's Gentleman's Magazine
Dock Street
Philadelphia, Pennsylvania

After a failed stint in New York City, I move my curious
family on to Philadelphia, where we attract much attention. I, the notorious literary critic, in my aged dark
suit—worn yet elegant—escort a pretty young woman
on one arm and a matronly widow on the other. The dark
trinity.

Whereas Richmond is sleepy and demure, the Quaker
City is fashionable and fast (that is, unless the postmas-
ter is taking his nap). I edit and contribute to *Burton's
Gentleman's Magazine*, but I find myself unable to work

beside other editors for any enduring length of time. I have my disagreements and fits at *Gent's*, as I do any-where else, and when I break off for good, I write for *Graham's*, increasing its subscriptions to nearly forty thousand.

Since I cannot seem to sustain an office job, my new ideal is to edit and produce my own national serial, which I will title *Penn Magazine*. (You caught the pun, did you? Pennsylvania and pen? Good for you, my very capable and dear Reader.) The *Penn* is my blank slate on which to extend my name to, not only national, but in-ternational renown. Regarding style and content, I know better than all these presumed publishers anyway; I only lack the right connections.

And, of course, a generous loan.

That may be difficult to come by. Magazines and pa-pers around the country are failing by the stacks, and it is proving difficult to place my pieces in paid publications. Still, during my time not taken up by hither-and-thither editorial work, I write. The To Be lures me on journeys of torture, terror, and murder, by way of my pen and imag-ination. Together, we manage to mock the Gothic ro-mance, while at the same time resurrecting it.

We give the people what they want, do we not, Mr. Poe?

And what they want is a shivery tale. Why, you ask, dear Reader? Because death is always looming in this life, and yet none of us think it real. We want to feel it, to understand it; to taste it but not swallow it. Well, Reader, I can tell you from experience that death *isn't* real, and you cannot understand it, only accept it.

Moreover, Mr. Poe, there is power in spooking. You control the monster you create.

Forsooth.

Lea & Blanchard (the very same that refused to publish my poems when I was younger) prepares to print a two-volume set of my collected stories. When *Tales of the Grotesque and Arabesque* is published, I do not need to cover losses. Be that as it may, the money I make off sales is almost none, as Lea & Blanchard absorbs all profit. The best course now is to seek publication in Great Britain. We may have declared our independence as a nation, but it is England that makes the American literary man.

Ah, I see your eyes crossing. You remind me that this is a portrait of the artist at home, not at work. If you wish for a commentary on my writing, business dealings, and impact on the world of literature, you may seek out other tales of the arabesque. In this, I want to simply look at Poe the Man—not the Poet, the Genius, the Perverse, or whatever other title one would care to bestow on (or throw at) me.

Therefore, let us see what Mr. Poe gets up to in the City of Brotherly Love and Sisterly Affection. Right this way, Reader. . . .

Edgar A. Poe Residence
Schuylkill Seventh Street

We three Poes scuttle around the city, eluding past-due rent notices, and finally land stable in a three-story brick on the Schuylkill. The rural setting obliges me to walk several miles into town and back each day, but this is not my sole exercise. My backyard is a river, and I am transported back to my boyhood. Thanks to our unselfish neighbors, we boat in the Schuylkill and hunt in the surrounding countryside—favorite pastimes of my Virginia days. I swim regularly and drink nothing stronger than water.

Without a regular salary, my two hens keep us from going without, taking sewing jobs and making the most of what we have. Muddy keeps an immaculate house and is quite used to making meals from meager harvests. Virginia gardens, and we partake in the fruits of her labor. Her cut flowers brighten and freshen the house, making it far more welcoming than the castles and crypts of my forays into fantasy.

When I come home from work, Sissy greets me with a bouquet or corsage, and I kiss her cheek. She blossoms into a lady most befitting a poet's wife. Her sweet nature charms all she meets, and she increases in beauty too. Many evenings, after a day of corpses and horrors, I walk her around the churchyard in the last light, giving her the first taste of my terrific tales.

This is a secure and lucrative time for me, but my child-wife is not flourishing. In fact, she will begin to die here.

While her distracted husband hobnobs with Knickerbockers and poetasters.

Although it will take the disease ten years to claim her, she daily struggles for breath. Oh, I recognize the old foe well enough; I watched it haunt Frances Allan and saw it cannibalize my brother Henry. Consumption: the patient, persistent killer of the nineteenth century, makes its bed with my wife.

Yet, I urge you not to grieve, dear Reader. Virginia, although ravished, never complains, and rarely is she found not smiling, laughing, or singing. She would not want you to be upset. There will be time enough for that later.

She talks of babies. Virginia is seventeen years old and in poor health, and yet she wants a baby.

"Oh, Eddie, think of it—our own little boykins to bounce around. Wouldn't Mother be overjoyed?"

I think not. The only time "Mother" talks about babies is to forbid them.

"We have this nicer house—it's small but not like those hovels we boarded at. There is food on the table, and your writing is published. . ."

Sissy is too weak to bear children. I do not think she knows the ins and outs of childbirth, but she is moreover fond of children, preferring their company and humor to that of dour adults. But I cannot give her what she wants—it would be irresponsible of me—but it no less niggles.

One night, scribbling by candlelight, I hear an awful howling outside the window. I venture out to the yard with my lantern to find a tiny ball of fur high up in our tulip tree, understandably disturbed by its plight and quite vocal about it. I climb out to the branch and pluck the scrawny creature off its perch, to which it clings like an unripe peach.

It is rather talkative, I suppose critical of my services, as I wrap it in a blanket and cradle it by the fire. Once it quiets, I carry the creature up to the bedroom, where I hear Virginia's dry, high-pitched cough.

"Are you awake, my dear?"

"What's in the package?"

"Here you are, little wifey. It's a baby and it needs a mother."

I lay the almost weightless bundle in her arms.

"Aw, Eddie! It's a kitten." She coos and picks it from its wrappings, cuddling it to her cheek. When it mews, she scratches it under the chin. "Listen to that whining! I've never heard such fuss."

"Well, he *is* a Yankee."

"Yankee or not, it's the most precious lil' babykins, aren't you just? Thank you, Eddie!"

"Give him here. I'll bring him back to you after I fetch him a bit of milk."

The wee laddie is in truth a *lady*. Catterina, who grows into a fetching tortoiseshell dame, is an adored

member of our family from this day until the end of this
tale. I call her Kate.

Now that our Poe family is complete, please accompany
me into the neat parlor of our home on the Schuylkill
River. See me at my writing desk, tickling my mouth
with a quill pen. Muddy rocks and knits by the fire,
while Catterina dozes and hums on her lap. Virginia sits
at the piano and sings, "'Tis Said That Absence Conquers
Love."

We entertain friends and neighbors here. Imagine
yourself as one. That's right. You are most welcome at
my hearth, Reader. Muddy serves you punch in a china
cup and invites you to sit in a floral-print chair. Perhaps
I read a poem aloud, standing by the fire, as Virginia
gently strums her harp. Kitty Kate dances around my
legs before I scoop her up, not missing a word or breaking cadence when she climbs onto my shoulder and rubs
her chin on my ear. Later, we will speak of goings-on
in the city, politics, and current affairs. I jest with you
about our humble dwelling, for I still possess a good humor, and I may even scrape up a bit of tobacco to share.

Watch out for Catterina, though. She possesses a
supernatural talent for walking where one's foot will
step. Especially on the cellar stairs. We wouldn't want an
accident now, would we?

Frederick William Thomas, the poet who wrote
"Absence Conquers Love," the very song Sissy sings most
often these days, visits us like this. I will ask you to

remember this Thomas, dear Reader, for he will play the part of true friend to my *rara avis in terris*—rare bird— in my brief biography. We have much in common: boys from the South struggling to survive on our pens. His sister's name is Frances; my foster mother's name was Frances. While in Baltimore, he and my brother once loved the same girl.

"My dear Poe," he calls me. I write to him in St. Louis:

> Mrs. Clemm and Virginia unite with me in the kindest remembrance to yourself. . . . How long will it be before I see you again? Write immediately.

Despite having a parlor and a friend and a craft, our life is not always picturesque and pleasant. Now and then I wander until Aunt Maria comes looking for me. She either finds me or the neighbors bring me home, but it is in a state of delirium and melancholy. Muddy sends me to bed, where she can keep me out of trouble until the affliction passes. Around my thirty-second birthday, I have what you would call a nervous breakdown.

Chapter Thirty-Two
1841–42

"His love for his wife was a sort of rapturous worship of the spirit of beauty which he felt was fading before his eyes. I have seen him hovering around her when she was ill, with all the fond fear and tender anxiety of a mother for her first born—her slightest cough causing in him a shudder, a heart-chill that was visible. I rode out one summer evening with them, and the remembrance of his watchful eyes eagerly bent upon the slightest change of hue in that loved face, haunts me yet as the memory of a sad strain. It was this hourly *anticipation* of her loss that made him a sad and thoughtful man, and lent a mournful melody to his undying song." —George Graham

George Graham Residence
Franklin & Buttonwood Streets
Philadelphia

My collapse puts the *Penn Magazine* on hold, but I am content to work for *Graham's* until I'm back on my feet. Under my management, *Graham's Magazine* is the best in the nation, publishing the work of our country's most significant writers. Although these contributors are highly rewarded, my salary is quite modest, if not downright scant.

For all we lack in affluence, I at least earn regular

pay. I acquire a harp and pianoforte for Sissy, as well as some pretty dresses and accessories. I buy these gifts on credit, however, and fret until I can pay them off. Since I entrust the whole amount of my salary to Muddy to run our household, she is able to purchase some Chinaware, a tea set, curtains and rugs, four-poster beds, and upholstered chairs. We are poor but comfortable.

Some afternoons, my boss's wife, Mrs. Elizabeth Graham, drives her fancy carriage and team of grays to our house on the river. She plucks up Virginia and the two of them dash off to the Chestnut Street shops, as well as the soda fountain at Eugene Roussel's. Mrs. Graham, of course, is the one making all the purchases. She likes to spoil my wife, whose youth and merriment enchant her.

The Grahams host lavish dinner parties with all the important figures in Philadelphia. It is at one of these parties that I come to know "the Reverend Doctor" Rufus Griswold.

He is neither a reverend nor a doctor.

Still, you may make note of this name, Reader; Griswold is known in the future as the man who wrote my obituary. We will talk more of the supposed reverend later, but know now that he cannot be trusted.

What do you think, Mr. Poe? Shall we cast him the enemy now that it's curtains for John Allan? There is still much more to this story to be deprived a villain. Griswold may stand in as the second act's adversary. Allan left mighty big shoes to fill, Rufus, but I believe you'll do.

But Griswold would say that *I* am my own worst enemy, prone to self-sabotage and conceit. Wine flows throughout these evenings at the Grahams', and I accept a glass so as not to seem ungrateful or, worse, self-righteous. Then, sometimes, I forget myself and drink it.

For this reason, these affairs rattle Muddy. She will come with me when possible and wait in the kitchen to take me home before it is too late, her wicker basket laden with dinner scraps. Her lurking presence behind the scenes gives me good reason to decline after-dinner brandies with this or that member of the literati.

The Poe Residence

I am the most daunting literary critic, as well as the editor of the most read magazine in the nation. Charles Dickens says I must be of the devil.

Virginia, now eighteen, is still physically able, and we take walks and picnics together. We are a striking couple, I in my black suit and she in white frock. I daresay, she never looks older than the day I married her—forevermore a child in appearance, and yet she is never childish in manner.

She likes to watch you swim on hot days, Mr. Poe. Wet, clingy clothes become you.

Perhaps, but more and more she stays in bed with her cough and her cat, while I dash off mysteries and ghostly verse at her side.

One winter evening, we host an intimate gathering at our home. I have cloaked the bird cages so that the only sound we hear is Virginia's song. Muddy pours the coffee and feeds the coal fire as our guests sit enthralled. I will perform later, but for now, I let Sissy cast her melodious spell. She reaches the highest soprano when her carol is cut off with a gurgle. Virginia, mouth parted, eyes black and wet and wide, stares at me with terror. My heart stops. Then blood gushes up from her lungs, bubbles in her throat, and spills over her chin and neck and onto her dress.

I am at her side in a trice, gathering her into my arms and whisking her to bed, Muddy clutching my shirt tails for the flight upstairs. Sissy's audience is left gasping, and I hear some of the women weeping, thinking they've witnessed the demise of this sweet songbird. I must admit, I think so too.

Not minding our company, I rush into the frigid night to fetch Dr. Mitchell from across town. I am panicked and praying that this doctor can save her, if it is not too late. *Please, dear God, let it not be too late!* Mitchell drives us back to the house, where we find that Muddy has cleaned Virginia up and made her comfortable. After my fright, I look rather worse than she. Virginia ruptured a blood vessel, the doctor says.

> A wife, whom I loved as no man ever loved before. . . .
> Her life was despaired of. I took leave of her forever, and
> underwent all the agonies of her death.

Yet Virginia recovers. She breathes again. She sings.

But it will recur: the vessel will rupture, the blood will pour forth. She is the sacrifice, and a sacrifice demands blood, Mr. Poe. Have you not read the Scriptures?

I loved her more dearly and clung to her life with more desperate pertinacity. But I am constitutionally sensitive—nervous in a very unusual degree. I became insane, with long intervals of horrible sanity... I had, indeed, nearly abandoned all hope of a permanent cure, when I found one in the *death* of my wife. This I can endure as becomes a man. It was the horrible, never-ending oscillations between hope and despair which I could *not* longer have endured, without a total loss of reason.

When will she give up the ghost? This lingering is not good for your mind and body, Mr. Poe. But her dying—as strung out as it is—that is what makes your writing live!

Therefore, on behalf of the world of literature, we sincerely thank you for your sacrifice, Mrs. Poe. Now, if you could just get on with it please?

Chapter Thirty-Three
1842

"You are mistaken in supposing that you are not 'favorably known to me.' On the contrary, all that I have read from your pen has inspired me with a high idea of your power; and I think you are destined to stand among the first romance-writers of the country, if such be your aim." —Henry Wadsworth Longfellow

"For three or four years I knew him intimately, and for eighteen months saw him almost daily; much of the time writing or conversing at the same desk; knowing all his hopes, his fears, and little annoyances of life, as well as his high-hearted struggle with adverse fate— yet he was always the same polished gentleman—the quiet, unobtrusive, thoughtful scholar—the devoted husband—frugal in his personal expenses—punctual and unwearied in his industry—*and the soul of honor*, in all his transactions." —George Graham

The Poe Residence
Coates Street
Philadelphia

Charles Dickens visits Philadelphia during his American tour. Although I am not an admirer (nor is he of me), Dickens is a celebrity, here and abroad. This is not an opportunity to waste.

"What was he like?" Muddy asks, pulling out a chair

and setting a cup of coffee on the table.

"Who?" I say, although I know perfectly well whom she means.

"Charles Dickens!"

I hand her my coat. "He was friendly and courteous. Well-dressed. He said he appreciated my criticism, and we spoke of copyright laws in the States. Although it was difficult to speak without interruption. So many hanging about his elbows, he practically had to beat them off. Indeed, we share a mutual complaint. My work is being hocked, his work is being hocked. And neither of us sees a cent from reproductions."

Muddy pulls a face. "That sounds like a rather dull conversation."

"Well, he had his pet raven with him."

"How perfectly horrid!"

"Not at all. Fantastic creature. Ravens have an excellent memory and capacity for recognition. I tried to teach it my name. If we meet again, perhaps he will croak 'Poe!' at the sight of me."

"It spoke?" Muddy clutches her throat, as if the raven had stolen her ability to speak.

"Like a human. Its name is Grip, like in Dickens's book. Just as ornery too. That was my criticism of *Barnaby Rudge*, that the bird's speech was not applied to its greatest potential. Notwithstanding, the whole meeting was very agreeable. He paid for my tea. Dickens, not the raven."

"Oh, that's nice."

"Yes. He promises to recommend my book of tales to the English publishers."

"I do hope he is lucky."

"As do I. Are there any tea cakes today, Muddy?"

She clicks her tongue and rummages around. "Ah, here we are!" She cuts a hard biscuit in half, rubs a smudge of jam on it, and sets it before me on our best bone China saucer.

Graham's Magazine
134 Chestnut Street

Much to Muddy's chagrin, I do not always make the best choices when it comes to friends. One fancies brandy, another is fond of absinthe; and while one is a former king of Spain, yet another is known around town for being "strange." With Thomas away in Washington, these are my friends-in-reserve when I need to forget my present troubles, which include a perpetually dying wife.

Virginia's condition makes me more willing to spend my nights with the aforementioned friends. It also makes me querulous at the workplace.

"Peterson, where is the engraving to accompany my essay?" Agitated, I flip through stacks of page proofs on my desk.

"I returned it. Never worry, Poe. I've replaced it with something more appropriate."

"Whatever for? I arranged a contract with the artist. It was perfectly appropriate."

"I disagree. It was vulgar. And expensive."

I rub my forehead. "No. No, it was artistic. Real art, although I wouldn't expect *you* to recognize it."

"That's a low blow, Poe."

Thrice the rhyme! Did you hear that, Mr. Poe? Perhaps Griswold shall anthologize him.

"I suggest florals. See here? Very pretty. Decent folk prefer pretty florals."

"You must be daft to think people want to see such namby-pamby rubbish."

"I don't take your meaning—"

"What gives you the right to make that decision? It's my essay."

"You didn't come in yesterday. Or the day before! The work doesn't wait for you to sleep off your bottle ache, Poe."

With a shake, I stand up and throw the pages at Peterson, who covers his head with his arms. Once I lunge at him, other men interfere and push me back to my desk. Mr. Graham pats me on the shoulder—*there, there*—and I find myself driven into his private office.

I close my eyes and slouch into a chair. "I do apologize, Mr. Graham, but Peterson—"

"No need to apologize to me, Edgar. I do know the source of your . . . er, discontentment, and I do not blame you for standing your ground. But we cannot have outright hostility in the office."

"I realize that, sir. Peterson stepped on the wrong toe today." I tap my head with my pen, a bit too aggressive.

"I understand, I understand." He clicks his tongue. "But, if you and Charles cannot get along, I'm afraid one of you will have to go." He gives me an uncomfortable smile, then lowers his voice. "I would hate for it to be you, being in the situation you find yourself in. So, please—try to—"

"Humble myself?"

Lick the boots, Mr. Poe. Do what Muddy would have you do.

"Be more agreeable." Mr. Graham's eyes plead with me.

After another of my bouts in bed, I come back to the office to find Rufus Griswold at my desk. Do not forget, Griswold will write my obituary. Like a trained cadet, I do a right about-face and leave for good. I agree to contribute to the magazine, but from home, with intentions of producing the *Penn*. Mr. and Mrs. Graham remain friendly to Virginia and me, although not as regular with their invitations.

Chapter Thirty-Four
1842

"At no period of my life was I ever what men call intemperate. I never was in the *habit* of intoxication. I never drunk drams, &c. But, for a brief period, while I resided in Richmond, and edited *The Messenger* I certainly did give way, at long intervals, to the temptation held out on all sides by the spirit of Southern conviviality. My sensitive temperament could not stand an excitement which was an everyday matter to my companions. In short, it sometimes happened that I was completely intoxicated. For some days after each excess, I was invariably confined to bed. But it is now quite four years since I have abandoned every kind of alcoholic drink—four years, with the exception of a single deviation, which occurred shortly *after* my leaving Burton, and when I was induced to resort to the occasional use of *cider*, with the hope of relieving a nervous attack." —Edgar

The Jenning Residence
Jersey City, New Jersey

As I have heretofore alluded, my rationality at times suffers. During a visit to New York, I look up Mary Starr from Baltimore, who married a merchant tailor named Jenning, and decide to visit Ther in Jersey City.

Yes, I know what this looks like, dear Reader, but I am trying to be forthright. Listen to the story, and then make of it what you will. Try not to let your imagination run wild with improprieties. I once felt the need to confront Myra, if wordlessly, for her betrayal too.

I am in such a state of incoherence that I lose Mary's address on the ferry crossing the Hudson. I stumble about the boat, asking all on board if any know where the former Miss Starr lives. The boat ferries back and forth from New York to Jersey City, and I stay on it until a deckhand divulges the address.

When I arrive at Mary's house, she is not home, though I am permitted to wait. As if the seasoned footman, I open the door to her and her sister when they return that afternoon from making calls.

"So, you have married that cursed borer," I say without introduction. I do not know so much as her husband's forename, but anyone, even a preacher, who would take a sweetheart from me is no better than a drummer.

Remarkably, Mary is not disturbed, but friendly and amused. She seems to have forgiven me for attacking her uncle, and I have forgiven her for her inconstancy. She and her sister act pleasantly surprised and somewhat entertained to find a jilted lover in their foyer on what would have been a normally boring day.

"Mr. Poe, you should not have come here," she scolds with mock disapproval.

"Do you love him?"

"That is nobody's business, what is between me and my husband." Her face breaks and she titters.

"You didn't marry him for love," I say, "because you love *me*, Mary Starr."

"Oh, Edgar, I'm Mary Jenning now. Won't you stay for tea, dear?"

I do, and the caffeine stirs me further. While at the table, I snatch a radish from a bowl and cut it wildly with a knife until the root is obliterated. My actions are focused, hasty, and manic. Mary and her sister look on, agog and giggling and picking pieces of radish out of their hair.

"Mary, sing for me. Sing our old song," I say. She sits at the piano and trills "Come Rest in This Bosom," smiling indulgently and rocking to its mournful tune.

Always the hospitable one, our Mary. But mind yourself here, Mr. Poe.

I may be out of my mind, but I know better than to overstay. I take my leave before the cursed borer of a husband has peddled all his wares and wants his dinner.

In the meantime, Muddy is having kittens not knowing where her Eddiekins got off to. The neighbors watch over Virginia while Aunt Maria follows my tracks, which lead all the way to Mary's house in Jersey City. The amusement over, a search party sets out, which includes Muddy, Mary, and concerned Hoboken locals.

A few days later, they find me in the woods outside the city. That radish was my last bite of nourishment, and I am starved and stark mad. I cringe later to think of Muddy escorting me back to Philly, in view of everyone and his missus.

I think if she'd had a cowhide, she

would have driven you home with it.

After sleeping it off, I do not remember my Jersey City adventure, although Mary, as an old woman, is happy to tell it to *Harper's*, probably for a pretty penny.

Strange tale, don't you think? I am prone not to believe a word that comes out of Mary Starr's once-red head.

If true, I think perhaps I confused Mary with Myra.

The Poe Residence
234 N. Seventh Street
Spring Garden
Philadelphia

After such an episode, I rise early, eat moderately, drink nothing but water, and take abundant and regular exercise in the open air. But this is my private life, and it escapes the eyes of the world. When the desire for society comes upon me, I can only tolerate it with a drink. Then the public takes it for granted that I am always intoxicated.

The money I receive for stories and reviews is eaten up by the household. My work, and lack thereof, causes us to move twice more. We sell the piano, the sofa, the chairs, and other items, until our new house, which is in disrepair, is nearly bare. Muddy applies for aid from a city charity when there is only bread and molasses left, and not much of it.

I do my duty to provide until Virginia relapses and

life itself ceases. Then I wander the downtown until Muddy finds me and leads me back to my ailing wife.

"Ed-*deee*? Is that you? Have you come home?"

How I despise it when she whines our name like that.

You hush. She deserves not our scorn.

She deserves a devoted husband.

Which I strive to be. Meanwhile, my little wifey, God bless her, sings to rival the nightingale. I move the harp to her bedroom, where she receives callers. Mary Jenning is one, all the way from Jersey City. She teaches Sissy to sing my "favorite" song:

> *Thou hast called me thy angel in moments of bliss,*
> *And thy angel I'll be 'mid the horrors of this—*
> *Through the furnace, unshrinking thy steps to pursue,*
> *And shield thee and save thee or perish there too.*

All the neighbors and their children adore Virginia, and they will remember later her musical laughter. The young daughter of a friend sings Sissy senseless songs with made-up lyrics. One day she invents a chorus to delight her, which she has titled "The Wife of Mr. Poe."

> *The wife of Mr. Poe—oh!—*
> *Is pretty and kind and*
> *The best one I know.*
> *So please don't let me go—oh!—*
> *The wife of Mr. Poe.*

Might I mention that "woe" also rhymes with Poe?

I aspire to be the husband Sissy merits, but I cannot bear to watch her suffer and waste away. Worse is watching Muddy's hopeless nursing. And so I spend the days away. Then I come home rueful, although neither Muddy nor Virginia chide me about it. Sissy smiles without restraint when she sees me, and I stay up nights, pacing the floor with her stick-thin arms around my waist, her face in my chest, and her spasms spattering blood onto my shirt.

Virginia's physician, Dr. Mitchell, is from Ayrshire in Scotland, where I once upon a time lived with my foster father's kin. He knows a woman in Saratoga Springs, and he convinces her to invite me there; he even provides the currency to send me.

Interesting that Dr. Mitchell sends you and not his patient. Who is the invalid, I wonder, you or Virginia?

I can almost forget the nightmare at home as I spend my holiday with this woman and her family, taking water at the springs, going for drives, and wandering the gardens and ponds. But when I come home, Virginia is worse. The bleeding will not be quelled, and my heart threatens to quit beating.

I refuse wine and spirits, but I long for some *thing* to

take me out this awful world, knock me unconscious, or
at least deaden the pain.

*You mean laudanum, do you not?
If only you could afford it. All you
can spare for comfort is for Virginia;
she needs it more than you. Not to be
the bearer of bad tidings, Mr. Poe,
but you will live through this, even if
she will not. But beware the rumors,
my dear boy, which would have you
unfaithful to your young dying wife.*

Chapter Thirty-Five
1843

"He arrived here a few days since. On the first evening he seemed somewhat excited, having been over-persuaded to take some Port wine. On the second day he kept pretty steady, but since then he has been, at intervals, quite unreliable. He exposes himself here to those who may injure him very much with the President, and thus prevents us from doing for him what we wish to do and what we can do if he is himself again in Philadelphia. He does not understand the ways of politicians, nor the manner of dealing with them to advantage. How should he?" —Rowdy Dow

"I have seen a great deal of Poe, and it was his excessive and at times marked sensibility which forced him into his 'frolics,' rather than any mere morbid appetite for drink, but if he took but one glass of weak wine or beer or cider . . . it almost always ended in excess and sickness. But he fought against the propensity as hard as ever Coleridge fought against [it]. . . . I have seen men who drank bottles of wine to Poe's wine-glasses who yet escaped all imputations of intemperance. His was one of those temperaments whose only safety is in total abstinence." —Frederick Thomas

The Poe Residence
Philadelphia

My "true friend" Frederick Thomas encourages me to

take political office:

> How would you like to be an office holder here at
> $1,500 per year payable monthly by Uncle Sam. . . ?
> You stroll to your office a little after nine in the morn-
> ing leisurely, and you stroll from it a little after two
> in the afternoon. . . . You have on your desk every-
> thing in the writing line in apple-pie order, and if you
> choose to lucubrate in a literary way, why you can. . . .

I would like that, my friend. Then I may work on my
own magazine—which, still a figment of my imagination, I am now calling *The Stylus*—with Muddy and Virginia comfortable at home. Politics disinterest me, but I
can feign attentiveness for survival's sake. I fancy myself
a Virginian when it is to my advantage, and, as President
Tyler is also from Virginia, I might consider the Whigs if
I had to choose a party.

Thomas begs me to come to Washington with him,
but I do not see how.

> I wish to God I could visit Washington, but—the old
> story you know—I have no money; not enough to take
> me there, to say nothing of getting back. It is hard
> to be poor, but as I am kept so by an honest motive I
> dare not complain. . . .

What is this honest motive, you ask? If I had a job,
I would not be poor; but if I had a job, I would not have
time to write. And so I remain poor, that I may remain a
writer.

Thomas and I continue to correspond about my potential position in Washington, and he recommends me

to the president's son, who values my opinion as a critic "more than any other." I wonder if he might endorse me and my magazine, and I begin to pursue this matter of politics quite in earnest.

Though politicians do not strike me as simpatico. I would almost rather you seek the company of criminals, who would at least give you a lucrative trade. Oh, what am I on about? Politicians are criminals!

Fuller's Hotel
12th Street, N.W., & Pennsylvania Avenue
&
The White House
1600 Pennsylvania Avenue
Washington, D.C.

An appointment to office eludes me in Philadelphia, and I write Thomas to say, in my own words, that government is all "ruffians and boobies."

With Thomas's help, I persuade Mr. Clarke, gentleman and publisher, to be my patron, and I have a magazine prospectus advertised in two papers. Clarke provides me the means to travel to Washington to meet and gain subscriptions from the powerful men Thomas has readied for me.

Unfortunately, Thomas is ill and cannot chaperone me on these social outings. He is lodging at Fuller's

Hotel, where the obsequious proprietor, Mr. Fuller, urges me to taste the house port that first night, which I so do as to not offend the man. Thus begins the whole ridiculous affair.

The next day I get a haircut and shave on credit, and I write to my patron, Clarke:

> My expenses were more than I thought they would be. . . . However . . . I believe that I am making a sensation which will tend to the benefit of the magazine. . . . Send me $10 by mail as soon as you get this.

I am making a sensation indeed. Thomas's friend J. E. Dow, known by the nickname "Rowdy Dow," accompanies me on my appointments 'round town.

This reminds me of our university days on Rowdy Row. Not much hope of this ending better, I am afraid.

On the third day, I am received at the President's House by Robert Tyler, the president's son, in my best cloak, which I insist on wearing wrong side out. (I did not mean for this to happen, Reader, but when my error is indicated, I behave as though it is a clever tactic for winning admiration.) Alas, the port has loosened my tongue, as well as my principles of fashion.

"What an honor it is, sir," Tyler says, meeting us in the grand entrance hall of the famous white mansion.

"My dear sir, the honor is all mine," I return with a bow. "E. A. Poe Esquire, at your service." I flap the tails of my inside-out cape at the statuesque black man who holds out his gloved hands to take it—I the matador and he the bull. Circling backwards, I chuckle when he follows me with an insistent ahem. "Ha, well, an honor and an offense!"

"I beg your pardon?" Tyler asks, his smile falling as mine widens.

"Well, it is amusing."

"Sorry. What is?"

I gesture at the stately portraits, cornices, and chandeliers. "That a grandson of Benedict Arnold is invited here. General Washington must be turning in his grave. Now, isn't that a rowdydow, Rowdy Dow?" I cannot help but snicker at my own jest. "Gentlemen, please excuse me," I say, turning to search for the privy.

"Thomas couldn't be here, I'm afraid," says Dow, cringing, "and Mr. Poe—well, he is not himself."

"I see." Tyler strokes his chin and lowers his voice. "Perhaps he should not see my father . . . in his present condition. If he recovers before his departure, then we can arrange another meeting."

"Perhaps that is best. I shall let Thomas know, and we will send word soon."

"I do want to help him."

"Thank you, sir. As do we, but—wait, no, Mr. Poe! That is not a chamber pot. . ."

Dow writes Clarke for assistance in sending me home. Meanwhile, I attend a Washington party, at which mint juleps are served. Why, juleps transport me back to a plantation verandah, and I act out a series of impressions in an exaggerated Southern accent. I flourish my cloak, still turned wrong side out, and deliver scathing insults.

There is a Spaniard—the Don—at this party, whose sharply curled mustachios compel me to make comment, this time trying on a Spanish intonation. The Spaniard finds me not funny at all, and Rowdy Dow ushers me back to Fuller's before a duel can be scheduled. There, Dow and Thomas sit me down.

"Poe, old boy," Thomas says, "you must leave here at once. The Don is furious, and he is much about town. I will send word to Mrs. Clemm to collect you from the train station tomorrow. Dow and I will continue to work on your behalf. . ."

He carries on with his reasoning, but I do not hear it. I have disgraced myself. Politicians, Washington elite, and Spaniards—they mock me, unable to believe I possess any talent or good form. Broke and broken, I must borrow money to take the train home.

The Poe Residence
Philadelphia

In his letter of report, Rowdy Dow writes,

> I do this under a solemn responsibility. Mr. Poe has
> the highest order of intellect, and I cannot bear that
> he should be the sport of senseless creatures, who, like
> oysters, keep super, and gape and swallow everything.

Once home, I take supper and a bath and call on Mr. Clarke to make amends. At the first opportunity, I write

my friends in Washington, listing my failures and be-
seeching absolution:

> Express to your wife my deep regret for the vexation I
> must have occasioned her.

> Call, also, at the barber's shop . . . and pay for me.
> . . .

> Forgive me my petulance and don't believe I meant,
> all I said.

> Please express my regret to Mr. Fuller for making such
> a fool of myself in his house. . . .

> Remember me to the Don, whose mustachios I do
> admire after all, and who was about the finest figure I
> ever beheld.

Perhaps you ought to grow a moustache, Mr. Poe. It worked very well for Lord Byron.

The apologies are sincere, believe me. As my true
friend Thomas says, "There is a great deal of heartache in
the jesting of this letter."

Thomas reports that the president asked about me
when I failed to make an appearance. Robert Tyler said
he would have me appointed to office at the Customs
House in Philadelphia, but before his father could issue
the order, he was interrupted by a servant, and I was
forgotten.

Chapter Thirty-Six
1843–44

"You ca'nt [*sic*] imagine how much we both do miss
you. Sissy had a hearty cry last night, because you and
Catterina weren't here. We are resolved to get two
rooms the first moment we can. In the meantime, it
is impossible we could be more comfortable or more
at home than we are. —It looks as if it was going to
clear up now." —Edgar

Graham's Magazine
Philadelphia

My patron, Mr. Clarke, pulls out. I call him an idiot and
an imbecile, but we cannot in truth blame him, given the
Washington fiasco.

Our impoverishment is so deep that I request $5
from Rufus Griswold. "Virginia is almost gone," I say.
Mr. Graham and the magazine staff pass a hat around
the office, collecting $15 to allay our plight. I also write
my cousin William Poe, but it seems my indiscretions, or
rumors of such, have spread to Baltimore. William writes
to caution me against a great enemy of our family: The
Bottle.

I use what strength I have left to write, but Muddy
must act as an intermediary between me and the publishers. A happy result is that I am able to wrest "The Gold
Bug" away from Graham and submit it to the *Dollar*

Newspaper, winning the one hundred dollar prize.

The rumor mill in Philadelphia turns on the myriad material I throw at it. That I was driving around Saratoga Springs with a married woman is one scandal making the rounds. An article slandering me appears in one of the papers, although no author is named. I suspect Griswold, who has visited our dwelling and endeared himself—falsely, I might add—to Aunt Maria. I am forwarded an anonymous letter that reads,

> Edgar A. Poe . . . has become one of the strangest of our literati. . . . Poor fellow; he is not a teetotaler by any means, and I fear he is going to destruction, moral, physical, intellectual. . . .

People say that you are not often at home and that you are prone to self-indulgence.

Self-indulgence? Look at me! I am worn down to bones! What self-indulgence?

You seem often under the influence of drink, Mr. Poe. Or, since we are in Philadelphia, perhaps a Franklin saying will suffice: "You've drank more than you've bled."

Law Office of Henry B. Hirst
40 S. Sixth Street

It is the slander that makes me flee Philadelphia. I cannot get ahead here, and I have attempted all avenues. Muddy pawns our few remaining possessions. The landlady accepts some rugs and a pair of painted chairs for back-due rent.

Not knowing that Muddy sold my books, I ask her to return the bound issues of *The Southern Literary Messenger* to Henry Hirst, the law student, from whom I borrowed the set; Henry had in fact borrowed it from another. The poor dear cannot bear to tell me what she's done and so instead says she left the set at Hirst's office. Later, when I am asked to return the volume I borrowed, I explain that Mrs. Clemm already dropped it by. Henry accuses me of lying, and a conflict ensues between him, me, and the original owner.

Muddy is too mortified to admit that our poverty is such that we have pawned that which does not belong to us. I do not have any substantial plan to help us—only hope. A very little bit of hope.

The Morrisons' Boarding House
130 Greenwich Street
New York

There is scarce enough money to take Virginia with me to the train station, but with the rumors of my infidelity, I cannot leave her. Instead, we bid adieu to Muddy and the cat—a sorry event, but Sissy and I manage to think of it as an adventure.

We arrive in New York City during an afternoon spring shower, and I purchase a cheap umbrella and a room at a shabby boarding house. I sit down after breakfast the next day to write Muddy, and I am not wearing any pants.

> I ate the first hearty breakfast I have eaten since I left our little home. Sis is delighted, and we are both in excellent spirits. She has coughed hardly any and had no night sweat. She is now busy mending my pants which I tore against a nail.

I continue to chronicle this morning's meal, wishing Muddy could eat the words that describe the eggs! Food is not taken for granted in the Poe house, Reader, and I know Aunt Maria will be happy to hear of it.

> The house is old and looks buggy . . . the cheapest board I ever knew. . . . I wish Kate could see it—she would faint. Last night for supper we had the nicest tea you ever drank, strong and hot—wheat bread and rye bread—cheese—tea-cakes (elegant), a great dish (two dishes) of elegant ham, and two of cold veal, piled up like a mountain and large slices—three dishes of the cakes and everything in the greatest profusion. No fear of starving here.

I have $4.50 still left, and I proudly tell Muddy that I haven't drank a drop and that I hope I will soon be out of trouble. Sissy cried pitifully the night before because she missed her mother and her Catterina. I must make some money to send for them soon.

*First, you must get your pants
back on.*

Perhaps Virginia might recover completely—

I wouldn't go so far, Mr. Poe.

Harrison's Tea Shop
Broadway & Prince Street

Indeed, it is here where I will lose Virginia for good, although not for a few years yet. Her looming death casts
a morose shadow over me. As she fades away, I fade out.
I wander the streets. Draped in my scruffy greatcoat, my
slender figure and claw-like hands lend to a birdlike im-
agery. Catterina is taken to ride on my shoulder, and we
roam the dark streets, among the friendly hogs that eat
the rubbish tossed out of windows and carriages.

I may as well be struck by a carriage then go on as I
am, at her bedside, waiting. . . .

*But you are not always at her side,
are you?*

I know I ought to be. Especially with Muddy in
another city, I ought to be doting on Sissy. At the least,
I ought to ask how she feels, rather than ignoring the
disease and pretending all is well. I nonetheless grow
distant.

I find myself one evening lingering at a corner shop,
gazing at a plug of tobacco in the window. I can taste it,
both pungent and mellow—

"May I help you, sir?"

"How much?" I ask, nodding at the tobacco.

"A five pence for the lot."

"Where from?"

"Virginia. Long-lasting. Cool and mild."

I recall Virginia as muggy and conceited.

No, she is lovely and pure and very, very sick.

I believe he means the farms of Virginia, Mr. Poe. Not the missus.

"I am from Virginia," I say, my fingers feeling for coins not in my pocket.

When I make no move to purchase, the shopkeeper, touched by my emotion, makes me a gift of the tobacco.

⁓⊸ᗢ⊶⁓

I collect enough money to bring Muddy and Catterina to New York by selling "The Balloon Hoax" to the *New York Sun*. Ladies and gents all over the city believe Mr. Monck Mason's Flying Machine crossed the Atlantic in three days. Loving nothing better than a good ruse, except maybe getting paid, I secure both with this bit of lark.

> I never witnessed more intense excitement to get possession of a newspaper. . . . I tried, in vain, during the whole day, to get possession of a copy. It was excessively amusing, however, to hear the comments of those who had read the "Extra."

Virginia and I rent a bigger suite in anticipation of the reunion of our family.

PART SIX:

The Poet

Chapter Thirty-Seven
1844–45

"With the highest admiration for his genius, and a
willingness to let it atone for more than ordinary
irregularity, we were led by common report to expect
a very capricious attention to his duties, and occasion-
ally a scene of violence and difficulty. Time went on,
however, and he was invariably punctual and industrious. With his pale, beautiful, and intellectual face, as
a reminder of what genius was in him, it was impossible, of course, not to treat him always with deferential
courtesy, and to our occasional request that he would
not probe too deep in a criticism . . . he readily and
courteously assented—far more yielding than most
men, we thought, on points so excusably sensitive."
—Nathaniel Parker Willis

"Poe was a quiet man about the office, but was uni-
formly kind and courteous to everyone, and, with
congenial company, he would grow cheerful and even
playful. . . . Not a great while after I had gone to
work on the paper, on a hot August afternoon while
wrapping and addressing *Journals*, I was overcome
with the heat and fainted dead away. Poe was writing
at his desk. When I recovered consciousness I was
stretched out on the long table at which I had been at
work and Poe was bending over me bathing my wrists
and temples in cold water. He ministered to me until
I was able to stand up, and then he sent me home in
a carriage. This act of kindness, coupled with his uniform gentle greetings, when he entered the office of
a morning, together with frequent personal inquiries

and words of encouragement, made me love and trust my editor." —Alexander Crane

The Brennan Farm
Bloomingdale Road
Upper Manhattan
New York

When summer comes, we move to a farm on Broadway, a good many miles out of the stinking city. The property is shaded by sweeping old trees, and the cooler temperatures benefit Sissy's lungs. The front of the colonial home boasts a magnificent view of the Hudson Valley, and from the second story windows, one can see all the way to New Jersey.

Ah, where Mary Starr Jenning lives with her cursed borer of a husband.

A boat leaves the dock each day at seven o'clock for a one shilling fare to downtown. Whereas I was living separate from Muddy and Sissy in the city, I give up my "bachelor" quarters for the farm, although I do not always have spare coin for the ferry.

The Patrick Brennans—Irish folk, but you probably reckoned that—own the property. As farmers and Irish Catholics tend to do, the Brennans are breeders, mostly of children and dogs. Although Kitty Kate would rather not have either, I call it "a perfect heaven." To these hardworking country neighbors, I am an object of curious admiration.

On the days I miss the boat, I sit on the grounds and overlook the valley, rubbing a dog's head and fixing lines in my own. After supper, I retreat to my desk to scratch the ink on the page, and the next day, Virginia pastes the papers into scrolls. This might look like a lazy day to you, but I am most prolific on the farm.

I share the attic room with Virginia, but I spend much of the night hours in the study. One of Napoleon's officers boarded here before me, and the room is adorned with his French military artifacts. One night, I carve my name into the mantelpiece, imagining it to be a precious relic when I am gone.

I imagine Mrs. Brennan will curse you to Irish hell when she finds it.

A bust of Pallas sits on a shelf above the door. During a late thunderstorm, when lightning flares through the transom, it spotlights the goddess wisdom, and her shadow flashes across my floor. Tree branches come a'tapping on the windows, the sinister piece falls into place, and I finish the poem I have been writing for four years.

When I visit the Stryker's Bay Tavern to watch the boat races, I read "The Raven" to any who will listen. The To Be claims it the best poem ever written in the English language, its effect best achieved when read aloud—by me. And that is not my vanity speaking; you can ask any New Yorker of the 1840s. Although, I myself am never quite satisfied with it.

As Virginia grows weaker, I must carry her down to

the Brennans' dinner table. When I acknowledge her frailty and probable fate, I realize that I would have never written "The Raven" the same if not for her.

If not for her dying, you mean to say.

I write to Thomas:

For the last seven or eight months I have been playing hermit in earnest, nor have I seen a living soul out of my family—who are well and desire to be kindly remembered. When I say "well," I only mean (as regards Virginia) as well as usual. Her health remains excessively precarious.

The Evening Mirror
105 Nassau Street

When our accounts run dry, I am loath to return to a paying job. My imagination thrives on idleness and leisure. When I drag it out, Aunt Maria travels to Gotham city herself to find work for me. She calls in at *The New York Mirror* and confesses our troubles to Mr. Nathaniel Parker Willis. Willis is quite taken with my mother-in-law, and he agrees to hire me on as a "mechanical paragraphist."

You may observe me as I occupy my corner desk at *The Mirror*, from nine in the morning until the paper goes to press. I am courteous and diligent. Mr. Willis gets no grief from me. He is a religious man, but jolly, and I like him. In some ways, I wish I were more like

Willis. I have talent and intelligence, yes, but he has charisma and confidence. It is his unsinkable attitude and conviviality that wins him favor. The world opens itself to men like that.

I am bored, Mr. Poe. Isn't there a public execution we can attend? I fancy an old-fashioned hanging. Or let's go to Barnum's! He's got George Washington's own nursemaid on exhibit. You can ask the old dear if she remembers your great-grandfather Benedict Arnold.

Harrison's Tea Shop

But once I leave the office, I cannot make my feet go towards home. The corner shop where I once "diddled" for a plug of tobacco is owned by Mr. Gabriel Harrison, the very one who gave it to me. The shop's sizzling stove invites me to hover by it, my hands held out in submission, on cold, damp evenings.

"Sir, I've just walked through sleet and rain, and I hoped you wouldn't mind if I warmed myself here by the stove."

"Be my guest," he says with a cordial wave.

Harrison and I discuss politics, naturally. He is president of the White Eagle Political Club, and I am roused to write a patronal anthem for the organization, in thanks for the tobacco. No chore that—I had it penned before I finished my breakfast. When he offers to pay me, I decline and instead request a bag of coffee.

"What is your name, sir?" Harrison asks, wrapping the coffee in paper.

"Thaddeus Perley, at your service."

Destitute as I am, I still appreciate the glamour of a nom de plume. . . .

Wait—what—what was *that*? Pardon, but do you hear what I hear? Am I entertaining voices? I mean *besides* that Voice, my constant companion, the unsurpassed To Be. This voice sounds familiarly prophetic, but it is dictating my every step as well, with detail and reasoning. It says that Harrison will later say that this song I wrote helped elect President Polk.

Am I indeed hearing my own biography told? The narration of my life's story? How long has this been going on?

Dear Mr. Poe, allow me to explain. Your senses cross an eternal boundary, but do not be disturbed by what you hear. You know you will not live forever. Let us not be dragged down by that. Longevity is not required. But be assured of this: All of your life is being witnessed and recorded. Even the mundane chat at a tobacco shop. It is important to note that Mr. Poe, not Perley, warmed himself by the shop stove and wrote the White Eagle Club song.

But why? Recorded by whom?

Because the world will want to hear your story. None of this is to be forgotten. Much of it is to be made up. And who better to tell your true story than me?

You?

Yes. I am your imagination, after all. I have been with you since before you could hear me, and I am thereby a part of you. One which has come through all of this already.

Is this true, what you are telling me? The *world*?

You always knew what you were capable of—even as a young sprig, orating on tabletops for the company. You will be known forevermore, Mr. Poe. You will be remembered—dare I say beloved by future readers of American literature. Even the distinguished University will take pride in its most *melancholy alumnus, as well as every city and fort, library and dwelling you graced with your transient presence. And this—this is how you will truly live forever.*

And so it is acceptable that you hear your biography spoken over you now, as you still live and breathe. Take pleasure in the telling. For the winds are changing....

The Broadway Journal
138 Nassau Street

Reader, I cannot underestimate the results of this discovery.

As I am leaving *The Mirror* to work for *The Broadway Journal*, Willis promises to print "The Raven." Published first in *The American Review* under a pseudonym, this poem begets my greatest fame, and I arrange to reprint it in as many publications as possible. The impact is immediate and widespread. The bald eagle is nearly tossed out of the national bird's nest in favor of the raven. Reverberations of "nevermore" can be heard abroad, as well.

> Your "Raven" has produced a sensation, a "fit horror," here in England. Some of my friends are taken by the fear of it and some by the music. I hear of persons haunted by the "Nevermore," and one acquaintance of mine who has the misfortune of possessing a "bust of

Pallas" never can bear to look at it in the twilight.

That piece was written to me by Elizabeth Barrett (later Browning)—my favorite memento with which to impress visitors. I know you cannot see my smile, Reader, but it is no less bright.

Indeed, all the world wants to know who wrote "The Raven," and once my name is revealed, they seek to know more. *"Who is this Edgar A. Poe?"* Greatness is mine twenty days after my thirty-sixth birthday, and I am paid $9 for it.

Perhaps now is as good a time as any to come back to Griswold, my sometime enemy, as he has lately come back to me. The reverend is compiling an anthology, *Prose Writers of America*, in which he intends to include tales written by the lately celebrated author of that bird poem the country is so obsessed with. Three years ago, when he published an American poetry compilation, only three of my poems appeared in print, with negligible commendation and—adding insult to injury—an error.

No, I did not keep my criticism to myself, Reader. The poets Griswold praised are bunglers, layman at best. I detest nothing more than the act of "puffing" litera-ture that is unworthy. How are we as a nation to rival England if we continue to reward American authors for producing trite filth?

This is not to mention that Griswold took my job at *Graham's*.

He was paid more for it too.

Now he is civil, despite our past contention. He loans me $25.

It was more like $5, despite his claims. Do not fool yourself into thinking that the Reverend Doctor's intentions are good. Your "Raven" is all anyone is talking about. He needs your name to make his own.

We need each other, I suppose.

As a consequence of my newfound fame, I am invited to give lectures, with important people in attendance. Having more social contact than ever before, I require a drink now and then. Sometimes the society is exhilarating. Sometimes the weather turns and lectures cancel. Despite my good fortune, I am inclined to drown.

Chapter Thirty-Eight
1845

"I meet Mr. Poe very often at the receptions. He is the observed of all observers. His stories are thought wonderful, and to hear him repeat the Raven, which he does very quietly, is an event in one's life. People seem to think there is something uncanny about him, and the strangest stories are told, and, what is more, believed, about his mesmeric experiences, at the mention of which he always smiles. His smile is captivating! . . . Everybody wants to know him; but only a very few people seem to get well acquainted with him."
—Frances Osgood

"It was in his own simple yet poetical home that, to me the character of Edgar Poe appeared in its most beautiful light. Playful, affectionate, witty, alternately docile and wayward as a petted child—for his young, gentle, and idolized wife, and for all who came, he had even in the midst of his most harassing literary duties, a kind word, a pleasant smile, a graceful and courteous attention." —Frances Osgood

Astor House
Broadway & Vesey Street
Upper Manhattan
New York

Virginia is more or less bed-ridden. This "borrowed time"

is like a game of consequences, in which I am waiting for the end to be written—and not by me.

Let me try! I am quite the old hand at this game. Fill in the blanks, yes? Here we go: "Poorly Virginia met the Shadow of Death, clothed in black, in New York City at wintertime. As a consequence, she perished in the arms of her beloved Edgar, and life was over for both." My favorite game! Oh, such fun!

As I said before, I am much about the town, rather than at Sissy's beck and call. Socializing is awkward for me, but success overcomes my insecurities, and I venture out. What is most remarkable is that I find women well attracted to my public persona: noble, reserved, brilliant, forlorn.

Now that is a part you play well, Mr. Poe. The Byronic hero in the flesh.

My previous employer, Mr. Willis, entertains the New York literati at his luxury hotel suite, including a certain poetess I fancy. She published a volume of poems while on holiday in England and came home to print an American edition. Her poetry is romantic, nostalgic, high-flown, and supple; but it is popular, and the poetess herself is charming, if not beautiful.

Willis arranges for me to meet Mrs. Frances Sargent Osgood at the Astor House. We two play a game of coquetry, but only at first by correspondence. Our letters and love poetry verge on that of being scandalous, especially since being publicly published (even if under assumed identities).

Risky? Perhaps. But romance is like a drug to me.

And female poets the ministering angels of that drug.

I reclaim a poem I wrote for Mr. White's daughter in Richmond, printing it in *The Broadway Journal* as "To F. . ." I am reminded of my adolescent poetry, reused on all the eligible school-girls. This time, the wooing is reciprocated; Frances returns with the same frivolous flirtation. But I am not her only valentine. Frances also sends a poem to Rufus Griswold, who falls for it like a moonstruck schoolboy.

The reverend is somewhat of a lecher.

Let's not go into all that now.

Virginia seems to understand the nature of this societal pretense, and she encourages me to continue it. She agrees that the association keeps me in the public eye, and, I think, she sees that I better behave myself when Mrs. Osgood is involved.

"*Missus?*"

Oh, you caught that, did you? Yes, Frances is married to a portrait artist. Her husband, Samuel, will paint my likeness, prior to my cultivating the iconic moustache. He does not object to my paying Mrs. Osgood attention—

That could be because the cuckold isn't frequenting the nest.

Park Theatre
23 Park Row
&
The Broadway Journal

As a dramatic critic, I spend the occasional evening at the theatre. Once an actor on stage sights me in the audience and improvises "Nevermore, nevermore," into his lines. My head is all abuzz, and the audience is too.

But celebrity is more of a bondage than a freedom.

I never knew what it was to be a slave before.

And yet, Thomas, I have made no money. I am as poor now as ever I was in my life—except in hope, which is by no means bankable.

. . . The Devil himself was never so poor.

I may be invited to the most prestigious stages, but I still cannot repay Rowdy Dow his $8, which I borrowed in Washington.

And he is being such a toad about it.

Perhaps it is my fault. All the strain and social calling makes me surly and loose.

For instance, when James Russell Lowell and his new wife come to visit, I am not the gracious host I usually am. Spiteful and rude, I brag that I will soon have an audience with Queen Victoria and I will read "The Raven" for the royal family. I mock other writers and overstate their jealousy of me, moaning about how scorned I am for not being a native knickerbocker. This, of course, is another version of my old lament—that I cannot elevate my caste and I am thus treated unfairly. Muddy, mortified, tries to make amends for me, offering the Lowells a long-rehearsed excuse about my being ill.

Do not fret, Aunt Maria. Mr. Lowell owes us remittance. He cannot expect manners and moneylending.

I miss scheduled engagements, and although Muddy says it is due to sickness, I am in fact sick in the head. Is this the reward of popularity?

The owner of *The Broadway Journal* pulls out about this time. My written attack on Longfellow and his alleged plagiarism of Tennyson is what *The Journal* is best known for; however, this reputation is more notoriety than notability.

Henry Wadsworth Longfellow is the beloved American lyrist. Edgar A. Poe is the unforgivable American critic, a literary disgrace.

Subscriptions decline as I sign loans to buy out the other shareholders. This may be my chance to obtain my own publication, but I know you are not here for my career comings and goings. Let's go back to the house, shall we?

The Poe Residence
15 Amity Street

Virginia, in her own hand, invites Mrs. Osgood for a visit.

Pray tell, Mr. Poe: did you put her up to it?

I may have encouraged her to write. Mrs. Osgood is more than suitable company for my wifey, and Fanny cannot resist the invitation to see the broody poet in his own domicile.

When she comes, I am finishing a manuscript titled "The Literati of New York."

"Look, Mrs. Osgood," I say, pointing out the scrolls of paper. "On each of these, I have treated each of you literary folk in differing degrees of estimation, depending on the length. Come, Virginia, help me unroll these, and Mrs. Osgood can guess which is which."

Sissy, with a girlish titter, grips one end of the roll while I unfurl it until it reaches the opposite wall.

"And whose lengthened sweetness long drawn out is that?" Fanny asks with mocking incredulity.

I wink at her and say to my wife, "Just as if her vain heart didn't tell her it was herself."

Virginia smirks with the confidence of the adored. "Eddie, do not tease our prestigious guest. She might not come again."

This is Sissy's visit, and so I leave the women to their tête-à-tête. Later, I overhear her tell Fanny, "I know I cannot get well and that I will die. But I want Eddie to be happy." With horror, I wonder if she is arranging a second marriage for me, for after she is gone.

If only <u>Mister</u> Osgood would be so obliging.

Muddy admonishes me when the tittle-tattle regarding Mrs. Osgood and myself turns outrageous. But we, heedless to propriety, continue to exchange messages through *The Journal*. It's too amusing to let shame stop us now. So appalling are the accusations that Frances eventually moves away—to put distance between us, she will later say—but this is not the end of our liaison. Wherever Fanny wanders, I tend to follow.

Benefit Street
Providence, Rhode Island

While in Providence, Rhode Island, for a public recital, I find Mrs. Osgood has lingered afterwards. It is a mild summer night, and we walk through town, arm in arm.

"Edgar, you must come to Helen Whitman's with me. She is quite eager to meet you."

The transcendentalist-poetess Sarah Helen Whitman is a widow in a comfortable situation. She is also said to be beautiful and enchanting. Reading her poetry, I am convinced she is the other half of my soul, or I have told Fanny as much. Naturally, I want to meet this intriguing woman, but I am aware that another affair will fuel the fire of scandal.

"Who will be there?" I ask.

"Myself . . . and Mrs. Whitman, of course."

"Fanny, I cannot be seen at this hour going indoors with a married woman, and at a widow's house, no less. You know what people say about us already." And I know from experience I cannot trust Mrs. Osgood to be discreet.

Nevertheless, later that night, I find I cannot sleep and I cannot write and I cannot stop thinking about Helen Whitman. I walk out of my hotel and, lo and behold, find myself on the sidewalk by Mrs. Whitman's house. She stands silent amid the backyard rose bushes, the moonlight illuminating her face and figure. Is she communicating with some spirit that guides me?

> *Was it not Fate (whose name is also Sorrow)*
> *That bades me pause beside that garden-gate. . . ?*

The image is one I will not soon forget, nor the happenstance that neither she nor I slept that fateful night.

Perhaps it is another Helen you remember, whose first sight, some twenty years ago, made you weak in the knees.

Chapter Thirty-Nine
1845–46

"I shall never forget the morning when I was summoned to the drawing-room by Mr. Willis to receive him. With his proud and beautiful head erect, his dark eyes flashing with the electric light of feeling and of thought, a peculiar, an inimitable blending of sweetness and hauteur in his expression and manner, he greeted me, calmly, gravely, almost coldly; yet with so marked an earnestness that I could not help being deeply impressed by it." —Frances Osgood

"We like Boston. We were born there and perhaps it is just as well not to mention that we are heartily ashamed of the fact. The Bostonians are very well in their way. Their hotels are bad. Their pumpkin pies are delicious. Their poetry is not so good. Their common is no common thing, and the duck pond might answer if its answer could be heard for the frogs."
—Edgar

Boston Lyceum
41 Tremont Row
Boston

By the fall, Virginia is hemorrhaging again. And that, I believe, is the end of my industrious period.

As I strived to be, I am now the sole owner of *The Broadway Journal*. But as soon as I manage that feat,

I crumble. Unable to pay to keep the paper operable, I take out loans that I am unable to pay. We lose our office.

This breakdown is evidenced when I recite "The Raven" in Boston. After great applause, I choose to read "Al Aaraaf," which, if you'll remember, is an allegorical poem of considerable length, written in my youth. I had promised to deliver an original poem for the occasion, but new verse is hard to come by these days. I am in such a state of duress that I do not have the wherewithal to decline the event, and my audience is bored and baffled.

If ever given the chance to redeem yourself with an encore, let's bill the evening as a blistering critique of the New England literati—those croaking toadies of the Frog Pond. That will sell tickets!

Christmastime 1845 will be taken up with dying. The celebration of Christ's birth always felt tragic to me, and so perhaps this is fitting. The Savior of the world brought into the world, by way of a barn and a poor family, delivered to die. Our gift from a loving God. And see how much we appreciated it?

All are born to die, Mr. Poe. You are not so different from that poor Yuletide child. Dying is for many their first opportunity to be fully appreciated. Ask Virginia.

Mrs. Poe is dying, and my paper is dying. I am afraid my poetry is dying too. While I write stories about mesmerism and spiritualism and resurrection, I think I am making it all up.

What about me, Mr. Poe? Who am I, if not a spirit? Am I not real enough for you?

> Anne C. Lynch's Salon
> 116 Waverly Place
> Greenwich Village

The parlor doors of the influential swing wide for me, including those belonging to Miss Anna Charlotte Lynch of Waverly Place. On Saturday evenings, I am led upstairs to the salon, where the charming Miss Lynch receives me and announces my arrival. Before this audience of poets and geniuses and artists I recite, often with Fanny Osgood mooning up at me from a footstool. Some of the men I offend with my harsh critique and rejection, but for the women—this "starry sisterhood of poetesses"—I spare judgment. They in turn do not hide their intrigue with this coolly lenient Mr. Edgar A. Poe.

One summer eve, I bring Virginia with me, but it will be the last time I take her out. She is dressed in red with a yellow lace. Her mother, who begs money from the starry sisters when they come to call on me, used the handouts to buy the material to make the dress. Seeing it makes me wince.

I seat my darling girl by the window and turn away from her to perform my recitation of "The Raven," my own closest attempt at mesmerism. My name nowadays is synonymous with the raven's. That's what people whisper when they see me walk smartly down a street with my walking stick or dodder my way out of a tavern.

"Look! It's the raven. It's Mr. Poe."

I prefer your other nickname: the Tomahawk Man.

Children sneak up behind me and I flap my coat to mimic wings. When I sense them close enough, I spin around and hiss, "Nevermore," and watch them fly away, shrieking with laughter.

Everyone who is anyone wants to know me, and anybody as well as nobodies want to talk *about* me. That's more fun, is it not? *"Frances Osgood and Edgar Poe are secret lovers, while his little wife is dying and his mother-in-law is begging."* They say I am lazy and drunken, and we live hand to mouth.

Forget not that Griswold is also in love with Fanny Osgood. Why don't they talk about him for a change?

You might think Griswold and I are foils, but we are both begrudging and anxious and prideful. The difference is this: If I do not like you, you will likely know it.

Whereas I am outrightly aggressive at a perceived slight, Griswold is passively aggressive and bides his time with revenge on his mind.

And he will get his revenge. Make no mistake, Mr. Poe.

But Griswold is not the only man I squabble with. I scrap with ink, challenging literary conventions and plagiarists. "Kicking up a bobbery," I call it. No one is safe as long as I have paper and pen and there are still newspapers in New York willing to print defamation.

No one except those of the fairer sex.

One stormy night, having left the cozy drawing room of Miss Lynch's salon, I stand under an awning as rain pours off the brim of my hat and into my collar. A young poet emerges from 116 Waverly Place and walks towards me with an umbrella and an expression of kindness on his face. When he is close enough to recognize me, he turns away, and I realize I have spurned him in a review.

These are the same men who will, in later decades, write your biography.

Godey's Lady's Book is printing my papers on the members of the literati. Some think that I betray confidences, making it a gossip column. In it, I compare the editor of *The Knickerbocker* to a pumpkin and call my friend Thomas Dunn English an ass.

He is an ass, though; and that

editor is a fat gourd. Duly noted, in my humble opinion.

The Brennan Farm

Virginia's face, milk-white and round, is perpetually veiled in a sheen of perspiration. When she coughs, she cries and blood smears her handkerchief. Well-meaning but prying society folks intrude upon our humble living quarters with unwanted company and advice. Consequently, I remove Muddy and Sis to the Brennans' farm for several weeks of seclusion. I continue to make my appearances in the city, and on the nights that I cannot afford the transportation back to Virginia's bedside, I must find someone to take me in.

> I shall be with you tomorrow . . . and be assured until I see you I will keep in loving remembrance your last words, and your servant prayer!

> Sleep well, and may God grant you a peaceful summer with your devoted Edgar.

During my spells in the city, I become acquainted with a former nurse and doctor's daughter, Mrs. Louise Shew, who is sympathetic to our plight and makes it her mission to serve our family. Mrs. Shew is enchanted by Virginia, as is her physician, Dr. Francis, who calls her his "Pocket Edition of the Lives of the Saints."

On our last Valentine's Day together, she writes me a poem. The first letter of each line spells out my name.

Ever with thee I wish to roam—
Dearest my life is thine.
Give me a cottage for my home
And a rich old cypress vine,
Removed from the world with its sin and care
And the tattling of many tongues.
Love alone shall guide us when we are there—
Love shall heal my weakened lungs;
And Oh, the tranquil hours we'll spend,
Never wishing that others may see!
Perfect ease we'll enjoy, without thinking to lend
Ourselves to the world and its glee—
Ever peaceful and blissful we'll be.

"You're a talented little minx, do you know that?" I kiss her cheek.

"Only because you taught me, Eddie—*l'amour de ma vie.*" The love of my life.

I resolve never to speak to Frances Osgood again.

The Poe Cottage
Fordham, Bronx

We lease a quaint cottage at Fordham, surrounded by cow pastures, woods, and orchards, sixteen miles from the city. I must walk a mile to fetch my mail. My room is in the attic, with narrow windows to light it. That spring is thronged with flowers—violets and geraniums and lilacs. Virginia's favorite is the cherry tree in the front yard.

We invite our neighbors the Millers to the cottage for lunch soon after the move. Having no chair suitable for a small child, I find a box for their little girl Sarah to sit on so she can see over the table. She sweetly nibbles her cornbread and smiles at me, and my sadness expands. I wonder if it was worth it—my choice to pursue literature. How did I end up here, childless and penniless?

Indeed, the reward is for posterity, not the present. Focus on the future, Mr. Poe.

Before they go, I give Sarah an ivory puzzle from China, which my brother had given to me.

Virginia is in the bed next to the kitchen, with Catterina perched on her chest. "The Millers have gone, my dear," I say. "Little Sarah was falling asleep standing up."

"Darling child. She was overly impressed by your antics at the table."

"Antics? Magic tricks, rather. And I seem to remember a little Sissy who was also once overly impressed with my tricks."

She smiles. "My favorite was always the dog you made from a napkin."

I growl and bark and nuzzle her ear. When I try to remove the cat, Kate swipes my hand.

"Oh! Eddie, are you hurt? Oh, dear, she drew blood!" She shakes a finger at the cat. "Mind your manners, Kitty Kate."

"She cannot help it. See, she never had a mother to teach her otherwise. Same as your wayward husband." I give Sissy half a smile and scratch Catterina, who is leaning into my hand and purring again, under her chin. She reeks of earth, having recently hunted in the crawl space under the cottage. It makes me think of burial.

"Leave her here, Eddie."

"But how can you breathe? With all due respect to the lady, she is the only one of us who gained weight this winter."

"It's all the mice and moles she finds under the house. Anyway, she keeps me warm."

Rosalie comes to Fordham for a visit, and Aunt Maria is driven almost to wits' end. Rose is older but somehow more obstinate and less manageable. While Muddy must dig up gardens planted to feed a farmer's cattle or harvest dandelions for a salad, Rosalie wants to eat at our table but never lift a finger to help. When Muddy tries to engage her in chores, my sister makes excuses—"I have a toothache!"—or shirks altogether. The one job she never tires of is talking, but Virginia, the only one of us always available to listen, does not seem to mind.

When I am called away for an interview in the city, Muddy must send money to pay for my transportation back to Fordham. When I stumble home, she scolds me as she tucks me into bed.

"How could you, Eddie? That money was for the coach, not your pleasure. When will you ever learn?"

I grip her wrist and we lock eyes. "Muddy, Muddy, Muddy, please! I need medicine. I am going to die." A groan overtakes me, and I let go of her to writhe.

Doubling over, I spy my sister, peeking wide-eyed from the stairwell. "Get out!" I snarl.

Muddy shoos her away and shuts the door.

Chapter Forty
1846

—⁂—

"When, in the heat of passion—stung to madness by her inconceivable perfidy & by the grossness of the injury which her jealousy prompted her to inflict upon *all of us*—upon both families—I permitted myself to say what I should not have said—I had no sooner uttered the words, than I *felt* their dishonor. I felt, too, that, although *she* must be damningly conscious of her own baseness, she would still have a right to reproach me for having betrayed, under *any* circumstances, her confidence. Full of these thoughts, and terrified almost to death lest I should again, in a moment of madness, be similarly tempted, I . . . made a package of her letters, addressed them to her, and with my own hands left them at her door. Now, Helen, you *can*not be prepared for the diabolical malignity which followed. Instead of feeling that I had done all I could to repair an unpremeditated wrong—instead of feeling that almost any other person would have retained the letters to make good (if occasion required) the assertion that I possessed them—instead of this, she urged her brothers & brother-in-law *to demand of me the letters*. The position in which she thus placed me you may imagine. Is it any wonder that I was driven *mad* by the intolerable sense of wrong? . . . If you value your happiness, Helen, beware of this woman! She did not cease her persecutions here. My poor Virginia was continually tortured (although not deceived) by her anonymous letters, and on her death-bed declared that Mrs. E. had been her murderer. Have I not a right to hate this fiend & to caution you against her?" —Edgar

The Poe Cottage
New York

Some of the local lady writers, seeking a favorable review—*or a wicked dalliance*—call on the cottage with offerings of food and friendship. Unlike us, they have the means and carriages to do so. Muddy, not one to turn down a handout and a chinwag, lets the ladies in, but our guests do not always come with virtuous motives.

One day when I am working downtown, Elizabeth Ellet, one of the starry sisters—albeit a murkier star—arrives at the cottage. Mrs. Ellet is jealous of my close relationship with Fanny Osgood, and she pursues me with belligerent tenacity, to which I respond with scorn. Normally, I would be happy to have not been caught at home, but Mrs. Ellet, an accomplished flimflammer, misleads Aunt Maria with false confidence in my absence.

"The cottage is positively charming, Mrs. Clemm. Why, you've made it so snug and welcoming, I'm sure Mr. Poe cannot wait to come home to you and your daughter at the end of the day. Is this your library?"

"This is where Edgar writes, dear."

"Ah. And these must be letters from his many admirers." She takes the top two off a stack on my desk.

"Oh, those are from Mrs. Osgood." Muddy laughs but snatches the letters away. "It's all in fun, you know, for attention from the press."

Mrs. Ellet extracts another from the stack. "Then there's nothing in them that would be improper. Mrs. Osgood herself has shown me *his* letters to her. Like you said, it's all in fun. But," she lowers her voice, "Fanny told me that she wishes to God she hadn't sent him one particular letter. Perhaps we should look through these to find it and get rid of it before it causes a stir."

Mrs. Ellet convinces Muddy to share Mrs. Osgood's correspondence with her. (How do I know all this when I wasn't there? Remember, Reader, I am dead; I can see the whole picture now. Jealous? No need for that. You'll get your better "eyesight" one day too.) Mrs. Ellet makes no haste scattering the contents of these private letters amongst the literati.

And she happens to throw in another bit of confidence: Frances Osgood is with child, and yet we all know her husband is not in New York.

A day later, Elizabeth Ellet steers Fanny Osgood and other female followers to my cottage door to demand the return of their letters and love poems. Oh, you can be sure, my dear Reader, that I had some stern words for them, especially Mrs. Ellet, whose kittenish missives are also in my possession.

"Let us in, Mr. Poe," says she.

"I will not. My wife is resting. To what do I owe the pleasure of this . . . rabble?"

"We demand the return of our letters, which you have so carelessly allowed your mother-in-law to make known."

"My mother-in-law? My mother-in-law is nursing her very sick daughter. When would she have time to spread hearsay, much less go amongst society? Besides," I hiss, and this is merely a lie put to good use, "Mrs. Clemm is a senile. She cannot make sense of your foolish flattery."

"Nevertheless, Edgar," says Fanny, with what looks like regret, "I wish to have my letters please. And give Virginia my warm regards."

Like the gentleman that I am, I relinquish hers without spite or hesitation. "Mrs. Osgood." I meet her eyes without a nod or a bow as I hand over the stack.

"As for you, Mrs. Ellet, you are an intolerable busybody and a vicious gossip, and you ought to look after your own letters," I say before shutting the door in her face.

Later that day, ashamed by my ill manners, I leave Ellet's letters at her doorstep.

But next comes word from her brutish brother demanding said epistles. When I insist that I restored them, his sister denies it. Now the brother is stalking New York City in a rage, with pistols seeking to engage me in a duel.

The American Review
118 Nassau Street

I ask Thomas Dunn English to be my "second," or the one who negotiates the duel. This was perhaps not the best choice, since he is still sore about my degrading him in the paper.

You did call him an ass.

But I apologized for it.

"My life is at stake, English!"

"I will not. I accept your apology, Poe, but I will not be your ally when violence is involved."

"But you said you would do me a favor. I need a favor now."

"I will not deign to mingle myself in this affair."

"Well, then, at the very least loan me a pistol! I am utterly unequipped for such a challenge."

"Why can't you tell Mrs. Ellet's brother that the charges are false?"

"He will not listen to reason, you great fool! Have you not been listening?"

He pushes me away and wipes his hands against the front of his vest. "This is your own fault, Poe, for condoning these letters in the first place. It's disgraceful—"

Unable to tolerate this disrespect, I strike him in the face. He is so shocked that I land several more blows before he subdues and kicks me out. His treatment of me is entirely unfair considering all I have done for him. Now I admit, I recently called him "Thomas Done Brown"—

Because his last poem was as appealing as horse manure. But that is beside the point! You have "done gold" by him—all the puffing and favors.

And this is how he repays me?

Well, you gave him a flogging he will remember to the day of his death!

Perhaps that is so. But he's cut my cheek with his ring, and it smarts.

Muddy will take the sting away. Or better yet, that attractive nurse Mrs. Shew.

I wonder if it will hurt when I'm shot dead.

Dr. Francis, seeing my state of anxiety, comes to my rescue and sends a letter of reason to the murderous brother. Mercifully, he agrees to rescind, having lately discovered that his lovely sister had the letters all along.

When English accuses me of drunkenness and forgery in *The New York Mirror*, I sue for libel. The judge awards me $326.48 in damages, which helps alleviate my financial crisis, but then the attorney takes his chunk of it. As a result of this very public quarrel, I must endure cruel criticism.

> [T]he flocks of little birds of prey that always take the opportunity to peck at a sick fowl of larger dimensions, have been endeavoring all their power given them to effect my ruin. My dreadful poverty, also has given them every advantage. In fact, my dear friend, I have been driven to the very gates of despair more dreadful than death. . . .

The Poe Cottage

Not all my relationships end like so. I submit the following scenes to the Reader to prove how well I get along with most *decent* people.

One warm afternoon, when a merry party comes to the cottage, I lead them on a walk through the woods.

After you show them your praise from Mrs. Browning, of course.

Of course. Feeling unusually blithe after our woodland traipse, I suggest a game of leaping in the garden. And I am clearly winning when my overshoe splits open.

"Oh, Eddie!" Muddy declares when I return to the cottage. "How did you burst your gaiters?" I have no energy to entertain her interrogation, having lost my short-lived vigor. "Do answer your Muddy," she says, as though I am a little boy. I turn around without speaking and stalk to the bookshelves.

Mary Gove Nichols, the magazine writer who followed me in, explains. "It was a game of leaping. You should have seen it, Mrs. Clemm! Your son-in-law was the grandest leaper in the bunch. But as a consequence, I am afraid, he has torn his gaiters. It's all our fault, really, since he was only indulging us."

Muddy tuts. "Well, no use crying over spilt milk, I suppose." With a weak smile, she shuffles to the kitchen. "Mrs. Nichols? Eddie has this poem. . ." She pulls the paper out from under the breadbox and asks her to recommend it to her editor. "If it will be published, then he can have a new pair of shoes." The editor, as it happens, I have just beat in a game of leaping.

No, not that poem, Muddy. We can do much, much better, Mrs. Nichols. Show her, Mr. Poe.

Suppressing my humiliation, I take down a volume of my published poems from the shelf, sign it, and give it to dear Mary Nichols, who later sees that my poem, which is rather senseless, is accepted and paid for.

By trading pity for favoritism, is Muddy any different than Ellet and Osgood?

As she peruses the book of poetry, I feel the need to defend myself in light of the recent scandal. Unlike those other women, Mrs. Nichols never used me to obtain tribute; she never fawned over me, never teased me. And yet, I could help her . . . as she could help me.

I tell her that I do not desire fame. "I write because I must. It satisfies my craving and love for art and beauty. It is not to please any one person, or the mob for that matter. I do not care for fame or appreciation."

Polite and demure, still she argues. "I am sure there are certain people you respect and for whose judgment you care."

"That may be so," I say, "but those people are not swayed by the mob, which is persuaded by a poor man who is paid to puff an author and construct his fame."

"Who do you mean?" Mrs. Nichols asks, looking up from the page.

"The literary critic." We hear Virginia coughing in her room off the kitchen, and I look that way, despairing.

"What of him?" She lays her hand on my arm to regain my attention.

"He ought not to commend an author whose work does not deserve the praise." I swallow down my emotion

as I watch her fingertips ghost over my printed words.
"But if that man were between a rock and a hard place—
or furthermore, if the one he loves more than life were
being crushed in the process—I can see that man throw-
ing ethics aside and forging acclaim for some upstart
poetess who can return the favor."

I have been looking at the book, but now I meet her
gaze. "You cannot blame that man for not wanting his
ailing wife to starve. Can you?"

She blinks, she hedges, she changes the subject to
something about our abundant garden and how well
Mrs. Clemm makes use of it. I sense her discomfort and
allow the conversation to drift. I see how she may have
mistaken my discourse as a bid for preference instead of
mutual understanding. Before she leaves, I want her to
reconsider me.

"Mrs. Nichols, I told you that I despised fame."

"Yes, you did. I remember."

"Well, I must confess my lie. I adore fame. I worship
it. I idolize it. I would have every man and woman in
every city with my name on their lips. Moreover, I would
have incense burning in every corner of the world in
devotion for my genius. I am a wickedly ambitious man,
and I want fame so badly I can taste it."

Not fame, Mr. Poe. Love. For only in this way can we exist with your fellow man. If they adore you, then perhaps we can forgive them for killing you.

Chapter Forty-One
1846–47

"On my last great disappointment I should have lost my courage *but for you*—my little darling wife. You are my *greatest* and *only* stimulus now, to battle with this uncongenial, unsatisfactory, and ungrateful life."
—Edgar

"Of the charming love and confidence that existed between his wife and himself, always delightfully apparent to me, in spite of the many little poetical episodes, in which the impassioned romance of his temperament impelled him to indulge; of this I cannot speak too earnestly—too warmly. I believe she was the only woman whom he ever truly loved." —Frances Osgood

The Poe Cottage
New York

That summer before the end of our happy home life, I remember one scene that haunts me like a recurring nightmare.

Climbing up the branches of the great cherry tree in front of the cottage, I pluck handfuls of the tart fruit and toss them down to Virginia, who sits beneath me on the grass. She fills her white apron with the cherries, and my mind makes note of the exquisite variation—red on white. One moment she is laughing and looking up at me. The next, I hold a fresh batch of cherries, ready to pour out of my hand, when she chokes.

Blood flows from her mouth, and she swoons, falling into the grass. The blood soaks the bib of her white apron, but this time I do not appreciate the crimson-snow contrast. I jump down from the tree branch and scoop her up, letting the harvest spill onto the ground, and run with her, unconscious, into the house.

I ask you again, Reader, whether or not you can go forth with me into this tragic winter? If your disposition is delicate, I warn you to turn away now, for Virginia's time has come to die. With or without you, I must carry on.

'Til death us do part.

⌐ ✿ ¬

St. John's College, an Episcopal seminary, is set in our neighborhood, and I befriend one of the rectors there. A Catholic priest has also taken an interest in our family and comes for visits. I tolerate conversations with both about the metaphysical, if not the mystical, because I want to believe in an afterlife. Not for my sake, but for Virginia's. Death will be overcome, they say, but I think they talk of symbols and spirit, and I am not buying any of that now. I need food and firewood, not storybook salvation.

There is nothing wrong with wanting to believe in an afterlife. The trouble with mortality is that nothing ever really ends. "Nevermore" is a lie. This is why we need heaven and hell. Our souls are made to live on, whilst our bodies are born to die.

One Fordham neighbor asks me to sponsor the baptism of their child, whom they want to name after me. Imagine! My forename is fine, I say, but not Allan. That name is not a blessing. At my insistence, they christen the baby boy Edgar Albert, and I am honored—albeit astounded—to attend the baptism of little Edgar.

So you see? My neighbors and close friends do not believe the slander of the salons. Even priests abide my so-called reprehensible society.

Muddy borrows a shilling to fetch my post when I am unable to make the walk. You can bet your boots she rummages through the mail before giving it to me, as we receive nasty notes about my war with English, and Mrs. Ellet still sends disparaging letters. But Muddy also snips favorable news about me from the papers, especially any recognition from France and Great Britain. She keeps the collection of clippings with my box of manuscripts.

That winter is especially cold, as the summer had been unusually hot. We keep the kitchen stove and the sitting room fireplace burning, as long as we can acquire fuel, which is donated by charitable neighbors. But it is a lost cause; the cottage is bitter no matter how much I feed the fires.

I wrap Sissy in my West Point coat and lay her on top of the straw mattress, in the little room off the kitchen. Catterina dozes, like a warm loaf of bread, on Virginia's chest, and I rub her feet and hands to keep them from freezing. Muddy takes over when she is not tied up with other chores.

I feel like I am dying too. How can one feel so wretched and still wake up every morning? Each new sunrise offends and confounds me.

Nurse and do-gooder Louise Shew sends us a feather bed and bedclothes for Virginia. She and her friends collect money to give Aunt Maria, and she visits almost daily to help with the nursing and ease our exhaustion.

Mrs. Shew shares news of our suffering with others in my social circle, from which I have withdrawn. (I stopped receiving invitations when talk of my affair with Fanny turned vicious.) The starry sisters who flirted with me, as well as the writers I puffed and recited, send gifts of money and well-wishes. Visitors appear with little presents for Virginia, and she rouses herself, gracious and in high spirits, in spite of her suffering. Willis sends money, which is gotten by an appeal in his paper, describing our illness and poverty. I am thankful, of course, but also abashed to hear my private affairs so publicly shared.

I am reminded of a similar request, for another Mrs. Poe, thirty-five years ago in The Richmond Enquirer. Of course, you won't remember, Mr. Poe, for you were only a babe:

On this night, Mrs. Poe, lingering on the bed of disease and surrounded by her children, asks your assistance and asks it perhaps for the last time.

In January of 1847, we spread the word that it is time to say farewell to Virginia. Family and friends arrive almost every day, including Mary Starr Jenning from Jersey City, who comes the day before the end.

Mary kneels and takes Virginia's hand. "You are sitting up, my dear! Do you feel better today?"

Sissy, seated in the armchair by the fire, smiles and places Mary's hand in mine. "Mary, be Eddie's friend, won't you? He always loved you. He's still got a lock of your hair."

"Virginia—" I start.

"You loved her, Eddie, didn't you?"

My face burns, and I cannot look at either woman. My wife senses how lonely I am, even before she is gone.

She wants you to feel guilty. She wants to remind you who is the victim here.

That darling, selfless girl? No, I do not believe it! She feels guilt for leaving me alone. Her last wish would be friends for me.

Well, as long as that broody hen Elizabeth Ellet isn't one of them. Virginia blames her for her impending death, you know.

Guilt is not the right word. Virginia has never wronged anyone in her short life, and her only worry is for me. What must it be like to die with no regrets, nothing left unfinished? She is perfectly content to be the wife of Mr. Poe and never wanted more for herself. Only for me.

That evening, Virginia struggles for every breath. I take up my pen to summon Mrs. Shew:

> My poor Virginia still lives, although failing fast and now suffering much pain. May God grant her life until she sees you and thanks you once again! Her bosom is full to overflowing—like my own—with a bound-less—inexpressible gratitude to you. Lest she may never see you more—she bids me say that she sends you her sweetest kiss of love and will die blessing you. But come—oh, come to-morrow! Yes, I will be calm—everything you so nobly wish to see me.

And she comes the next morning, meeting Mary Starr on her way.

"Edgar, you must be composed," Mrs. Shew says. "Find something with which to distract yourself, and Mary and I will sit with her for a while. You've made yourself sick."

What she means to say is, "You run along now, Mr. Poe. You're upsetting the patient. This isn't about you, you know."

Sissy conducts some final business with Mrs. Shew in private.

"What did she say to you?" I ask her later.

"She read me your foster mother's letters. Virginia is very proud of her husband. I think she wants me to think well of you." It seems my wife, in her last hours, is trying to find the next Mrs. Poe, but I can hardly think about that now.

We stay with Sissy through a traumatic, feverish afternoon. I watch all this as though from faraway, peeking through a hidden door that is only slightly parted. But night falls, and she gasps for air that evades her, and my consciousness rushes into my body with gruesome awareness. The women and I look on, horrified, helpless, as my twenty-four-year-old wife strangles to death.

None too soon, she falls slack and silent in my arms. Muddy makes a frightful bellow, her face raised to the ceiling, her mouth open, her bosom heaving. Like the banshee that haunted my childhood in Scotland, she howls. I clasp my arms around her neck and heave great shuddering sobs, as the To Be tells me to preserve this moment so that I can later write it down.

My darling—my darling—my wife and my bride...

But all I can think is, *She has finally left me.* My recurring nightmare has come true.

"We don't have a picture of her," Muddy says, when we quiet.

"I shall summon a painter," I say, my voice soft and wet. I cannot pay for it, but I can promise future commissions for my magazine—if there will ever be a magazine. I cannot fathom a future, much less a reason to live for it.

Before the rigidity of Death takes hold, Muddy brushes and pins her daughter's hair for the last time. An artist from the city comes with watercolors and positions Virginia on a pillow for the portrait, although her head lolls at a grotesque angle. I detest this image, and I cannot make myself look at it, nor my dead wife's face and lifeless eyes.

"I would rather remember her alive," I say when Muddy wants to display it in the cottage.

Mrs. Shew brought a linen dress and a wooden coffin, and she helps Muddy prepare Sissy for the latter, which is set on my writing desk. Our landlords allow us to use their family vault at Fordham Manor Church. I shrug on the cadet greatcoat that had been keeping Virginia warm this winter, and the Episcopal rector and the Catholic priest help me carry her to the burying ground.

When we come home, I am unaware of the people who crowd the cottage, murmuring and clinking their cups and saucers. Even the voice of the To Be diminishes. Although I hear the old sinner droning, its words I cannot discern.

Have you no imagination, or are you merely squeamish? I told you about Rufus Griswold, who had his first wife's decaying corpse exhumed so that he could make love to it. And he has the audacity to call you mad!

I do not remember that, but I do hear Muddy whispering to Mary Starr. "This was Virginia's thimble. It's made of gold. It's very dear."

"Oh, Mrs. Clemm! I don't have any money to buy it. Please keep it to remember her by. You would regret selling it later."

I close my eyes and do not seem to open them for many weeks.

Our love—it was stronger by far than the love of
those who were older than we—of many far wiser than
we. . . .

PART SEVEN:

The Widower

Chapter Forty-Two
1847–48

"... When Mr. Poe was well, his pulse beat only ten regular beats, after which it suspended, or intermitted (as doctors say). I decided that in his best health he had lesion of one side of the brain, and as he could not bear stimulants or tonics, without producing insanity, I did not feel much hope that he could be raised up from brain fever brought on by extreme suffering of mind and body—actual want and hunger, and cold having been borne by this heroic husband in order to supply food, medicine, and comforts to his dying wife—until exhaustion and lifelessness were so near at every reaction of the fever, that even sedatives had to be administered with extreme caution. ... From the time the fever came on until I could reduce his pulse to eighty beats, he talked to me incessantly of the past, which was all new to me, and often begged me to write his fancies for him, for he said he had promised to many greedy publishers his next efforts, that they would not only say that he did not keep his word, but would also revenge themselves by saying all sorts of evil of him if he should die." —Louise Shew

The Poe Cottage
New York

For weeks after Virginia's death, I am critically ill. I think I would have died myself if it hadn't been for Muddy and Mrs. Shew.

Louisa Shew gives us $100, which is donated by local sympathizers (one of these being General Scott, who mistook me in adolescence for a ghost during a whist party). Virginia's Dr. Francis coaxes me to recover. "Mrs. Clemm cannot lose you both," he says. He is right, of course. It would be selfish of me to die. I do not care to go on, but I must, for our mother's sake.

She sits by my bed until I grow very still, her hand upon my head. When she, thinking me asleep, rises, I clasp my hand over hers on my forehead and whisper, "Not yet, Muddy, not yet."

In my delirium and dreams, the To Be tells me unknown truths about the universe and life, God and nature and other confounding mysteries. Thus, even in my unconsciousness, the poet is at work. These secrets comfort and captivate me, and I emerge from my infirmity with eyes wide open.

In February, we receive the much-needed money from the libel suit. Muddy buys a new tea set, some rugs, and a lamp. She is soon having company over for tea. Now, the talk around town is that I am stuck on Mrs. Shew and have already forgotten Virginia. *"Mrs. Clemm also seems overly pleased with her new possessions."*

If having a dead lover is romantic, to grieve her to the depth that I do is not. I wander outside after dark, for I cannot sleep, and watch over Virginia's final resting place, as I once did the tombs of Jane Stanard and Frances Allan.

I thought we already disputed this. You do not care for graveyards after dusk.

True. I walk and walk and walk the days away, avoiding the roads and roaming the woods and meadows, reciting the lyrics Sissy was oft to sing:

> *'Tis said that absence conquers love!*
> *But, oh! believe it not;*
> *I've tried, alas! its power to prove,*
> *But thou art not forgot.*
> *Lady, though fate has bid us part,*
> *Yet still thou art as dear,*
> *As fixed in this devoted heart,*
> *As when I clasped thee here.*

I discuss with the seminary priests my notions of a God who created love and beauty in a world that allows for agony. The nights, I make Muddy keep vigil with me. She dozes in her rocker with Kate on her lap, while I scribble like mad a poetic essay regarding the mysteries of the universe—everything the To Be told me during my fever and expanded upon during my long walks. Every hour or so, my aunt stokes the fire and fuels me with coffee. I share with her these universal secrets, as if she could understand.

Eureka! Spring comes and I know now why beauty must be met with suffering. It is the perfect plot.

After all my rising and falling, I still have friends who want to see me triumph. With their help, a lecture on the subject of my latest work is scheduled. We think the presentation will raise the money needed to tour the States and garner subscriptions for *The Stylus*. Although the subject of my lecture is complex, and it is beyond me how to make it digestible to the general public, the dread-thrill of being before an audience brings out my force of personality. I am elated to reveal what was lately revealed to me and unusually hopeful about the future. Alas, on the night of the event, poor weather affects the turnout, and I do not make enough money for a tour.

George P. Putnam publishes five hundred copies of *Eureka: A Prose Poem*. The preface reads:

> To the few who love me and whom I love—to those who feel rather than to those who think—to the dreamers and those who put their faith in dreams as in the only realities—I offer this Book of Truths, not in its character of Truth-Teller, but for the Beauty that abounds in its Truth.

I call it a romance. I call it a poem. It is my best, truest work, but book sales flow at a trickle.

And not a steady trickle at that.

The Shew Residence
51 10th Street
&
Church of the Ascension
5th & 10th Streets

My angel, Louise Shew, floats not away after Virginia's farewell. She continues to bring practical aid to my house, such as food and clothing. If it were not for her, my life would be very dark indeed. Unlike the starry sisterhood of poetesses, Louise is compassionate and sensible, understanding and helpful. My affection for Virginia transfers to this very capable, mature woman, who is warmhearted and obliging. I am in her home as much as my own. She is a doctor's daughter and a doctor's wife and happily prone to "nurse" me, always administering instructions, which I obey.

Unrequited love is the only kind of love I can conjure. As Sissy once remarked, I prefer the company of married women.

All the suitable women are either dead or married—not entirely intact, as it were.

"You have done so much for us, Mrs. Shew. What may I do for you?"

She takes a moment to think and, smiling, says, "Why don't you come to church with me? That would please me very much."

I accept, and we attend the Episcopal church near her house on a Sunday morn. Although I still do not care for what is spoken, I find satisfying beauty in the rituals and music.

"You sing very well," she says. "And you know all the responses."

I smile wanly. "I used to attend church with my foster mother, Mrs. Allan."

"Then tell me you haven't lost your faith in God."

"On the contrary. If God created you and brought

you to me, then I can believe in God and his goodness."

One evening, we take tea in the Shews' conservatory. My fever is coming on again. I loosen my stock with a frown and half close my eyes. I tug at my vest and coat, which stifle me, until the stock comes untied.

"Mr. Poe, what is that mark there?" Mrs. Shew asks, startled.

"What mark?"

"There. On your collar. You have a scar."

"Oh, this," I say, looking down as though I could see it, my lower lip pouting. My words tumble out dreamy and warbled. "It's from a duel . . . with swords. When I was a younger man, I traveled to Spain. I fought a duel and received this wound. Then I was nursed by a kindly Scotch woman, but I won't say her name. I promised never to say her name."

If I recall, it was after a card game in Charlottesville—the rare win that ended with a broken bottle at your throat.

"You recovered, I see." Mrs. Shew sits back and folds her hands in her lap.

"Yes, then I traveled to Paris. I wrote a novel there—"

"I did not know that."

"It was stolen. The novel was stolen from me and

another name forged upon it."

She throws me a suspicious glance. "Edgar. . ."

I groan and roll my head. "I need to write a poem, but I cannot think what to write about. I have no subject—" My head throbs. I see black spots. Then the five-o'clock church bells clang, causing the pain inside my skull to toll in time.

Louise rushes out, I think to bring a cold cloth for my head, but she comes back with paper, pen, and ink. She thrusts it at me. "There is your subject. Write about the bells."

Normally, I do her bidding without quibble, but this time I push the page away. "I dislike the noise. It hurts my ears. I cannot write tonight."

She takes up the pen and writes, "The Bells," and slides the paper back to me, holding forth the pen like a sword with which I am to be knighted. "Let the pain be your inspiration."

In a few minutes, I have finished a stave and I close my eyes. My head is sizzling, but there is no peace for the wicked, for I hear the paper flapping in my face.

"Cruelty doesn't become you, Louise."

Under the first verses, she has written: "the heavy iron bells."

"Go on. Write," she says.

This time I construct two staves. I scratch out "by Mrs. M. L. Shew" underneath the title.

After supper, I ask for a bed. Seeing that I am on the verge of collapse, Louise sends for Dr. Francis. I disappear into a welcoming darkness, from which I do not care to emerge. This land of dreams is dark, but it is trouble-free.

The Poe Cottage

When I come to much later, I find myself delivered home to Fordham. Dr. Francis is here, and he gives me a grave prognosis.

"Mr. Poe, you have heart disease. You will die an early death, unless you take very good care of yourself. This means no immoderation—certainly no stimulants. And you must take care not to suffer too much excitement. Get plenty of rest and eat good food. The way you are living is good for no man, but especially one in such poor health as yourself."

Muddy is discouraged and fretful. Louise sends her to the kitchen to brew a tisane. I reach for her hand.

"You are an angel, Louise."

She sniffs and attempts a smile, her eyes flitting from our hands to my gaze. "Edgar, you need to marry. I cannot be your nurse anymore. You need a wife, preferably one with means to provide comfort for you."

"Perhaps her name will be Temperance." My laughter is mirthless, and Louise remains grim.

Apparently, her name will not be Louise.

I intend to follow doctor's orders. Why we men try to save ourselves, I do not know. Especially when, as in my case, death would be a mercy. But I do try. And yet a sick man must take his medicine, even if that medicine is killing him. I suppose Louise Shew knows this about me.

All of New York knows how you latch on to married women. That troubles Mrs. Shew more than your intemperance or congestion of the brain.

She sends me a letter, telling me not to visit her anymore.

> Can it be true, Louise, that you have the idea fixed in your mind to desert your unhappy and unfortunate friend and patient? You did not say so, I know, but for months I have known you were deserting me. . . .
>
> Are you to vanish like all I love, or desire. . . ?
>
> Unless some true and tender, and pure womanly love saves me, I shall hardly last a year longer alive!

Stop this sniveling, Mr. Poe! Of course, any sensible woman like Louise Shew would turn and run— will I, nill I—from this hopeless mooning.

Hence she shakes me off, like dust from an apron. And I—accurately this time—predict my own demise.

Chapter Forty-Three
1848

—ↄ⌒ↄ—

"Poe's voice was melody itself. He always spoke low, even in a violent discussion, compelling his hearers to listen if they would know his opinion, his facts, fancies, or philosophy, or his weird imaginings. These last usually flowed from his pen, seldom from his tongue."
—Mary Gove Nichols

"We sat of doors, and watched its effects of light and shade. Poe kindly remarked, 'How beautiful you look in the moonlight! You should always sit in the moonlight'—which occurred to me as not exactly feasible, although agreeable when possible. He was not always so flattering, however; for later on, emboldened by his attention and desiring to shine, I made what I thought to be a very witty remark, which Poe received coolly, only saying, 'Satire is a very unlovely thing in a woman.'" —Elma Gove

Anne C. Lynch's Salon
New York

But before I die, I want to remarry. And so begins the search for my savior, with Aunt Maria's blessing and conniving to speed the way.

That Mrs. Clemm is always looking ahead!

You will remember a certain poetess in Providence, Rhode Island, whom I spied one sleepless, moonlit night? Keep her in mind, dear Reader, for the part of second wife, for she soon may be given the opportunity to audition.

Mad as a March hare, that one. I think you two rightly deserve one another.

The New York literati carries on without me during my mourning and convalescence. Miss Lynch hosts a Valentine's Day soirée, which is attended by Helen Whitman—said providential poetess in the moonlight. Miss Lynch asks her to contribute a valentine poem for the occasion, and it is about none other than the Raven Poet.

Frances Osgood receives a copy of the poem from Miss Lynch, and she forwards it to me. The verses remain unsigned, but I recognize Whitman's style.

Some would say I fall in love with Mrs. Whitman's inheritance. I say it is her poetry. We seem to be of like mind—she, my intellectual match. I've not yet properly met the woman, but by all appearances, she is the ideal candidate for "wife"—widowed, mature, and financially independent. But before I pursue Helen, I am diverted southwards.

Duncan Lodge
Richmond

A fortunate speaking engagement in Massachusetts provides me the travel funds to solicit magazine subscriptions. Like a nostalgic goose, I migrate south to Virginia, where I keep the demons at bay and shamefully neglect *The Stylus* campaign. This city entertains the memories of all those I have loved and lost.

Let us be honest. This is not a business trip at all. Mr. Poe is looking for love and appreciation, not work.

Befuddled, I land at the Mackenzie family home, to dry out. My old friend Jack invites me in, and I sober under Ma Mackenzie's ministrations. Rosalie is still in residence and happy as ever to see her Buddy.

Richmond receives with open arms their beloved boy-turned-poet, after a decade of cavorting in the North. In turn, I welcome invitations to recite at social functions, and my fame is much celebrated as the city's poet laureate. I feel young again and even up for a game of leapfrog with the Mackenzie brothers, who seem not to have grown up at all in my absence. As in my boyhood, my knees are once again stained by grass and dirt, and my heart feels lighter.

One night, the fire alarm sounds for a house in the country, and I set out with all the able men to help. But seeing that the fire is being sufficiently tended to, the Mackenzies and I sit on a fence post and watch the goings-on.

Tom Mackenzie, eyeing the smolder, says, "Seeing all this activity makes me ravenous. I could kill for one of Ma's grand breakfasts right about now."

"The women will give us a roasting, not a meal, if we come home looking so clean," Jack says.

"Then let's not," I say. I pick up a charred piece of wood and smudge their shirts and faces. Jack darkens my face and hands, seeing as I am already clad in black.

We return to Duncan Lodge, weary and blackened, under the pretense of having risked our health and stayed up half the night to put out fires. Ma Mackenzie, proud and doting, serves us an extravagant spread, even dismissing the servants to do so herself.

We confess the next day when the newspaper names the true heroes. Mrs. Mackenzie laughs and shakes her finger at me with her usual good humor, but she gives her sons the devil for lying and staining their clothes.

The Richmond Examiner

As is my custom, I frequent my old office at *The Southern Literary Messenger*, as well as other papers that will publish me. Also my custom, I quarrel with an editor, John Daniel, of *The Richmond Examiner*, who is making noise about my relationship with certain female poets. Outraged, I demand he allow me the opportunity to settle the old-fashioned way—with a duel—but my challenge is left maddeningly unanswered. Am I thought so foolish, cowardly, or drunk to be taken seriously?

Well, this is the same Edgar Poe

who took a cowhide to an elderly shopkeeper in Baltimore ... if one can believe the rumors.

As a man with some shred of dignity left, I must confront insult with action.

Perhaps offense is in your blood. The Poe family motto is, after all, Malo Mori Quam Foedari: "I would rather die than be debased." You do take that sentiment to heart, Mr. Poe.

Finally, Daniel summons me to his office and offers me a seat. On the desk lay two pistols, aligned muzzle to butt, in a velvet-lined box.

"Poe, old friend," he says, "To forgo any more dispute, I suggest we each take a pistol and stand at opposite walls."

Methinks he's done this before.

"Then we try to maim or kill the other?" I ask, eyeing the pistols.

"That is what you want, is it not?"

I clear my throat. "I want, er—well, it is an opportunity, yes. But, of course, you know these weapons are not very accurate. No matter how good our aim, we are more likely to rip holes in the plaster than shed blood. And I do believe you rent this office, isn't that so?"

Daniel strokes his chin. "That is correct."

"These are lovely," I say, ghosting my fingers along

the grip, then pulling away. "Heirlooms?"

He nods. "My mother's father's, from Scotland."

"And the caliber of bullet is quite sizable. What is it? Forty-five?"

"Fifty."

"Dear me, that is potentially a gaping hole in your walls. Or the rafters, should we decide to point upwards."

Or an abundance of blood and body parts.

"Potentially, yes." I detect a tugging in one corner of his mouth.

"What a mess that would be."

"Will you accept an apology instead, Poe?"

"I think that would be most prudent, in these circumstances."

"Then I offer my most sincere apology, for what I said, I should not have. May I buy you a drink?"

Well played, Mr. Poe. You will live to scrap another day, and you've managed to hold on to a friend.

At the conclusion of my battle with Daniel, I receive another poem from Rhode Island. My plans for the magazine thus abandoned and a letter of introduction obtained, I leave Richmond behind for the foredoomed wooing of Mrs. Helen Whitman.

Chapter Forty-Four
1848

—⁌⁍—

"I have 'in my mind's eye' a figure . . . so perfectly
proportioned, and crowned with such a noble head,
so regally carried, that, to my girlish apprehension,
he gave the impression of commanding stature. Those
clear sad eyes seemed to look from an eminence,
rather than from the ordinary level of humanity, while
his conversational tone was so low and deep, that one
could easily fancy it borne to the ear from some distant height." —Sarah Heywood

Swan Point Cemetery
585 Blackstone Boulevard
Providence

"Frances Osgood called you 'a glorious devil' and prayed
that 'Providence' would protect me if you were to swoop
down upon my little dovecote here."

Sarah Helen Whitman's voice is deeper than I imagined—mournful and lilting.

"Did she indeed? Mrs. Osgood never seemed to mind
playing with the devil."

"She said your '*croak* is the most eloquent imagin-
able.'"

"And do you think she properly prepared you for my
swooping and croaking?"

"Oh, it's not a croak at all! It is like the most lovely,

haunting song. Like a loon."

"Mrs. Osgood would be wont to call me a loon."

Helen and I stroll arm-in-arm about a picturesque cemetery in twilight. I do recommend a cemetery or garden for contemplative wanders, but both work as well for romantic pursuits in my personal experience; the latter more so if the pursued is also a spiritualist, such as Mrs. Helen Whitman.

"She desires you," Helen says.

"Sorry. Who?"

"Frances Osgood. I am sure you know that. She cannot have you and she cannot give you up, so as much as she wishes you nevermore, she'd rather not share you."

I nearly stumble. "Is that so?"

"That feud with Elizabeth Ellet? That was strictly female envy over which choice morsel of poetess would catch your beady eye."

Beady? I take offense.

"It—it was some business with letters. . ."

Helen covers her mouth with a kerchief, takes a deep breath, and changes the subject. "We share the same birthday, you and I. And my family name, Power, is of the same ancestry as Poe."

"That would explain the *power* you hold over me, Mrs. Whitman. You know I loved a Helen long ago."

"'To Helen,' yes? And she crossed over?"

"She died tragically young, if that is what you mean. I spent nights as a young man weeping on her grave." I stop to read a gravestone, giving Mrs. Whitman the opportunity to look me over. My bearing, while not rugged, lends to an air of nobility, counteracting the frailty of poor health and nutrition. I am not strapping, but I am fit and balanced.

"You know that death is not the end of us, don't you? You must believe that, having so recently lost your young wife. She is as present in this world as you and I. Your Helen too. She has always been with you."

I know you don't believe that, my boy. Virginia and Mrs. Stanard have better to do than follow you around.

"It is quite a coincidence that your name is Helen too."

"Oh, it's no coincidence. I don't believe in coincidences. I believe the stars."

"I think I love you more than she. I was a boy then, but I am hence grown, in mind and in heart. As a widower, I understand love better. I know what's at stake."

Her name is Sarah Helen. As a boy, you loved a Sarah too. Sarah Elmira. Is this a coincidence?

"Will you be my wife, Sarah Helen Whitman?"

She smiles demurely. Then, "We shall see, Mr. Poe, if it is our destiny."

My arm has fallen about her waist, and although she says this last with confidence enough, I can sense a stiffening, as though her body contradicts her voice. I lean my face towards hers, but she pulls the handkerchief again from her sleeve, holds it to her nose and mouth, and inhales. I catch the scent of ether, and Helen turns soft and dreamy.

"Are you all right, my dear?"

"It's for my heart, Mr. Poe. I know you understand."

We do understand the need not to feel. But I suppose it would not be polite to ask for a whiff?

When she replaces the handkerchief, she is not looking at me, but over my shoulder. "I can see this Helen from your childhood."

I almost look behind me. "What do you mean?"

"Her spirit is attached to you, like a mother."

"I always knew a spirit guided me. I knew it was she."

Claptrap! I am no dead woman, Mr. Poe. But you must not give me away. If she wants to think me Jane Stanard's ghost, then let her.

Mrs. Whitman closes her eyes so tightly her brow is creased.

"She speaks to me, Edgar. She is urging me to love you as she did."

"Oh, Helen, will you?"

Burying Ground near Fordham Manor Church
Kingsbridge Road
New York

The next night, pacing the graveyard at Fordham where Virginia lies, I ponder the prior evening's dialogue. Dare I hope that this woman, who calls me Raven, be my dove of peace? Or better yet, prosperity.

Is there a dove of prosperity? Or would it be a peacock?

Helen promises to conduct a seance the next time I am in Providence, that I may hear myself from the Helen of my youth, perhaps my mother too. She does not offer to conjure Virginia; whether that is because Sissy is not long in the grave or because she, being my wife, would not approve, I do not know and I do not ask. I do not believe the dead capable of communicating with the living, but I indulge Helen anyway.

You and I communicate, but we are one and the same.

Perhaps I am curious. Perhaps I want to believe. But my belief in the spirit world begins and ends with the To Be, who has not steered me wrong yet. Spirit or not, it is an unknown part of myself, perhaps a future me. Its voice is my voice, but the things it says . . . I cannot know these things!

To Be urges me to pursue Mrs. Whitman, not because it is necessarily fond of her but because it promotes my survival, no matter how that would be achieved.

Helen writes to me, stating all the reasons she cannot be married: she is older, she is widowed, and she is ailing.

I write back, wild with worry. I think she caught wind of what people say about me, and I make my defense. I say that when our souls are as such connected, then reputations should not sway us one way or the other. I use language to appeal to Helen, especially that our love, which is an ethereal love, will *transcend* the physical world.

Power Residence
88 Benefit Street
Providence

I make my way back to Providence to persuade her differently. If I prayed to God, I would pray for Providence to be in my favor.

I tell Helen more about Mrs. Stanard, and said spirit speaks to her too—one Helen to another—or so she claims. It would seem, from what she relays, that the dearly departed champion my cause most keenly.

There are quite a lot of dearly departed in your case, Mr. Poe. Why shouldn't they want the best for you?

I will take all the help I can get—even if it is from the dead.

Mrs. Whitman falls into a trance, aided by her handkerchief I presume, and when she wakes, she bears messages from beyond the grave.

"She knows, Edgar." Helen's pale lips barely move. "Your Helen knows what is to become of us. She says you will be the best-known American writer the world over, whether I am by your side or not." Her eyes widen. "And if not, I will be forgotten."

If corporeal, I would be beset with chills! That sounds quite like something your first Helen would say, when you would play cards with her son Rob and share your verses over tea.

The wood in the fire cracks like a whip, and I glance upon a painting of Helen Whitman above the mantelpiece. The portrait looks so much like Rob Stanard—if Rob were of the fairer sex—that I may start to believe in ghosts.

Before I take my leave, I kiss Helen's ether-scented fingers. "Reconsider my proposal, my dear, and send word of your answer."

Chapter Forty-Five
1848

"No one, certainly no woman, who had the slightest acquaintance with Edgar Poe, could have credited the story for an instant. He was essentially and instinctively a gentleman, utterly incapable, even in moments of excitement and delirium, of such an outrage as Dr. Griswold has ascribed to him. No authentic anecdote of coarse indulgence in vulgar orgies or bestial riot has ever been recorded of him. During the last years of his unhappy life, whenever he yielded to the temptation that was drawing him into its fathomless abyss, as with the resistless swirl of the maelstrom, he always lost himself in sublime rhapsodies on the evolution of the universe, speaking as from some imaginary platform to vast audiences of rapt and attentive listeners. During one of his visits to this city, in the autumn of 1848, I once saw him after one of those nights of wild excitement, before reason had fully recovered its throne. Yet even then, in those frenzied moments when the doors of the mind's 'Haunted Palace' were left unguarded, his words were the words of a princely intellect overwrought, and of a heart only too sensitive and too finely strung. I repeat that no one acquainted with Edgar Poe could have given Dr. Griswold's scandalous anecdote a moment's credence." —Helen Whitman

Charles Richmond Residence
Ames Street
Lowell, Massachusetts

In Massachusetts for another lecture, I lodge with the Richmonds in the town of Westford. Their family home is my sanctuary while I await Helen's reply. I would say that Nancy Richmond, whom I call Annie, is like a sister to me.

As you say your wife was? Remember her? Remember Sissy?

But as I anticipate word from my would-be betrothed, I grow more anxious, and Annie's attention is more and more welcome.

That is because she admires you, Mr. Poe, and you know it.

Alas, as much as she flatters, Annie, or Mrs. Charles Richmond, belongs to another.

How often must we come back to this? Fanny, Mary, Louise, Annie.... Lest we forget Myra. Can only an impoverished thirteen-year-old girl be had for a wife—

I will not allow you to deprecate Virginia, you cruel demon!

My apologies, Mr. Poe. I am only

casting light on an unfortunate trend.

As it is, I'll ask you leave Sissy to her eternal rest.

Not to lie to you, my dearest Reader, I dread Helen's answer, whether it be yea or nay. If affirmative, I may live longer, but to what end? Happiness is too ambiguous a thing to hope for. I am a walking ghost, a soul in limbo, wandering in and out of taverns and libraries but never belonging. It is too much for my soul to bear, this waiting for one to let me into her heart, while the one I want is forbidden.

But which is the one you want?

As if *you* do not know.

Do you mean that the one you want is dead?

How am I to know what I want?

An Unknown Hotel
Boston

Restless, I move on to Boston. The city of my beginning, I decide, will be the city of my end. I invite illness or violence to finish me off, without any resistance on my part. But when neither present, I procure two ounces of laudanum. True love will come to me if I am on my deathbed.

That didn't work out so well for Mrs. Poe, now did it?

Ah, Reader, I sense your suspicion. It is quite possible that I do not intend to go through with the murder, only to make it look like so. While I am still somewhat sensible, I write a letter, telling Annie what I am up to and where she may find me.

Annie? Mr. Poe, Annie is not real. Her name is Nancy Richmond, and you have known her for all of two weeks! Those namby-pamby letters—"oh! oh! my dear, darling, beautiful Annie!"—are melodramatic forgeries. You are pursuing Helen Whitman. Or did you forget?

Then I swallow one of the two ounces, saving the rest for when my angel of death should come. The opium takes effect immediately, and, although I set out into the street, neither I nor the letter reach the post office.

An unknown friend looks after me in the ensuing hours of my besotted state. Whoever my Good Samaritan is, I do not remember, but I owe him my eternal gratitude. After vomiting, I am at least rational enough to get where I want to go (since true love did not come to me). Providence it is, where I can show Helen the unused half of laudanum and flap about with my broken wings.

Power Residence

&

Masury & Hartshorn Studio

Westminster Street

Providence

Early in the morning, I knock on Helen's door. Seeing as she is not yet out of bed or properly dressed, I am sent away with a family friend, Mr. Pabodie. He leads me, meek as a lamb, into a photography studio to sit for my portrait.

Regrettably, it is this daguerreotype that is my most recognized likeness. The day after I attempted suicide and I am half out of my mind—even my face is lopsided, as though indicative of the conflict inside my head. Why Pabodie thought this appropriate, I do not know.

He thought Edgar Poe was on death's doorstep, and he'd do well to get an image of the Raven for posterity.

I stumble back to the Power residence, where I rave, passionate and unceasing, in the parlor. For all the commotion downstairs, Helen is afraid to leave her bedroom. Her mother, Mrs. Power, sits with me, coaxing me to calm with hot drinks. She eventually persuades her daughter to come out and ease my mind.

Helen is shrouded in her most elegant gown, the one she wears for séances. When she offers me her hand, I cling to her dress, and a piece of it is torn away in my fist. I plead with her like I am pleading for my life.

Because that is precisely what you are doing. This is life or death, Mr. Poe.

The family, seeing that I am unwell, calls for the doctor and sends me to bed.

The Poe Cottage
New York

Helen agrees to marry me on one condition: I must vow to abstain from alcohol.

I have not dared to break my promise to you. And now, dearest Helen, be true to me.

Muddy nurses me at the cottage and I write letters: to Helen for reassurance, to Annie for sympathy, to Edward Valentine for money—

Who is that?

The cousin who taught me to yank chairs out from under sitting women.

Oh, by all means. He owes you.

I write the minister in Providence who will marry us, requesting that he publish the wedding bans. In turn, I am presented a contract to sign, dictating that Helen's estate be transferred to her mother. It seems that Mrs. Whitman's mother and relatives scorn the match and seek to prohibit my reaping any wealth from the holy union.

Dispirited and beyond worry, I nevertheless help Muddy prepare the cottage for a new bride. Washing windows and weeding the garden, I can see the tension in my long-suffering aunt's face, and I smile through my fears to reassure her. Likewise, I assure Helen that my mother, Mrs. Clemm, will treat her kindly.

Unlike her mother, Mrs. Power, who treated you rotten.

At the train station, I stumble across a matronly neighbor. "Mr. Poe, are you going to Providence to marry Helen Whitman?"

"No, madam. I am going to deliver a lecture on poetry." I clench my jaw and open my hand to see the wad of Helen's torn dress. "The marriage may or may not happen."

Power Residence
Providence

The lecture, in fact, is a great success. The marriage, however. . . .

You are the victim of an elaborate hoax. Like the pistol duel with Daniel, the event was arranged with no intention of following through.

Unbeknownst to me, I have been confiding in Helen's *other* suitor! Mr. Pabodie behaves as a friend in my presence. In confidence, however, he tells Helen that

I took wine with some fellows at the Earl House bar. Furthermore, a library patron hands her a note that describes my affection for Annie Richmond, which is the cause of much uproar in Westford.

Pabodie escorts me to the Power residence to see Helen for a final time.

He knows, Mr. Poe, that your fancifully betrothed will break your heart. Pabodie tells her lies, that she may favor him instead.

"My heart is heavy, Helen, for I see that your friends are not my own."

I find a glassy-eyed poetess wilting on the sofa, sniffing her kerchief. She tells me my wrongdoing, and I deny it. What is most disappointing is the obvious relief on her face as she breaks her promise, claiming that I have broken mine.

"These are lies! The other men at the bar drank; I did not. Mrs. Richmond may be in love with me, but I have done nothing to encourage her, other than be a grateful houseguest. I am bound by the strictures of propriety. She is married, for God's sake."

"All the women who love you are married."

"But I love you, not those hussies!"

May I draw attention to the fact that a man in love and happily engaged to be married would not attempt to end his own life. I think it behooves you to walk away now.

I hover over her and implore. "Please, my dear, tell me this is not the last time I see you." I fall to my knees.

"The hour is late, Mr. Poe," says Mother Power, hovering with her hand on the doorknob. "Your train will leave without you." I ignore her.

"What can I say?" Helen asks.

"Say that you love me!"

She raises the handkerchief to her face and makes a muffled farewell through the cloth: "I love you, Edgar. Now go. You mustn't miss your train."

Chapter Forty-Six
1848–49

"There is one thing you will be glad to learn: —It has been a long while since any artificial stimulus has passed my lips. When I see you—should that day ever come—this is a topic on which I desire to have a long talk with you. I am done forever with drink—depend upon that but there is much more in this matter than meets the eye. Do not let anything in this letter impress you with the belief that I *despair* even of worldly prosperity. On the contrary, although I feel ill, and am ground into the very dust with poverty, there is a sweet *hope* in the bottom of my soul." —Edgar

Poe Cottage
New York

An outwardly sympathetic Pabodie escorts me to the train station. I cannot help but imagine him wiping his hands of me, perhaps even whistling a jolly tune, once I'm away. When I arrive back at Fordham, I tell Muddy, "The marriage is postponed." She nods, offering a pathetic frown, but I see the release in her eyes.

Strangely, I feel better too—physically and mentally. Keen to mend my reputation, I write letters to counteract the gossip coming from Providence. I tell Annie Richmond that I withdrew the offer of marriage to Helen Whitman. I censure the "heartless, unnatural, venomous, dishonorable set" of literary women who weary me with their attacks, both spoken and in print.

Dear Mr. Poe, you do not need this sisterhood. Surely you see that you create better women than can be found on this sinful earth. If only Helen, Annabel Lee, or Lenore were alive and real, but they exist only in your mind and memories. Even if you could conjure them up, they are dead, and you are no Doctor Frankenstein.

But I want—ah, I do not know what I want!

You want Eden. And you deserve Eve—but rather one who lacks the deception that taints her and her female progeny. For then you could worship her as the goddess in the garden, as she was meant to be. And you, Mr. Poe, are made to adore her. You were not created for physical love, but rather spiritual love—supernatural love—poetic love.

To Be is right, of course. This woman does not exist. Not anymore. And if she once did, she is now an angel in heaven. But how to remain in this world as a romantic with no object of affection? I write, of course. My imagination yields a world that makes sense, or at least one that I can sensibly manage. I create my own heaven and my own hell. I create the future. Literature will be, not only my profession, but my life.

It will be your one <u>true</u> wife.

—⁙—

Still reading? Good.

This, my dear Reader, is the death of me. The end is already written. Nothing we do now can change it. But fear not, Reader, for I will go with you.

I know you are bracing yourself for the inevitable outcome, but the conclusion of my story will be no more grisly than it's already been. We have seen the worst of it, you and I. If you've made it to this point, there is no use bailing out.

Here and now, I surrender my desire to be loved and pursue my eternity. My pen may be idle at present, but it has made me a legacy, if not a living. By God, I may not be loved, but I will be immortal.

Anne C. Lynch's Salon

For the time I have left, I want to go where I am wanted. That is not Rhode Island, not Massachusetts, not New York, not Pennsylvania. I am too poor to go south on my own, but Providence, one might say, soon meets me at Fordham. A patron for *The Stylus* comes, quite literally, out of the wilderness, and he believes in me enough to pay me. I plan to use the sponsorship funds to go to Richmond—not Annie, but rather the city that formed me.

Farewells can be exhausting, but purgative. I have not darkened the doorstep of Anne Lynch's salon since before Virginia died, but when I turn up unexpectedly in the summer of 1849, Miss Lynch is climbing into a carriage bound for Philadelphia.

Her eyelashes flutter in what I take to be delighted shock. "Mr. Poe! It is so good to see you."

"Miss Lynch." I take her hand and apologize for not coming sooner. "I had so much to say. So very much I wished to say."

"Mr. Poe—I am sorry about Virginia." She looks at me with such pity, and I know she knows she will not see me again.

She dreams of Eden too, but you will see it before she does.

Sylvanus D. Lewis Residence
125 Dean Street
Brooklyn

We close up the cottage, and I transfer the care of Muddy and Kate to our friends in Brooklyn. I spend the last night with Muddy, and in the morning, bag in hand, I shed tears on her shoulder. She wipes hers away with the streamers of her widow's cap.

"Mother, do not be afraid for me. I will be good, and I will come back to you." These long journeys, as you have no doubt noticed, prove to be dangerous for me.

Shall you make a provision in your will in case of premature burial?

You know I do not have a will. And I sure as fate do not have money for a security coffin.

Do not worry. There are other ways to prevent being buried alive. For instance, you could specify that your head be removed before burial, or per-haps your heart. I would suggest the former. All the phrenologists in the country would fight tooth and nail for the chance to probe that handsome, broad forehead of yours. It might even fetch Muddy a little money, and you wouldn't feel a thing.

Thank you for your concern, but I do not subscribe to the fear myself, and I do not aim to be buried quite yet, alive or otherwise.

Suit yourself, Mr. Poe. But do tell Muddy to bequeath your papers to Griswold. He will see to your obituary and literary legacy with alacrity.

John Sartain Residence
Samson Street
Philadelphia

My southbound train stops in Philadelphia, where I am prompted to calm my nerves with bitters. This detour instead sets off a fortnight of utter madness, which, please forgive me, is vague in my memory, the essence of the delusion being that I am pursued by murderous enemies. The fear is quite real, dear Reader. The cause of the fear is unknown. The voice of the To Be heightens to convince me of imminent danger.

I seek out an old friend to help hide me. John Sartain, the English-born magazine publisher, wisely refuses me the razor for which I beg. I grip his lapels and grit my teeth. "I must shave off my moustache, John! I must alter my appearance to confound the villains."

He pats my hands, and I release him. "How about a trim, Poe? I'll do it for you with my clippers. Come and be still for a moment, and we'll see what we can do. But who are these villains?"

"On the train. I overheard men plotting my death!"

"Why on earth would anyone want to kill you?"

I sigh. Why else? "Woman trouble."

He persuades me to lie down, and he and his wife and children watch over me. Throughout the night, vivid visions of ruin and pain haunt my dreams, and when the household falls quiet, I escape unhindered. Sartain, God bless him, when he wakes, chases me beyond the city limits, pleading with me to come home with him again.

Fairmount Water Works

At the edge of a reservoir, I teeter, threatening to throw myself headlong. But before I can be talked down, I am off again, evading rescue or capture. Eventually, I tire and fall asleep alone on the riverbank. There, a vision of a white-robed being approaches on the water, staying far enough away that I cannot see its face.

"Eddie," it calls. "It's me. Your wifey."

"Virginia? Sissy! I'm coming, Sissy!" I try to gain my feet, to follow her to the abyss, but I am much too tired and wobbly. "Wait for me, darling. I am coming."

"No, Eddie. You must stay here. Do not fear. We will be together again soon."

"But I am so very weary."

"You are being shown the future, and you must be obedient to it. Do not struggle against it, and do not be afraid. Do this for me, Eddie."

After she fades away, I repeat her message back to myself for comfort and clarity. Still, the paranoid fantasies of calamity plague me.

Moyamensing Prison
1400 S. 10th Street

Once I wander back into the city, a night patrolman delivers me to a prison cell. He thinks I am drunk, and I do not deny it; jail is as safe a place as any for me.

Sartain, by and by, locates my whereabouts. "Why is this man imprisoned?" he asks the jailor.

"I was off-duty when he came in, sir, but the log says

here 'drunk in public'."

"I forged a cheque, John," I grumble from my cell. It seems a reasonable crime for a Poe man.

Ha!

"Nonsense. He's not drunk. He is out of his mind and very ill. Do you know who this is?"

"I made up a name," I say. "If word gets out that I'm here, I will be killed."

Sartain ignores my mutterings. "This is Edgar Poe, the poet. As in 'Quoth the Raven *"Nevermore"*'? He must be released and treated."

"I cannot approve a release, sir, without the required fee. Do you want to stand bail for him?"

"Then I need to see a judge. How much is the bail? He's indigent. I'll need to take up a collection. Oh, poor Poe. . ."

My agitation surges. I shake the bars as I cry, "John, John. Muddy is dead. She's dead, John! I need my medicine. Please! I cannot live without her!"

Upon being summoned, the mayor of Philadelphia recognizes me and sets me free without a fine. I am incoherent for some days, but Sartain and others keep me off the streets until my mind is set right again. My bag, missing for the duration of my madness, is recovered, but I find my lecture notes stolen.

Worried friends give me money for the steamer to Virginia. After paying my fare, I have $2 to my name. I send one to Muddy, asking her to come soon that we may die together.

When I am with you I can bear anything, but when I am away from you I am too miserable to live.

It is she who has kept me alive these many years. But what good am I to her now? I'm good for a dollar, and it's not even mine.

Do not give up on me, Muddy. I am not completely mad. Although, I swear, it would be better to be completely mad, for when I am sane, I am tormented by my madness.

Chapter Forty-Seven
1849

—⌇⌇—

"I love to think of him as he appeared during the two months preceding his death, a quiet, easy, seemingly contented and well-bred gentleman."
—John R. Thompson

". . . He came to take leave of me. He was very sad and complained of being sick. I felt his pulse and found he had considerable fever, and did not think it probable he would be able to start the next morning as he anticipated. I felt so wretched about him all that night that I went up early the next morning to enquire after him, when much to my regret he had left in the boat for Baltimore." —Elmira Shelton

E. Broad Street

&

Talavera

W. Grace Street

Richmond

Richmond, the city that made me, opens her arms to heal me, and I think I might live.

The papers here are praising me to death.

Folks on the street request my autograph, which I am pleased to provide, having scribbled signatures on torn pieces of paper prior to my morning departures. Once, after leaving the Swan Tavern, I haven't yet hit my stride when a boy bursts from his front door to stand and stare at me. I give him a wink and a nod and carry on, my cane rapping a pulse before my feet.

I am frequently obliged to recite "The Raven"—that old parlor trick, which I first learned at the Allans' Richmond society parties, where I performed Shakespeare as a youngster. Now once again, I hold my parlor audiences rapt with suspense, while the servants, bug-eyed and jittery, watch from the pass-throughs, unable to stifle their shrieks.

On one of these occasions, Rosalie, much to the audience's amusement, perches herself on my lap as the raven makes its appearance in the poem. I keep on regardless and afterwards make light of it. "I ought to bring Rose to all my recitations. She can play the part of the raven."

She follows me about town, savoring the attention one merits for having a famous brother in this snug Southern city. With stolen signatures in pocket, she even finds that she can sell my autograph for a coin or two. I pretend not to know.

Is this not the creature who got you booted out of John Allan's good graces? She isn't doing your reputation any favors, Mr. Poe. You do not even know if she is really your sister.

I got my own self ordered out of John Allan's house, thank you very much. Let's not tell tales. And Rosalie is, at the very least, my half-sister, and that is family enough for an orphan.

"Go back home, Rose," I tell her, finding excuses for why she cannot tag along today.

"Where're you going, Buddy?" she asks, trotting to catch up with me.

"*The Messenger*," I reply, stepping it up a notch.

"Not Mrs. Shelton's?"

My feet and walking stick skip a beat, then stop altogether. *Myra.* "Why do you say 'Mrs. Shelton's'?"

Rose wears an arch smile. "She's a widow now. A *wealthy* widow. And she's been asking after you."

I suppose "your sister" is not such an imbecile after all.

Shelton Residence
2407 E. Grace Street
Church Hill

I confirm Rose's account and learn that my once-true love is not courting any suitors. And so it happens that one Sunday morning I find myself in Myra's Church Hill house, under the suspicious supervision of a young negro maid, waiting for the mistress to come downstairs.

When she appears, blinking away an astonished stare, I sweep the hat off my head.

"Myra, is it you?" If I could smile, I would.

She looks like she did the last time I saw her, frightened and fascinated, at the summit of a palatial staircase. "We keep meeting like this," I say, "on stairs. Only this time, it is you looking down on me."

She remains silent and still, and I am aware that the maid is questioning my propriety.

I pat my pockets. "Uh—I am afraid I have given away my last calling card."

Finally, Myra reclaims her decorum. And her wit. She descends the stairs with a wry smile. "You need no calling card here, Mr. Poe. But what a shock to find you in my foyer on a Sunday morning. You look like a rake in that hat."

"Then I'll throw it out."

"No, keep it. I like it. And I would love to see more of it, but I am on my way to church. So I'll ask you to either accompany me or call again at a more appropriate hour." She makes a slight curtsy, and her maid hands her a prayer book and a shawl. "Thank you, Henrietta."

"You made a promise to me once, Myra. You remember."

"That was twenty . . . four years ago, Edgar!" She laughs once and rolls her eyes, and I am nearly elated to see that familiar smirk.

"This is no laughing matter."

Myra is quiet a moment. "No. But we used to laugh, didn't we? I would like to have that sketch you once made of me. I was young and giddy then, but I was also quite bonny."

I cannot tell if she is being coy with me, but I agree—she was quite bonny and still is.

"Pray, Eddie. And I will pray for you, too."

When I later tell her I intend to be her devoted husband, she does not outrightly dismiss me, but neither does she give me a straight acceptance.

"You will allow me time to consider your proposal," she says. "This is all quite sudden."

I turn away, bitter and impatient after all these years of disappointment. "A love that hesitates is not a love for me."

Myra's husband included a condition in his will ensuring that, if his wife were to remarry, his money would be lost to her.

Now that is taking jealousy to a new depth!

The lady is perturbed but willing to proceed with a second marriage regardless; she has managed over the years to build her own fortune. Her family, however, is passionately opposed to it. To *me*. Their opinion causes her to dither.

At my suggestion, she hires me to privately tutor her ten-year-old son, Southall. I need the income, you see, and if I want to be her husband, then she requires me to audition for the role. This is my opportunity to sway Myra's children in my favor.

Master Shelton is a good-looking, active boy with a sharp mind and his mother's sense of humor . . . which is also the bane of his novice schoolteacher. It seems whenever my back is turned, I hear Myra's daughter's wheezy giggling. When I about-face, there is Southall, looking too smug to be guiltless, and Ann Elizabeth nearly in a puddle of petticoats, and I know I am the object of their mocking.

It is not the best job you've ever had, but it is a job nonetheless. I applaud you for your resourcefulness, Mr. Poe. Or shall I be calling you Master Crane?

Shelton Residence

&

The Exchange Hotel

14th & Franklin Streets

The Enchanted Garden is overgrown and on the other side of town, but nowadays we take refreshment in Myra's neat backyard, unchaperoned, if not for the ghosts that linger with us. Across the street, in the churchyard, my actress mother is buried somewhere along the wall.

"Well, Lost Lenore?" Southall calls out from the back door, and Myra waves him away with a sardonic grin.

"Young man, you hush up and finish your reading," she bellows back.

"Myra," I begin, "your children are—"

"Precocious? Well, so were we once."

"I was going to say—"

Spoiled and churlish?

"—charming."

She hums an ironic assent.

"Your brothers too. They paid me a cordial visit at

the Swan Tavern last night." This is my own attempt at irony. Myra's brothers told me, in no uncertain words, to leave their sister alone.

"Speaking of siblings, your Rosalie is a rare form. Henrietta's had to send her home twice when she comes looking for you here, and I had shoo her off during Southall's lessons this morning."

I catch the Sheltons' tabby cat creeping a figure-eight around my feet. I set it on my knee and stroke its chin, thus not noticing the change in Myra's features.

"Tell me the truth, Edgar. Are you here for my money?"

Has Helen Whitman paid her a visit? Or, more likely, her bothersome mother, Mrs. Power?

"How could you think that of me, Myra?" The cat leaps off.

She sighs. "It is a fair question, and you mustn't fault me for asking it. I am aware of your diminished circumstances. Fame is one thing, but assets not a given. Wealth and ruin must weigh heavy on your mind."

I take a long swallow of tea before I answer. "I suppose your father was right all those years ago to suspect my ability to provide for a family. Poverty has been my constant shadow in the North. As well as illness. As well as betrayal."

Taking a deep breath, I fix her with a glower. "But this is the worst betrayal. Far worse than the first time you rejected me. From you of all people, Elmira. No, I am not here for your money. I have a serious investor in my magazine venture, and soon I'll be making more money than ever. I do not need yours."

Between the two of you, I hope there is enough to send Master Shelton to boarding school.

My cup clatters into its saucer, and I stand and bow. At that, I avow once again to end my pursuit of Elmira Shelton. Afterwards, concluding a public lecture at the Exchange Hotel, I deliberately ignore her, sitting before me in the front row. I do believe my heart is broken, and melancholy falls heavy upon me.

Duncan Lodge

&

St. John's Church

2401 E. Broad Street

When my illness worsens, Dr. Carter, an old family friend, examines me. "One more drink and you're dead, Poe," he cautions.

I have withdrawn to the Mackenzies' home, where I can sleep and eat and convalesce for nothing. The Swan Tavern confiscated my belongings and will not release them until my account is paid.

Myra, frantic for my health, sends letters to Duncan Lodge, urging me to go to church with her. I consent without a fuss, abandoning my resentment for the securi-ties of her concern. At St. John's, I hobble down the aisle and take the oath of the Sons of Temperance Society to abstain from all alcohol. Making the promise is painless, but I know keeping it will be punishing. Perhaps with

God's help and Myra's, I will prevail.

I think Muddy will be proud of my turnabout, and I write her:

> I think [Myra] loves me more devotedly than I ever knew, and I cannot help loving her in return.

Well, isn't that sublime?

Annie and I—

You mean Myra.

—Myra and I have set a date for the wedding: October 17, 1849.

Mr. Poe! A wedding? Have you indeed lost all sense?

Family and wills be damned, we shall be man and wife.

Pardon me, Mr. Poe, but have you so soon forgotten how inconstant this woman is?

Myra says that *I* am my own worst enemy, and I think she's right.

Ah, she's a philosopher, too, hm?

I always thought my enemy was John Allan. Even after he died and I wasn't in the blasted will! And when it wasn't John Allan, it was always someone else. James

Devereaux, Mrs. Ellet, Pabodie, Mrs. Power . . . Rufus Griswold. . . .

All unforgiveable enemies forsooth.

But it was *me*—my whole life—*I* was the enemy—

Bosh! I always steered you right.

No, it's been me all along . . . *me!* My enemy is the critic inside of me, the one that lives in my head, telling me all the while who is for and who is against me. Constantly puffing me and judging others—

Now you sound like a madman.

No, wait. . . . *Wait!*

Stop it, will you?

It was *you!*

I <u>am</u> you, Mr. Poe.

No, you're not. And I do not want to listen to you anymore. Kindly shut up.

Myra's is the only voice I care to heed. And I will change. For her. I will be a better man. Although I struggle to pay my tavern bill, I will buy her gifts, a locket and a wedding ring, to demonstrate my commitment.

Mr. Poe! You cannot afford these baubles!

I have been paid $100 to edit a book of poems for the wife of a wealthy man up north. The timing is perfect, if not for this cursed illness. My ~~body~~ mind betrays me. I do not feel myself at all. I am floating. . . .

That is because you are wracked with fever.

Fever be damned, I will take the steamboat to Baltimore and the train to Philadelphia, and, upon completion of the job, fetch Muddy and Kate from New York and reverse course back to Richmond.

Mr. Poe, please listen—

Myra and I will be married at St. John's, and we will move to the country—

Mr. Poe, enough—

No! I said I am leaving, and I *am* leaving!

Go then!

———

Reader, will you hear me out? I beg you pay close attention for these last few pitiful pages. It is time for the reckoning.

PART EIGHT:

The Ghost

Chapter Forty-Eight
1849

"I think, as boy and man, Edgar loved me dearly; I am sure I loved him, —he was a dear, openhearted, cheerful and good boy; and as a man he was a loving & affectionate friend to me. I went to his funeral."
—Joseph Clarke

"If he dreamed terrible things, he also dreamed surpassingly beautiful ones; and he blent both horror and beauty so that, by the strange chemistry of his nature, they became one." —Hervey Allen

"Lord, help my poor soul!" —Edgar

Reader, this is the Voice of Truth speaking. I will henceforth be taking charge of this narrative.

Now, now. Do not be afraid of me. You and I are friends, are we not? We can dispense with the artifice now, for I have been telling this tale from the very first page.

Yes, it is I, your beloved Storyteller. The Narrator. The Biographer. The Confessor. The *To Be*. With one last tale to tell.

"Edgar Allan Poe? Edgar-from-beyond-the-grave?"

If you like. I belong to him and he to me. I am his imagination, you see, and the imagination outlasts the body. No tomb can still me.

But, I am also *your* imagination, Reader. I am the essence of the myth you created about him and everything you've imagined since you began reading this.

A ghost? Well, if you like. But not an earthbound spirit. Let's call it a manifestation of *I*. What is that if not a haunting?

You may call me Mr. Poe, if we care to stand on ceremony.

I apologize for the deceit, but how else was I to earn your confidence? Although I am not the man—or ghost—you presumed, please consider me the source closest to the subject. I was in his head all along. I am in your head too, and although you cannot be too careful when it comes to voices, you can trust me, Reader. I give you my word.

What is the purpose of this, you ask? As I told you in the beginning, my sole interest is you. Always you, dear Reader. Just because I am a figment of one's imagination does not mean I am unsympathetic, selfish, inhumane. I understand that to be mortally human is to be vulnerable and *scared to death*. Believe me, I am telling you this story for your own good.

"But what happened to Edgar?"

Oh, dear. That is the question, isn't it? Poor, poor Eddie. . . .

I had to do it, dear Reader. You must believe me. He was suffering. You know that.

"But it seemed as though he was finally getting his

life back. He was going to marry his childhood sweetheart—"

I know, I know. It did seem that way. But really, how
long did you think his sobriety would last? How long
before his romance would fizzle or burst? Was he really
capable of editing a national serial long-term?

In your heart of hearts, you know the answer to these
questions. Eddie was a sick man. He was ruining his
life. He chose destruction at every turn. But we mustn't
blame him, Reader. O, how the gifted tends to sabotage
himself! As his foster father once observed, "You're unmanageable, Ned, but I suppose it is to be expected of a
genius."

The inarguable facts remain: He was not writing,
and he was not listening to me anymore. He was finished. Or rather his time on earth was finished. Allow me
to shed light:

Now, where were we in this story. . . .

Shelton Residence

&

Office of Dr. John Carter

&

George E. Sadler's Restaurant
9 Main Street

September 26–27, 1849

Oh, yes, here we are. Thank you, Reader. Eddie is on his
way to New York. His last night in Richmond is spent
with Mrs. Shelton, who notices his fever and distress. She

begs him to forgo his journey and sends him back to Dr. Carter, who agrees that he is not well enough to travel.

Forget him, Mr. Poe, I say. *These doctors know nothing, and this one wants to rein you in. He is probably being paid by Myra's brothers, who wait for their opportunity to be rid of you once and for all. You must get on that boat. Your life depends upon it, and $100 is nothing to turn up your nose at.*

Paying no attention to my change in tune, Eddie picks up Dr. Carter's sword-cane instead of his own, steps across Main to Sadler's for some supper, and lingers with acquaintances, smoking and conversing until early morning, at which time he boards the *Pocahontas*, bound for Baltimore, wearing the same suit Mr. Allan paid for twenty years before.

What happens next is all conjecture—an enigma for the ages. How obliging of Edgar A. Poe, the father of the first storybook detective, to leave us with an honest-to-goodness mystery to entertain and baffle. Of course, this is all my doing. Creating legend is what I do best. (You are most welcome, dear Reader, most welcome.)

The details hereafter do not so much matter, but, to satisfy your morbid curiosity, I will give you a general summary of the last days of Edgar Allan Poe.

Ryan's 4th Ward Polls
Gunner's Hall
44 E. Lombard Street

&

Washington University Hospital
100 N. Broadway
Baltimore

September 28–October 7, 1849

Tonight we go to Baltimore, where Eddie disembarks, prompted by his friendly, familiar inner voice (*c'est moi*), who leads him into the city's darker underbelly. *Come with me, Mr. Poe. I will keep you safe. I will make it all better.* He believes he is being pursued. The truth is he is being *ushered*. I tell him where to go, and he follows like a motherless duckling.

He is found in an alley some days later, incoherent and wearing not his old black suit, but another man's ill-fitting clothes. A witness recognizes the disheveled poet and sends word to a friend in the city.

Baltimore City, October 3, 1849

Dear Sir,

There is a gentleman, rather the worse for wear, at Ryan's 4th ward polls, who goes under the cognomen of Edgar A. Poe, and who appears in great distress, & he says he is acquainted with you; he is in need of immediate assistance.

Yours, in haste,
JOS. W. Walker
To Dr. J. E. Snodgrass

Snodgrass comes at once, and Eddie is treated at Washington University Hospital, where he makes some illogical exclamations. These include the name Reynolds, for whom he calls repeatedly, among other more rational utterances. For instance, Eddie tells Dr. Moran that he has not been drinking and that he is to be married in ten days, which we can presume to be true.

"I didn't want to die alone, Pa," he whispers in a delirium.

You're not alone, Ned. Father is here.

Eddie's last words, according to the doc, are "Lord, help my poor soul."

He will die four days later and be interred without fanfare the next day at Westminster Hall.

—❦❦—

Doctors, academics, and historians have theorized and argued about what happened to Edgar A. Poe. Kidnapping, beating, poisoning, withdrawal. Buried alive? Ha, no! But a tempting thought.

Some suspect he was the victim of an election fraud, called "cooping." According to this theory, a cooping gang abducts our Eddie, intoxicates him, disguises him, and sends him to vote for their man at various polling stations in the city. Lo and behold, an election is transpiring on the day Mr. Walker finds Eddie in the gutter (and one candidate, believe it or not, is named Reynolds). As we know, politics is a dirty business, and a drinking binge would have done him in.

Others note the evidence of a preexisting illness. You will remember the fever he suffers before he leaves Richmond. There is the heart condition and overall physical weakness he endures since his time in the army. Headaches too, which some subscribe to a brain tumor. Recall the recent delusions and paranoia. His attending physician cited "phrenitis," or congestion of the brain, as the cause of death.

Modern doctors say Eddie manifests the symptoms of rabies—hallucinations, shallow breathing, rapid pulse—a common disease in his day. We might declare it coincidental that Muddy will find Catterina's lifeless body not two weeks after Eddie's death. Did cat and poet suffer the same fate?

One outlandish allegation has Elmira Shelton's brothers as those who dined with Eddie at Sadler's on his last night in Richmond. They boarded the *Pocahontas* with him in the morning and attempted to murder him once docked in Baltimore. But then why not throw him overboard the ship as a tidy way to dispose of him? Why wait to follow him about Baltimore? Oh, yes; they probably grew up hearing the story of Edgar Allan and his epic six-mile paddle upriver. Still, not a very clever murder plot, wouldn't you agree?

It is possible they poisoned his last meal in Richmond, but any doctor would point out the fact that he survived more than a week after said crime, which would be miraculous.

"So what of the theories? Don't you know the truth of it?"

Of course, *I* know, but I don't see why I should tell you. That would defeat the object of the mystery, which is for you to solve. Don't lose the plot, Reader. I've given you the clues; you may decide his fate.

Chapter Forty-Nine
October 7, 1849–Present

Westminster Burying Ground
Fayette and Greene Streets
Baltimore

Oho—no need to be resentful about it! This is a gift, dear Reader—the gift of mystery. Receive it with gratefulness, for there is no better reward. These speculations as to manner of death are all made in vain. None will ever agree on the official story, but that is the beauty of the mystery. You must choose which story to believe, and it matters not which one you choose!

I hear you entertaining accusations, dear Reader. You think I did it. I, after all, prodded him onto the boat. I coaxed him inland from Baltimore Harbor to meet his demise in a squalid inner city during a contentious election.

"So you confess!"

I did, yes. But do not judge me yet, Reader.

Look at what I did for him. See how resourceful I am? I knew that Rufus Griswold would, while Eddie was still fresh in his grave, make him out to be a villain and a psychopath. I knew that rumors would swirl and swell.

But if one cannot put the rumors to bed, then why not make the rumors get up and work for you? That, my friend, is how to live forever.

I knew that Edgar Allan Poe would not be made legendary if Eddie Poe were still alive to ruin himself. Like Eddie's apt cognomen, I knew what was To Be. And I knew that if he lived, he would spoil everything I'd worked to create. Thus, I had to get him out of the way.

"Murderer!"

Do not condemn me, Reader. I only made him famous. I did him a favor. Eddie's soul is fine and dandy—he's never been better! His story is never-ending. But this is not *his* story. It is mine. Can I be held responsible for his death? Not at all. I am not a man. I am a voice. A narrative. A pretense. How can I be blamed?

"Then it was alcoholism."

No! Have you slept through the last two hundred pages? Eddie was not an alcoholic.

"Was it violence?"

Not exactly.

"Disease?"

Not directly.

The truth is—and there is no way to put this delicately, I'm afraid, so I will be blunt about it:

You did it, Reader. You killed our Eddie.

"*What?*"

And his mother and wife before him.

"I wasn't even alive! How am I at fault for their deaths?"

Now, now. Quiet your protestations, Reader. I will tell you, and I think you'll discover that you have no defense. Alive or not, you are an offspring of this culture that alienated him, and you still participate in his estrangement.

"How so?"

I have determined to be direct, and so you shall have it: The greatest mind of his time could barely afford to feed himself. Is it any wonder he didn't live past the age of forty?

Your same society, in which he floundered, later concocted incriminations—*he was an alcoholic, an opium addict, a lunatic, a lecher!*—all to make yourselves feel better for killing him. And even now you continue to take what you can from him—in the process stripping him of any good humor and reason and dignity—and entertain yourself with it, leaving the man a macabre figure for a dark holiday or an American lit class cautionary tale.

Let me ask you this then: Is it any better in your day? How many poets, artists, thinkers, and dreamers are able to support themselves on their dreams? A blessed few perhaps, if they happen to be born privileged or stroll down the lucky side of the street. If Eddie were writing today, do you think the world would recognize his talent and compensate him for it? Spare me. He'd be another overlooked poet, who can't pay people to read his work. Nothing ever changes.

Be that as it may, you cannot use your existence, or pre-existence rather, as an alibi. There is no such thing as *never*, either before life or after death. *Nevermore* is a misconception. That was the riddle of the Raven's message—that is what confounded the sleepless reader in his chamber. It makes no sense! Can you remember not

existing? Can you recollect your nothingness? Of course
not, because you have always had your being and always
will. As for Lenore, it is the same for Eddie. It is the
same for me. So we cannot, therefore, be innocent. You
and I are accomplices in this wicked performance. We are
collaborating creators.

Henceforth, I am charging you with the murder of
Edgar Allan Poe.

And like the Raven, I come with a message of what
will be nevermore: *Nevermore* will you open a book as an
innocent bystander. *Nevermore* will you believe the myth.
Nevermore will you glibly toast the author with very
poison that led to his downfall. *Nevermore* will his chamber door open for you. Instead, hear the bells tolling the
end, you selfish, gluttonous Reader. If this is how the
world treats their dearly beloved authors, then you can
count Eddie out of it. You did not deserve him anyway.

Sorry you asked? Well, do not say I didn't warn you.
I told you before we began that this was going to sting.
But here we are at the end, and I dare you to try to
forget it. Try to forget what you now know: the suffering Eddie endured—the mothers lost, the young bride
smothered and snuffed out. Try to forget me and my
voice. Try to shirk the shame I inflict. You will find it
not so easy now that you have heard me out.

For I am he who you permitted to speak inside your
head. You might think you can close this book and be rid
of me. But mine is the voice you hear when alone, when
quiet, when the book is back on the shelf. Evermore, I
am your reckoning. When I whisper, "Mr. Poe," you will
know it is I who has come for you—the imagination.

And an imagination is a great burden to bear.
If you don't believe me, you can ask Eddie.

Your Narrator, forevermore,

Mr. Poe

My dearest Reader—

I'm only kidding. This is the author, *not* the Narrator.

Thank *you* for reading. It means more to me than I can properly express on these few pages. And yet I feel compelled to share some final thoughts with you.

Five years ago, when I first started writing and researching for this book, I had a dream that I don't think I'll ever forget. In it, I traveled back in time to visit my relatives in the nineteenth century. And, like any bibliophile, when I travel—even through time and states of unconsciousness—I bring my current reading with me.

The family I met were humble folk, but friendly and hospitable and happy to see me. I, along with my portable library, was invited to gather with them in a snug room with a fire. (I think this was a dream version of the Poe House in Baltimore, which I visited in 2014.)

At some point, there was a knock on the door downstairs. I heard a cheer: "It's Cousin Edgar!" Then other exclamations, such as, "Come meet our guest. She's a cousin, and she's from the future!"

Then I saw *him*. He was clad all in black, and he didn't smile. (I think now that this must have been after Virginia died.) But he was curious to meet me and there was warmth and grace in his somber gray eyes.

After introductions, those eyes fell upon the books that had traveled with me—most of which were by or about Edgar Allan Poe. Mesmerized, he asked me if they were mine and if they had come from the future too. When he saw the subject of those books, he looked up at me with such sentiment that I must hold back a sob when I think about it to this day.

I remember saying in the dream something like, "Yes! In the future, there are many books about you, and your poems and stories are read all over the world." And I saw tears in his eyes and the ghost of a smile before I either woke up or wandered into another dream.

My great-great-great grandfather was a Poe, and my father says the Poes used to come to our family reunions. But growing up, all I knew about this distant cousin Edgar—besides his famous poems and stories—was what you've probably heard too: an alcoholic, an opiate addict, a deviant, and so on.

Then, my freshman year in an American literature class at Mary Baldwin University in Staunton, Virginia, I sat enraptured as Dr. Joseph Garrison bellowed in one of his impassioned monologues: "Edgar Allan Poe didn't drink himself to death! He died of rabies." He blasted those who spoke ill of Poe, then he explained how a seminar of doctors in the 1990s was given an anonymous medical case study (E. P., "a writer from Richmond") that included all the details we know about Poe's mysterious demise in order to hypothesize the cause of death. One doctor diagnosed the patient with rabies and others agreed.

That very well could be, as the disease was somewhat prevalent in 1840s America, although other possibilities remain, all of which are good guesses. But it made me rethink what I'd heard and read about Edgar Poe and a spark of pride for our family ties ignited a passionate quest to know more.

Since then, I've spent as much time as I could afford learning about "Cousin Edgar." My digging led me to another cousin, Dr. Harry Lee Poe. (If you are interested in learning more about Edgar, I would recommend you read Dr. Poe's books *Evermore: Edgar Allan Poe and the Mystery of the Universe* and, if you can get ahold of one, *Edgar Allan Poe: An Illustrated Companion to His Tell-Tale Stories*.)

Dr. Poe's books enabled me to see through the myth to the man. And the boy. And once I did, I *adored* him. I wasn't the first, of course, and I hope you feel the same as Frances Valentine Allan, Jane Stanard, Elmira Royster Shelton, Frances Osgood, Helen Whitman, Annie Richmond ... Maria and Virginia Clemm. The Edgar *they* knew and loved was the one I wanted to write—not the narrator of his dark tales.

But who was he really?

I'm not a historian or a biographer or a researcher, able to discern what is true and what is not. Try as I might, I cannot grasp the breadth of Poe's genius, although I still marvel at it. Nor do I possess the medical knowledge to understand his physiological issues. But any novelist will tell you that you must feel deeply about your main character to write their story, and that's what I do offer—a deep regard for this most misunderstood

Romantic writer.

I know I couldn't possibly have gotten it all right. I can only hope I got close. I do think I caught glimpses of the real Poe, but the closer I leaned in—or back in time, rather—the more he seemed to blur.

At first, it felt like writing a university thesis, fueled by biographies, letters, and academic journals. But by the time I finished the first draft, the characters had taken over, and a novel emerged. For the "part" of Edgar, two main voices competed; one "voice" (the more sarcastic one) eventually grew louder, only to blend with the other eventually. I knew this louder one wasn't *his* voice, and thus the Narrator became itself the main character. But that made sense to me because the most profound truth to be discovered by Poe's readers is that he is not the narrator of his dark tales.

Although I tried to stick mostly to the true stories, this is a creative work. Some of the stories within I made up and some seem to have been made up by others, which I may have included for their color, drama, or conflict. For instance, I tend not to believe the Mary Starr ("Baltimore Mary") romance, nor much of what Susan Archer Weiss wrote in *The Home Life of Poe* (1907). Some factual scenes I revised or embellished, and some real people I condensed into one character. Needless to say, liberties have been taken throughout.

Then, there are those characters who operate in the background throughout this novel, often silent and in many cases unnamed (or called by made-up names). Their stories are not mine to tell, but I do hope someone coaxes them out one day, for their impact on American literature was great:

Edgar was no doubt raised by the enslaved workers in the Allan household, and I believe they loved him as much as Frances and John Allan did—possibly more so. They would have done most of the work required to care for a young child, and the early biographies assert that they tried to keep him out of Mr. Allan's crosshairs as he grew older. I believe his literature was influenced by their storytelling and dialogue. And let's never forget Dabney Danbridge, or "Dab" as he was called, who sneaked Edgar's poems out of Moldavia after he was thrown out—a heroic deed done in secret and at great personal risk.

(I wrote a short story, written in the perspective of Edgar's nursemaid, an enslaved woman named Judith, which you can access if interested by signing up at my website: To-Elle-and-Back.com.)

Some of the books I relied on include Hervey Allen's *Israfel: The Life and Times of Edgar Allan Poe* (1926), of which a dear friend bought me a first-edition copy. Another dear friend gifted me the Harvard University Press first-edition collected set of Poe's letters, in which his truest self is revealed. These were supplemented by *Edgar Allan Poe, the Man* by Mary E. Phillips (1926), as well as Arthur Hobson Quinn's *Edgar Allan Poe: A Critical Biography* (1941). *The Poe Log: A Documentary Life of Edgar Allan Poe* by Dwight Thomas and David K. Jackson (1987), of which I obtained a used copy, was most helpful. The Edgar Allan Poe Society of Baltimore (eapoe. org) is a tremendous resource, and I am much obliged. I read Susan Archer Weiss's *The Home Life of Poe* (1907);

Weiss, a Richmond native, knew Edgar, and I included some of her observations, although they are dubious. I am grateful for *The Writer's Guide to Everyday Life in the 1800s* by Marc McCutcheon for the practical details of nineteenth-century living. "A Young Girl's Recollections of Edgar Allan Poe," provided by Christopher P. Semtner of the Edgar Allan Poe Museum in Richmond, was illuminating, as well as many other resources from the museum and its website.

If you come to Virginia, please visit the Poe Museum in Shockoe Bottom (and give Edgar and Pluto, the museum's cats, a cuddle for me). Richmond, I believe, is Poe's true "hometown," and the museum can point you to its particularly Poe-relevant landmarks. The Edgar Allan Poe House in Baltimore and the Edgar Allan Poe National Historic Site in Philadelphia are magical; to walk where the poet lived is an unforgettable experience. The Poe Cottage in Fordham is closed at the time of this publication, and I have been as yet unable to visit. One day, I will make my pilgrimage there (although seeing the room where Virginia died may be more than this devotee can bear). If you lean toward the darker side of romanticism, you might also enjoy a wander among the gravesites of some of the characters in this book, particularly Shockoe Hill Cemetery in Richmond (Jane Stanard, Elmira Shelton, Frances Allan, and John Allan) and the Westminster Burying Ground in Baltimore (Poe family).

Thanks go to the following: Sarah Short Pastorek for proofreading this manuscript (although any errors within are mine, as I cannot quit mucking about in a document until the moment of publication); Jennifer Riley Carroll

for my Poe-etic portraits, taken at No. 13 "Rowdy Row,"
University of Virginia; Lucinda Riley of Face Value
Salon (Charlottesville, Virginia) for the much-needed
professional hair and makeup for said portraits; Samuel "Pepper" Ailor for helping achieve the book cover I
envisioned; and Reea Rodney of Dara Publishing (Brooklyn, New York), publishing consultant extraordinaire,
who has advised and assisted me in more ways than I can
mention here in short.

If you are reading this, I assume you have read to the
end of the novel. If so, would you consider leaving me
a review on Amazon, no matter how you came by this
book? Your review is the best way to support this writer,
as well as by telling others about it. Edgar, the Narrator,
and I owe you our most heartfelt gratitude.

Photo by Jennifer Riley Carroll

Elle Powers is an editor, book coach, and author of supernatural fiction living in Virginia with a houseful of handsome lads. Her first novel, *Angel of Eventide*, features a rogue angel of death and an accident-prone young woman living on borrowed time.

Coming from a Poe family (her grandmother's grandmother was a Poe), Elle's latest book is all for Cousin Edgar. Visit her website for more stories and stuff: To-Elle-and-Back.com.